PRAISE FOR E|

MW00414633

Dangerous Play

"Hart Kipness knows her territory the way Messi knows the pitch. *Dangerous Play* is a surefire winner."
—Reed Farrel Coleman, *New York Times* bestselling author of *Blind to Midnight*

"Crime comes to the Olympics in the captivating new Kate Green thriller. With a flair for conveying the complexity of friendships, and a meticulous eye for anything sports, Elise Hart Kipness delivers another big win."
—Tessa Wegert, author of *Devils at the Door*

"Hart Kipness writes with impressive authority and specificity about the worlds of sports and sports reporting, and her skillful treatment of the human relationships at the heart of the mystery makes this a must-read thriller!"
—Sarah Stewart Taylor, author of the Maggie D'arcy series

Lights Out

"*Lights Out* is a thriller that starts at breakneck pace and never lets up. Kate Green is a great character—you'll want her to be your best friend, but she already has one, and she has to answer the question: Is she a murderer? In this striking debut, Elise Hart Kipness writes with heart, empathy, and psychological insight into evil that exists where you least expect it. She has created a main character who is real and warm and tough and faced with the biggest mystery of all: Who in her world can she trust? You don't have to love sports to love this book, but either way, Kipness's inside knowledge will pull you right in."
—Luanne Rice, *New York Times* bestselling author of *The Shadow Box*

"With a TV sports reporter protagonist, *Lights Out* blasts onto the thriller scene with something completely new and exciting for seasoned readers of the genre. The book is teeming with plausible suspects, each with a compelling motive and secrets they'd kill to keep, but always returns to the question of whether or not we truly know what those closest to us are capable of. This is fast-paced suspense you'll want to read in just a couple of sittings, and with an ending that hints at more intriguing layers of our protagonist's story to come, I can't wait to see what Elise Hart Kipness delivers next!"

—Megan Collins, author of *Thicker Than Water* and *The Family Plot*

"When a basketball superstar is murdered in his gated home, all eyes look to his wife and circle of insiders for possible suspects. Drawing on her experience as a national sports reporter and longtime resident of suburban Connecticut, Elise Hart Kipness takes us inside both worlds in this scandalous, page-turning thriller!"

—Wendy Walker, international bestselling author

"What a fantastic debut! A unique protagonist, an interesting setting, and a story that grabs you from the beginning and keeps on building. I couldn't put this book down and read it in one sitting!"

—Chad Zunker, Amazon Charts bestselling author of *Family Money*

"Elise Hart Kipness's debut novel, *Lights Out*, is the kind of gripping, tightly paced domestic suspense mystery sure to delight fans of the genre as well as general readers. Set in the high-stakes world of professional sports, the book pits an appealing female protagonist against an increasingly slippery killer who will stop at nothing to evade capture. Elise Hart Kipness is a writer we are sure to hear more from in the future!"

—Carole Lawrence, acclaimed author of *Cleopatra's Dagger*

"*Lights Out* is a seminal triumph in mystery writing, as original as it is polished. Elise Hart Kipness's sterling debut takes us inside the world of professional sports on the one hand and a female reporter cracking that particular glass ceiling on the other. A crime thriller of rare depth and societal implications, *Lights Out* shoots straight and hits the bull's-eye dead center."

—Jon Land, *USA Today* bestselling author

DANGEROUS
PLAY

ALSO BY ELISE HART KIPNESS

Lights Out

DANGEROUS
PLAY

ELISE HART
KIPNESS

THOMAS & MERCER

Text copyright © 2024 by Elise Hart Kipness

Published by Thomas & Mercer, Seattle

www.apub.com

Amazon, the Amazon logo, and Thomas & Mercer are trademarks of Amazon.com, Inc., or its affiliates.

ISBN-13: 9781662512681 (paperback)
ISBN-13: 9781662512674 (digital)

Cover design by Caroline Teagle Johnson
Cover image: © photoc / Plainpicture; © Josh Hawley / Getty; © ilbusca / Getty; © Mona Makela Photography / Getty

Printed in the United States of America

To my extraordinary sons, Justin and Ryan, for their support, encouragement, and late-night video calls. And, always, to my husband, Rob, who continues to support me in everything I do.

CHAPTER 1

Standing on the field at Yankee Stadium, I stare into the camera lens and continue my live Olympic television report, trying to ignore the brutal Bronx summer heat and the trickle of sweat it's inducing.

"In just a few hours, the United States Women's National Team will play in a do-or-die soccer match as they fight for Olympic gold. But drama, both on and off the field, has plagued them." I decide to skip over the gory details of the girl drama: The tears. The anger. The accusations. The soap opera of it all. Instead, I focus on the matchup and the dire situation the players find themselves in.

I move the microphone closer to my lips as a crowd of young girls, draped in red, white, and blue with stars painted on their cheeks, screams from the stands. Rock star–sighting kind of screams. Boy band screams. They jump up and down, arms lifted high, and chant, "USA. USA."

My cameraman, Bill Salvatore, gives me the signal to throw to a commercial break. I promise an interview with the team's head coach when we return.

Bill picks up my MAC powder in his nicotine-stained hands and steps over to me, a cigarette dangling from his mouth. He bends his lanky body down and dabs powder on my forehead.

"Talk about full service." I laugh.

"Your forehead is so shiny it could break my lens." He winks, handing me the makeup.

"Ha ha ha." I take the compact, open it, and study the mirror as another member of the crew signals sixty seconds. I inspect my reflection. My normally fair skin boasts a bit of color from the sun. It's helped along by the foundation I shellacked across my skin, which feels like someone squirted glue on my cheeks. I dab a little powder against my nose, a spot Bill missed, and then check my eyes. My black mascara is holding up, outlining my blue eyes in a way I like to think sends a bit of a Greenwich Village vibe. I smooth a few loose strands of hair against the tight ponytail I opted for, given the humidity.

"This assignment suits you." Bill studies me as he takes a long drag of his cigarette and turns his sunburned face in the other direction to blow the smoke away from me. What Bill really means is that he's glad to see I'm moving forward after a crazy person tried to kill me this past November when I inserted myself into the middle of a murder investigation. An investigation, he believes, I should have steered clear of.

I ignore the undertone and tell him covering soccer does agree with me.

I mean, who better to cover women's Olympic soccer than a former Olympic gold medalist? I had my doubts I'd land the assignment. It's one of the highest-rated events. And I haven't been one of the highest-rated employees this year. Still, it makes sense. *You were teammates with the head coach,* my boss said when handing out the assignment. It's a good thing he doesn't know the other stuff.

I even scored an invite to the NetWorld Media Corporation box. NetWorld is the conglomerate that owns my station, along with dozens of other media outlets around the world. Yes, I will have to hobnob a bit with the brass, but I hear they have excellent hors d'oeuvres up there.

Coach Savannah Baker approaches from across the field, where she was taking the players through warm-up drills. She holds her head high as she jogs toward us, not appearing impacted by the brutal Bronx heat and humidity, unlike the rest of us mere mortals.

"The studio decided to play another round of commercials," Bill says, stepping away from the camera. "Two more minutes."

"You're running late?" Savannah folds her graceful arms across her chest, clearly displeased. I could remind her that product placement made her a household name and that the commercials contribute to her high salary. But she knows that. She just wants to be contrary. While, at nineteen years old, I was a member of the gold medal team with one or two memorable moments, including a winning goal in the group stages, Savannah—Savy to her teammates—was the face of the team. Our Mia Hamm. Captain of the red, white, and blue. Her magnetic brown eyes graced boxes of cereal. Her shining ashen hair swished for shampoo endorsements. Her flawless peach skin glowed for makeup ads.

"This is taking too long." She draws out the word *long* in her southern drawl.

"One minute," I say.

She glares at me. Savannah Baker is all southern charm and smiles until she's not. In fact, she's probably one of the most complicated people I know. She also hates wasting time, which she considers this interview to be. I guess at this moment, I shouldn't begrudge her that assumption, seeing as she's coaching what could be her final Olympic game. *Pressure's on, Coach Baker,* I think.

"Ten seconds," Bill says, taking another puff of his cigarette.

"God, what an awful habit," Savannah says with scorn. She turns to me. "How can you stand it?"

"It beats his driving," I respond, thinking about how Bill bobbed around the cars on the Bruckner, like we were playing chicken. Bill flicks his cigarette onto the ground and stubs it out. The Yankee security will kick him out if he doesn't pick it up later. Or if I don't.

Savannah straightens her shoulders and puts away any sign of irritation. The camera light turns red. We are live.

"Welcome back." I smile. "Joining me is the women's head coach, Savannah Baker."

"Thank you, Kate. Always nice to be with you." She flashes her sweetest smile and leans into her southern drawl, which often gets stronger when she's on camera.

3

"I guess the question on everyone's mind"—I also force a sweet smile across my lips, which hurts my cheeks—"is, How could one of the strongest teams in nearly a decade play so poorly over the last two games? And can you pull off a win today to save your Olympic dreams?"

She points her toe like a ballerina and pushes the ball of her foot into the grass. It's off camera. Barely perceptible. But I remember. That's her very small tell. I hold her gaze and wait for an answer. At least I didn't ask her about the *girl drama* from the first game, even though I know my boss wanted me to.

"Well, Kate, don't you go for the jugular." She laughs. "No, it's a fair question. You above anyone else know how rocky things get in soccer," she says, an underhanded swipe at my turbulent early years in the youth national program. But I'm not a teen anymore. And Savannah no longer intimidates me.

"Everything turns around," she continues. "And I feel like the team has really gelled in our last trainings. I'm confident we will win today and emerge stronger for it."

We finish up. Bill motions the all clear. Savannah hands me the microphone and turns without saying *thanks* or *bye* or *y'all*.

"I thought you were friends with the coach?" Bill says as he takes the microphone from me.

"We were *teammates*. Not friends. Sometimes there's a difference."

CHAPTER 2

The luxury boxes can only be accessed with special credentials, checked many times by multiple smiling employees dressed in black-and-white uniforms reminiscent of old-world fancy restaurants. To give the aura of prestige and affluence. It's not enough that the people paying for the boxes know the obscene cost; they need all their guests to understand it. To feel it. There's no *subtle* in stadium luxury boxes.

I stop at the door with PLATINUM BOX engraved on the ornate plaque and once again flash my invitation. "Welcome, Ms. Green." The uniformed woman opens the door for me. I step into a modern rectangular event space, with glossy wooden floors and oversize copper-wire chandeliers shaped into globes that glow and sparkle. But the most impressive feature is the view. Floor-to-ceiling glass panels provide an unobstructed panorama of the field.

As they say, the view is worth the price of admission, although I seem to be the only person gawking in the direction of the field. I can't help but feel this privilege is wasted on these spectators, a word I'm using loosely.

But I'm not here to stare down at the field. Or to judge. I have a mission—eat, grab food for the crew, say a couple of necessary hellos. And leave. This is definitely not my crowd. Speaking of people who don't belong—I recognize a figure lurking on the edge of the group, looking decidedly uncomfortable.

Charlie, my boss, with a Diet Coke in his hand, stands by himself, watching the television screen tuned to TRP Sports. I'm shocked he's here. He hates this stuff. The only possible explanation I can form for Charlie's presence is that he was summoned. If that's the case, it can't be good. Did the brass order him to come? And if so—why? It couldn't be for his scintillating personality. That's nonexistent. It's too much to contemplate on an empty stomach, and I make my move toward the food.

As if sensing my presence, Charlie turns. I step behind a group of women talking and pull out my phone, hoping to hide from him. Once he finds me, it will be all work and no eating. And I want to take advantage of this spread.

I count to twenty and then glance up, relieved to see Charlie once again staring at the screen. I walk to the windows and make a wide circle to avoid him and get to the food carts. The setup is themed: red, white, and blue melded with carnival. Food carts line the back wall, featuring Epcot-like cuisines and decor from around the world. Bonsai trees decorate the sushi cart, and large lobsters with black beady eyes sit in ice buckets next to trays of lobster rolls. A popcorn machine reminiscent of those from old-time movie theaters gurgles with smells of butter and salt that make my stomach rumble.

After a childhood of forced health food from my vegan mom and stepfather, who embraced the green living of Berkeley, California, with open arms, I take every opportunity to indulge in what they refer to as *junk food*. And what most of the world considers just food.

I study my options carefully, deciding on a Mexican food cart featuring a build-your-own-nachos station. The serving lady fills a bowl with homemade chips, pours warm cheese over it, and adds all the toppings—jalapeño peppers, sliced black olives, and chopped tomatoes. I move down the line and take a large helping of homemade guacamole, mixed right in front of me, and some hot salsa. It looks good.

I step up to one of three bars, with fancy uplighting. It smells like a frat party. A high-class frat party, if that's a thing. Microbrews replace kegs, and expensive-looking wines line the shelves. There's even a frozen-margarita station that would rival a Caribbean-island bar. Seeing as I'm working, I make the mature decision to skip the alcohol and order water, which comes in a fancy glass bottle.

I take my riches and make a beeline to the seating area that's farthest from Charlie: a tufted leather bench on the far end of the space, under one of the larger globe light fixtures. If only there were a pillar blocking the view, but all the seating areas are exposed. I sit down and turn my back against the crowd and, by extension, my boss.

I take a bite of the nachos and let the spice mix with the guacamole and cheese. I feel like I'm in heaven.

"There you are." Charlie sounds irritated, as if I've been hiding from him. Oh right. I have. *Busted.* He sits next to me and extends his thin lips into a grimace. Everything about Charlie is thin—from his nose to his lips to the ties he wears. "You should have pushed the coach on the girl drama," he says.

"Hello to you too," I respond, biting into another nacho.

"Why did you hold back?" He continues talking about the interview as if I didn't say anything. Charlie wouldn't recognize a social nicety if it smashed him over his head. Phrases like *How are you? Hope you had a nice weekend. Hello* all strike him as big wastes of his time. When I was married, he'd call the house and bark at my ex, *Is Kate there?* Without even saying hi. It drove my ex insane. Actually, in retrospect that's a good memory. I now revel in anything that irks my ex, as everything about him bothers me.

"I'm surprised you're here." I change the subject. "This doesn't strike me as your scene."

"Complete waste of my time." He reaches his narrow fingers into my nachos and takes one. "Summoned by the CEO himself." He grimaces and chews. "I'm assuming the same happened to you?"

His comment surprises me. I figured coming to the box was just a perk that came with the assignment. "One of the producers just told me to swing by and take advantage of the food."

"The producer may have relayed the information, but you don't just get an invite to the box for no reason. They don't *do* nice." My stomach suddenly sours, and I put the food down. Charlie doesn't seem to notice and continues to scold me for my interview with Savy.

"It's not just the sports," he says. "It's the *drama*. Viewers want that."

The girl drama happened two games ago, when the young striker, Quinn, criticized the players from the other team, saying they got *lucky* winning—that the USA was actually the better team. She was reprimanded. And scolded for her terrible sportsmanship. Quinn is always drama, and I did cover the story during the postgame. Even a little leading up to the second game. But the question today for the coach is whether the team will win and make it out of the group stage. And I'm not going to apologize for moving on.

"That was so two games ago," I respond, picking my plate back up. I am hungry, and the food is good. I'll deal with the mystery of my invite with a full stomach.

"If the US loses, *return* to the drama. It could have been the tipping point." He's wrong. These players fought tooth and nail to get here—training until their bones hurt, sacrificing every event in their orbits for one more practice or game or meeting. A few choice words did *not* tip the scale. But for me to tell Charlie, I'd need to stop eating, and I've regained my appetite. Besides, I doubt he'd hear me. Even though I am the former soccer player and he's a guy who just loved watching sports from the comfort of his couch.

A burst of laughter from the bar reaches us. An older well-coiffed woman with expensively highlighted hair giggles again while putting her hand on a younger man's chest in a flirtatious gesture. "What's that drama?" I ask Charlie, noticing nearly all the attendees in the vicinity watching. And whispering.

"That is our CEO's wife. Their marriage troubles would make headlines if her husband didn't control all the papers."

"And where is our intrepid boss?" I ask, looking around for Wyatt Hutchinson, who would be hard to miss. He sports shockingly blond-white hair and wears suits that range from white to beige. He goes for that 1920s old money vibe—even though his money is new. And tied to his flirtatious wife.

"Wish he'd show up already so I can get back to the station," Charlie grumbles and then segues into the game plan for the rest of the day. I'm to watch the match from the field, do a live halftime report, a wrap-up at the end of the game, and then get some interviews from the locker room for the morning anchors. Same game plan he laid out this morning. And one that will surely change minutes before he needs something else from me.

He continues: "After this game, TRP will switch to track and field and then gymnastics in the evening," Charlie says. "David's story," he adds, with what is either a twitch or a purposeful eyebrow raise. David Lopez is another reporter at my station. And, more recently, some-one I'm kind of sort of involved with. *Relationship* is not a word I'm comfortable using yet, but it might be the correct description. I study Charlie's face for signs of innuendo, but he's uncharacteristically hard to read.

"Finally," Charlie spits. I follow his gaze to two men walking toward the bar, gripping crystal glasses of whiskey. Wyatt Hutchinson glares at his wife at the bar and then walks past her, without so much as a nod.

"If I have to play nice, you do too." Charlie grabs my plate out of my hands and puts it on the table. "Let's go."

"What?"

"Please." He nearly chokes on the word. "I'm not good at this stuff."

"That's some impressive self-awareness." I'm surprisingly moved by his honesty. "Fine." I stand up, wondering if Charlie orchestrated my invite just so he didn't have to face the brass alone. Although that would require a certain level of guile that I'm not sure he's capable of. "But you owe me."

Charlie grunts and leads me toward the men.

"Ah . . . Charlie." Wyatt Hutchinson extends his hand and smiles, his white teeth bright against a salon-looking tan. "Good of you to come." *As if he had a choice.* "And if it isn't our very own soccer star," Hutchinson says as if I'm a prize he won at a carnival. "Call me Wyatt." He extends his hand to me and offers a firm handshake that I believe is meant to display his superiority, masculinity, or something. But I'm strong and match his grip. Dare I say, surpass it? He lets go quickly, his smile morphing into a sneer, and I smell booze mixed with mint on his breath. "We're just so incredibly happy to have our own soccer celebrity on staff," he repeats, then takes a sip from his crystal glass. "What do you think? The girls gonna pull out a win?" He says the word *girls* with derision in his voice.

"They certainly have the talent," I respond, realizing I was probably invited to be shown off like a trophy. A possession.

"I don't like the new striker." Wyatt's older son joins the conversation, hunched at the shoulders, as if to hide the fact that he's taller than his dad. "They shouldn't have sidelined the veteran—Gayle Adams. She was amazing," the son says.

I could talk x's and o's all day, but that's a pretty loaded statement. I don't necessarily disagree with him, but I also don't want to bash the team in front of the brass. I decide to evade. "You like soccer?" I ask.

"Big fan." He blushes a little.

"He was a big fan of yours growing up," his dad says, taunting his son. "So was his younger brother. Where is that boy?"

"Curls is over there." Junior points at the couch where a man sits talking to three women. Curls is certainly a fitting nickname for the youngest Hutchinson, who has a mass of curly dark hair. I read somewhere this Hutchinson opted out of the family business—he's a surgeon, I believe.

"Did you play soccer?" I ask Junior.

Wyatt gives a cruel laugh. "Junior wasn't a very sporty kid."

Junior hangs his head. Wyatt excuses himself and motions for Charlie to follow him, like he's summoning a dog. Hell, a dog might get a little more respect. The two walk over to a corner of the lounge, where Wyatt settles down, Charlie perching on the edge of a chair across from him.

"What's that about?" I ask Junior.

"I'm not really supposed to say—" He glances at his father.

I give Junior my best *you can trust me* look.

"I'm sorry. I'd like to tell you . . . really."

"Does it have to do with the first floor?" I persist. The first floor is slang for *my* floor at TRP Sports. The reporter/programming floor. And whenever corporate has concerns, heads tend to roll.

"Nothing's really determined—" he stammers, his eyes suggesting trouble. I always thought being an athlete was an unpredictable profession—job security based on the preferences of coaches and the unpredictability of injuries. But life as a television reporter makes athletics seem like a stable occupation. The turnover rate in television is obscene.

"Well, Mr. Hutchinson, if things are precarious—" I say, searching for the right word. "I better not slack off on my job." I mean it as a joke. Sort of.

"Kate, I can't tell you what's going on. But I assure you—*you* have nothing to worry about." He steps closer. "And please call me Junior."

I don't know if I feel relieved or anxious.

I steal a glance at Wyatt and Charlie—Wyatt seems angry, jabbing at the air with his index finger. Charlie sits in a defensive position, arms crossed over his chest, body leaning away from Wyatt. As much as I get annoyed at Charlie, he's good at his job. And he's a straight shooter. No bullshit in a business that is almost all bullshit.

I look up at Junior, who's watching me.

"I didn't say it would be pretty." He shrugs. "Just that you're safe."

CHAPTER 3

I bring Bill and the rest of the crew plates of food in nicely provided to-go bags, but don't partake in this feast. Junior's comments made me lose my appetite for a second time. That and the expression on Charlie's face when I left. He looked deflated.

As the whistle blows the start of the game, I forget about Charlie, the Hutchinsons, and the nachos. The view from the sidelines beats even the one from the luxury box because I don't just see the action—I hear it. It's almost like participating. Almost.

The first half of the game goes well for the U.S. National Team. Coach Baker even flashes a real smile in my halftime interview. Up 2–0, the players come out even stronger in the second half, their confidence showing in their play. With a minute left in the game, the US scores another goal. The crowd roars. Everyone stands. The air pulsates. Cheers echo through the stadium. Red, white, and blue flags and pom-poms bounce in the air. The referee blows the whistle, signaling the end of the game. Fireworks explode from the edges of the stands. Neil Diamond's "America" blasts through the speakers.

The US players rush Quinn Price, the twenty-one-year-old superstar striker whose three goals marked a career high with the national team. The striker Junior criticized in the luxury box. They hoist the brash, young player on their shoulders, her fingers flashing a heart sign to the crowd.

Bill and I stand at the ready. He has his camera on his shoulder, recording the celebration, which the TRP control room broadcasts live. I'm holding my wireless microphone, prepared to get the first interviews. A perk of being the station hosting the games. We jog across the field toward the huddle. The public relations officer nods to me and grabs Quinn, the player of the match, to speak with us.

I whisper into the microphone that I'm about to interview Quinn. In my ear, the studio producer says they are going to show highlights and then come back to me for the interview. I can hear the anchor describing the goals.

"I'm here." Quinn opens her arms wide to punctuate the point; then she flashes a peace sign to the camera, her other hand on her hip.

"This girl's a piece of work," the studio producer whispers in my ear. Quinn is all that and more—loud, dramatic, and unapologetic.

"Get ready. They're wrapping up and throwing to you. Five, four, three . . ."

I smile into the camera and welcome the world of sports to the celebration going on behind me. Quinn must realize that her first display in front of the camera wasn't actually shown. She repeats the "spontaneous" motion—peace sign into camera, hand on hip.

I don't know if I admire her bravado or feel embarrassed on her behalf. My kids claim I don't understand their generation—that Gen Z embraces boldness and rejects behavioral restraints. A part of me does envy Quinn's unencumbered manner. Back in the day, even the top women, like Sav, kept their confidence quiet. It showed in subtle displays, like a raised chin, a hard stare.

"What the hell is she doing?" the voice from the control room yells at me. I want to respond, but instead, I let my eyebrow lift a millimeter. There's a certain relationship you develop with the producer in the control room. If you're in sync, they can talk to you while you're talking. Or listening. If you're not in sync, well, it's like having a gerbil running around your brain while you're trying to gather your thoughts and sound articulate. This producer is one of my favorites. We are in sync.

"Quinn." I call her back to the interview. "Tell the audience how you're feeling," I prompt, although she clearly doesn't need my encouragement.

She looks at me, her mouth wide. "We are on our way to gold. You heard me. I predict it now. We are going to kill it." She puts her thumbs up.

"That's an audacious statement," I respond. Predicting gold goes against all kinds of superstitions. Not to mention placing a giant target on the team's back. If your competitors weren't already pumped up to beat you, they are now.

"We are a bold team. And no one's going to stop us now that we've found our groove." She blows a kiss to the camera as a few of her teammates come over. I wrap up and send it back to the studio as Bill signals that we are clear.

"This girl needs a dose of humility," Bill grumbles, lighting up a cigarette.

"That's one way to put it," I say, remembering how I felt when we made it past the group stages during the Olympics. It took all my energy to moderate my excitement. I wanted to scream. It was one of the most joyful events in my career. My last-minute goal propelled us to the win. In that moment—especially on a big stage like the Olympics—all the injuries, missed holidays, and coaches who didn't believe in me were replaced by pure and utter joy. A feeling only surpassed when we later went on to win it all to take home gold. I watch the women still celebrating on the field and feel a pang in my gut. I wish I was still out there.

My phone buzzes and takes me out of my self-pity. It's Charlie. Change of plan. Need locker room interviews now in addition to the morning.

"Guess who changed his mind," I say to Bill, showing him the text.

"Shocker," he replies.

I lift my hand to shield my eyes against the setting sun and steal a glance at the Yankee dugout.

"You're fangirling," Bill quips. "You are the only reporter I know who hasn't gone completely cynical."

Despite the July heat and humidity, I wouldn't trade this assignment for the world. I may have grown up in California, but I became a steadfast Yankee fan at an early age.

He snorts and takes a drag of his cigarette. "If you're done gawking, can we head to the locker room?"

"Fine," I grumble and follow Bill past the Argentina bench, where a few of the players remain. The goalie sits on the grass, arms wrapped around her legs—sobbing. She doesn't even bother to wipe the tears away. My heart goes out to her. I want to tell her it will be okay. That she'll get over it. But she won't. She already announced her plans to retire after this Olympics. That was the end of her career.

"It's just a game," Bill mutters, shaking his head.

"No, Bill," I say. "It's so much more."

There's a lot of commotion on the sidelines, and I'm not sure where to focus my attention. In front of us, Argentina's head coach huddles with the head referee. I tell Bill to discreetly shoot the women talking, sensing that might be something we'll need later. I don't understand why the two would be in the middle of what looks like a heated exchange. There wasn't a disputed call. And it wasn't a close game. What could that possibly be about?

Quinn walks past the Argentina goalie, points, and laughs. "Oh my God. Have some self-respect. Crying in public. I would never!"

The referee and Argentina's head coach both look up and stare at Quinn, aghast at the taunt. Then the Argentina head coach starts waving her arms at the ref. Bill and I exchange a look. We don't like mean. And Quinn is mean.

Meanwhile, by the tunnel, a group of players from the national team start to circle around Savy. A few of them hoist up a cooler of Gatorade. I nudge Bill. He starts shooting as the players dump the sticky liquid over Sav's head. She squeals as the blue beverage runs over her blonde hair, across her face, and down her top.

"Oh my!" She laughs. Her fake laugh. She wipes her eyes and puts her hands on her hips in mock anger. The girls giggle and run into the tunnel. Savy takes a towel from one of her assistant coaches and wipes her face. She glances down the sidelines, her eyes finding the Argentina head coach, still locked in a discussion with the referee. Is that worry that flashes across Sav's face? The expression lasts a millisecond, and then she disappears into the tunnel.

CHAPTER 4

About half the spectators settle in for a spontaneous party. With beer cups half-full and music blasting, fans continue their chant of "USA. USA. USA." It's still hot but no longer boiling. The sun dipping behind the stadium provides a slight reprieve from the blazing rays.

Out of the corner of my eye, I spot a group of young girls, fully clad in women's soccer paraphernalia, leaning over the stadium rails. They call out my name.

"Look at you." Bill nudges me with his elbow. "Go sign some autographs."

"You just want a chance to have another cigarette," I respond, but walk toward the young girls as Bill pulls out his lighter.

"Our coach says you were the best female left winger ever," one girl with delicate limbs and a shiny blonde ponytail gushes.

"Your coach is very kind." I smile, signing the pink soccer ball she hands me. "What position do you play?"

She blushes and tells me she's also a winger. I hand her back the ball as a loud voice shouts from behind her. I can't quite make out the words—but they're aggressive. And my name's part of it. The girls rush off, making a wide circle to avoid the man as he yells again. Louder. Clearer. Meaner.

"You're an embarrassment to sports—Kate Green."

He's a hefty man with his face painted the colors of the flag, beer in hand, mouth twisted. He repeats the insult. Then spits in my direction, the dribble hitting my cheek. I'm stunned and stand there frozen as he laughs. Bill runs over and yanks me away.

"Ignore him." Bill hands me a tissue as he pulls me in the other direction. "He's a moron."

I nod. But inside I feel the shame rising. While I don't deserve to be harassed, one could argue I brought the hate on myself. Last year I screwed up and got caught on a gotcha video cursing out an NBA player. An NBA player who goaded me into losing my temper. I was in a bad place—my son was recovering from a drug overdose. And objectively, the player was a complete jerk and deserved my wrath. Still, I shouldn't have done it. And I can't blame said jerk for the fact that I flew into a rage. I keep thinking the incident is behind me. Then I get spit on.

Bill looks over his shoulder at the stands, seeming more troubled than me. Before we get to the tunnel, he tells me to wait, and he jogs over to a police officer, then whispers and points at the man.

"You told him about the heckler?" I say as Bill returns.

"He spit on you, Kate. That's more than heckling," Bill replies. "Let's make sure he doesn't do anything worse."

In the past, I'd tell Bill he's being paranoid. But these days, you never know. I watch as a uniformed officer and two plainclothes officers approach the man. He pushes one of them, and they immediately tackle him, pulling his hands behind his back and securing handcuffs. He stares at me, venom in his eyes, and screams, "I'll get you for this."

I keep my expression neutral on the outside but feel a chill run up my spine.

Bill pulls my arm. "Let's go."

I shake off the growing sense of unease and focus on my task. Get to the locker room. Interview players. Feed the footage back to TRP's control room.

The excessive number of officers standing guard at the tunnel entrance feels welcoming at the moment. Three, backs to us, face the crowd, keeping watch behind aviator sunglasses. The other three officers face forward, two looking toward the field, heads moving like they are observing a tennis match. The third turns to us and studies our press badges. He waves us through, and I exhale, realizing how exposed I felt on the field.

If you were magically transported into this tunnel, it wouldn't even take you half a second to know where you were. Everything screams Yankees—from the blue-and-white walls to the giant logos to the plaques. And it's all done in such a way that suggests one has stepped onto sacred ground. Either that or, as Bill likes to say, I'm fangirling again.

We approach the Yankees locker room and are quickly waved by. The Yankees don't share their space with anyone, including Olympic soccer players—so we walk to the original Yankees visitors' locker room, which was taken over in recent years by New York City's soccer team, NYCFC. Visitors now relegated to a third, auxiliary locker room.

Bill anxiously taps his foot as two security officers take what feels like forever to let us inside. Finally, they open the door as champagne corks pop. Someone sprays the liquid around the room; it bounces off the plastic protecting the wooden lockers and hits the girls. Bill has covered his camera in plastic and put on a rain poncho to shield himself and his equipment. I'm just going to try the duck-and-cover method to avoid the celebratory alcohol getting spritzed through the room.

Ahhh, the moment. The utter joy. Music pulsating, players dancing, more champagne popping. Quinn strides into the room, spits out a wad of gum, and smashes it against a picture of Argentina's team taped to the wall next to the door. I study the image, now debased by a pink wad. The flippancy irritates me. Respect your opponents. Don't diminish them.

When I competed in the Olympics, our coach put up a picture of the French women's team by the locker room door to motivate us. France had beat us in the quarterfinals of the World Cup, two years before the Olympics. We were crushed. And the photo was there to remind us of how awful it feels to lose. To motivate.

But there's a line—and smashing gum into a photo of your opponent's faces crosses it. I scan the room, my eye catching the goalie, Hazel Silver. She shakes her head, her long microbraids pulled back in a thick ponytail. Hazel is old school. Captain of the team. Tough, intense, strong, but fair. Sportsmanship matters to her. Prove yourself on the pitch. And keep your mouth shut off it. She looks away, and the moment passes as Quinn jumps up on one of the benches.

"All right, you bitches, we did it," she yells, bending from the waist and circling her body so she addresses everyone. Someone flips on "Celebration" as Quinn dances from the bench, shimmying and twerking. A few players join in; others dance over the U.S. Women's National Team logo on the floor.

I spot Savy, blue-stained hair pulled into a ponytail, hugging the goalie coach. Savy looks past the woman she's embracing; our eyes meet, and she raises a brow in a *see, I told you we'd win* kind of motion. I tip my head, acknowledging her achievement.

Wrapped up in the emotion, I don't know whether I feel sad and nostalgic or joyous and excited. Probably all of the above. I remember the moment our Olympic team made it into the quarterfinals—the exhilaration. The release. Relief. Although I don't remember champagne popping. Or this big a celebration. We were focused on the next stage of competition.

"You all right?" Bill comes up next to me, cocking his head.

"Just a bit nostalgic," I respond. "But we don't have time for that." I laugh and take the plastic-covered microphone from him, suggesting we speak with Hazel, who will be a nice balance to Quinn and her antics.

We move along the edges of the room, our bodies pressed against the plastic-lined lockers. One of the many mysteries of locker rooms, to me, is who puts these plastic protectors up. I mean, the facility staff always has them in place in the winning team's facilities. And not in the losing team's room. Even when the games come down to a penalty kick. How do they manage to do that so quickly?

Hazel removes her AirPods as we approach. "You want to talk to me when there are so many more interesting players around?" She puts her hand on her hip.

"We do want to speak with you—*I* do."

She straightens her body. I start with the easy questions: How does it feel? What do you anticipate against your next opponent, China? Are the players ready for the next challenge?

She provides stock answers in a sedate tone. Hazel isn't the exuberant type. But she sounds completely detached when she proclaims that she's proud of how the team pulled together. I end the interview quickly, knowing none of these lifeless comments will make it on air. Bill moves off to get footage of the players line dancing. But I linger. I want to ask Hazel another question, off camera. Maybe offer a little advice—former player to player.

"Hazel." I step closer so she can hear me over the music. "I remember when my team got out of the group stages, we were ecstatic," I say to her. "Why aren't you more excited?"

She opens her almond-shaped eyes wide. "Isn't it obvious?" She juts her chin toward Quinn.

"You can't let her ruin this achievement for you," I say, wanting Hazel to enjoy her moment, especially because she's the backbone of the team.

"Her lack of sportsmanship really makes my blood boil." She looks toward Quinn. "And some of those players from Argentina are my teammates on Chelsea," she says, referring to her professional team. "They're my sisters. They deserve respect."

"I get it," I say, my mind flashing back to Quinn's taunts of the goalie. "But don't let Quinn destroy this for you. Enjoy your win. You never know when it will disappear."

She flinches as pity flickers through her eyes. She's remembering how my professional career came crashing to an end. I can still feel the despair and sadness that followed. Everything I worked and sacrificed for, gone in a split second.

It was at Mitchel Athletic Complex, my third year with New York Power. I'd been plagued with knee injuries, but always managed to fight my way back. We were playing Philadelphia. The game was tied in the second half. I was speeding past the opponents. I could sense a goal in my future, when a defender fouled me from behind. I went down, my knee twisting unnaturally. I heard the deafening pop. As the whistle blew and my teammates swarmed to give me a hand up, I thought to myself, *Maybe I'm actually all right.* I didn't feel any pain. Maybe I'd only imagined the pop. I gripped a teammate's hand and hoisted myself up. I heard a murmur on the field. My teammate's eyes filled with compassion mixed with horror as she stared down at my leg. It dangled from my knee. I felt a crushing, soul-sucking blow to my gut. In that moment, I knew I wouldn't come back from this injury. I remember falling back onto the turf, covering my face and willing myself not to cry in public. "Leave with dignity, Kate," I kept mumbling to myself. I'd have plenty of time for tears in the locker room.

"I know I shouldn't take playing for granted." Hazel watches me. "But you saw what she did to the picture of the Argentinian team." Hazel's voice fills with anger. "And it wasn't just the gum . . . Quinn's done other things."

"Like what?" I focus on Hazel.

"Did you see Argentina's head coach with the referee?"

"They seemed to be locked in a pretty heated exchange." I nod. "Which confused me because there weren't any controversial calls."

"There was something worse," Hazel says. "Much worse." She hesitates.

"What is it, Hazel?" I put my hand on her arm, hoping to reassure her.

"You have to promise that you won't report this," she says.

I promise. And I mean it.

"I'm trusting you, Kate," she replies. I hold her gaze as she debates what to do. Then she leans down to whisper in my ear. I hear myself gasp.

CHAPTER 5

I try to wrap my mind around what Hazel whispered. I knew Quinn was brazen. And mean. But what Hazel is accusing Quinn of goes a step beyond.

"Someone planted a threatening note in the Argentina goalie's backpack before the game," I whisper, to confirm what she said.

"Not only that, but the note smelled like it had been smeared with excrement," Hazel adds.

"Why do you think it was Quinn?" I ask.

"The wording on the note—'We know you'll fumble under pressure—*bitch*.'" Hazel folds her hands across her chest, glaring at me.

"The word *bitch* does scream Quinn. But she doesn't have an exclusive on that particular expletive," I say to Hazel, scanning the room for Quinn but no longer seeing her among her dancing teammates.

Hazel opens her eyes wide. "Who else uses the word—*bitches*—every other second?"

"Someone could be trying to frame her." I shrug my shoulders.

"Doubt it," Hazel says and puts her AirPods back in.

Bill waves. I start in his direction when I'm immobilized by a shrill scream near Hazel's locker. She hears it, too, and removes her AirPods, explaining the training room is on the other side of her locker.

We hear the cry again . . . screeching. I look around—no one else seems to have noticed. Except for Hazel and me, everyone else is in the middle of the locker room next to a speaker cranked up high.

The squeal comes a third time, followed by "*Oh my fucking God.*" Quinn. It's Quinn.

"Stupid crybaby," Hazel mutters and returns to her music.

Quinn is all drama. I agree. But something in Quinn's tone concerns me. She sounds scared. Terrified, actually. I scan the room again and notice Sav is also missing.

I approach the entrance to the training room and put my ear to the door. Nothing. Above the entrance a large sign with red letters warns: NO MEDIA BEYOND THIS POINT. I ignore it and pull the door open. The smell of Bengay hits me hard, along with swamp-like steam from earlier showers. I blink my eyes, trying to focus despite the dim, cloudy light. I take in the edges of the space, a rectangular room with physical therapy tables, stacks of tape, and ice baths. Those ice baths were brutal, and I shiver thinking about dunking my worn muscles into the frigid water, trying to fight the wear and tear on my body.

"Get out!" I immediately recognize Sav's voice and focus on where the words came from. Savy stands at the far end of the room, by one of the ice baths. The figure next to her appears to be Quinn.

"Don't come any closer," Sav shouts. "You shouldn't be in here at all. Get out, Kate." She keeps her face toward me. Quinn seems fixated on the ice bath. I move my eyes in the direction of Quinn's gaze and notice a colorful flutter in the water. Like fabric. I look back at Quinn and see she's shaking uncontrollably. Something is deeply wrong.

Again, I study the flutter in the tub and then notice an object hanging over the side. I gasp. The object is an arm. And it hangs limp.

"There's been some kind of accident," Sav says, with absolutely no sign of a southern accent. Such a strange thing for me to notice in the same moment I'm realizing there's a possible dead body in the ice bath in the women's locker room at the Olympics.

I walk quickly toward the bath, which is about fifteen feet away. Sav walks fast to block me. "She's not alive, Kate. There's been a tragic accident. Please go and let me handle this. No media."

"I'm not going to report this on television," I say, trying to discern why Savy seems so intent on getting me out of here.

"Go," Sav repeats. "Please, go." Again, no sign of her southern accent.

"Coach, let her check!" Quinn squeals. "Maybe she is alive. OMG! This can't be happening. I mean . . . here . . . today. It's my day."

Her level of narcissism is astounding. But her interruption gives me the opportunity to bypass Savy and reach the tub. I move quickly to Sav's left; she reaches for my sleeve, but I wiggle away and step up to the tub. I now see the arm belongs to a woman, her head bent forward, and I see a large bloody gash in the back of her head. She must be rich, because ornate dazzling bracelets of gold, diamonds, and gems adorn her wrist.

"Is she alive?" Quinn asks in a quivering voice.

The wrist feels plastic and cold in my hand. No pulse. I shake my head, and Quinn lets out a wail.

"Okay, Kate, we've determined she's not alive, now let me handle it. I'll call the police. Quinn and I came in here and just found her in the tub," Savy adds, even though I didn't ask for details.

I let go of the arm, and the body moves; the orange-and-pink silk dress flutters in the water, like a graceful fish. More jewels hug the neck; layers of delicate gold chains with bright stones wrapped around. My eyes move up the neck, taking in the red hair floating on the surface like electric currents. Her hair floats back to expose her face. Her lips form the shape of an O. Terror fills striking emerald eyes. I stare into those eyes and freeze. I haven't seen those brilliant green eyes since we were teenagers. But I'd never forget them. And all of a sudden, I understand why Savy was so desperate to get me out of the room. She recognizes those eyes too.

CHAPTER 6
THEN

Thirty years ago

U.S. Under-14 Women's National Identification Camp calls up one hundred girls for a training camp in Arizona on the Central University campus. Coaches will assess participants to select a roster for international tournament play in August. This group of girls will be made up of thirteen- and fourteen-year-olds.

Alexa Kane had the most expressive green eyes I'd ever seen. All her emotions shined from her eyes, often multiple feelings at once. My first encounter with Alexa came when we were both thirteen years old and among one hundred female soccer players invited to the U.S. Women's National Identification Camp.

The word *camp* was very misleading. Even at my age I knew the experience would be nothing like camp. Meaning not fun. These *camps* provided coaches the chance to observe the top-tier girls in the country.

I'd heard stories about the intensity. Coaches didn't just watch; they dissected every shot, movement, pass—deciding who among us would become part of the team to travel abroad that year. From one hundred girls down to eighteen. A brutal percentage would find themselves discarded. Dreams smashed. Hearts broken. Once I learned I'd gotten selected for the camp, I was determined to prove I belonged on the roster.

I remember the June evening when the invitation arrived. I was in our yard, which had long ago become a full-size soccer training facility, my parents generously removing the grill, volleyball net, and picnic table that had once graced the small grass lot. A goalie net sat against a white picket fence with targets to practice precise shots—top left, top right, and lower corners.

It was my stepfather who called me over that afternoon while I finished up agility training. I heard thunder in the distance but didn't give it much thought—rain or shine, I needed to complete my routine.

I jogged to my stepfather, who held out a towel, and I realized the rain had already started. I dried my cheeks while he waited; his smile lit up his whole face. But I was also confused—he had tears in his eyes.

"Is something wrong?" I asked, looking past him into the house, where my brother sat reading a book.

My stepfather shook his bald head. "Look at this." He handed me a thick envelope.

I took the envelope and examined the return address. My heart stopped.

"Go on," he encouraged.

I opened the envelope and removed the letter. My eyes rested on the emblem—U.S. Women's National Team. I glanced at my stepfather, who grinned. I read the first paragraph. Then read it again. Tears falling down my cheeks.

"Is this real?" I asked, breathless.

He laughed, picked me up, and spun me around despite how wet I was. "You did it, Kate. You're going to national camp."

My brother ran over and asked what the racket was about, and I showed him the letter. He whooped and screamed. We must have looked like crazy people to any neighbor peeking over our fence.

For dinner, Mom brought home pizza to celebrate. A big deal for my vegan-health-nut parents, who'd ordered a no-cheese salad pie for themselves. "You need to go to national camp more often." My brother smirked, taking a huge bite of the large cheese pizza he and I were sharing. We didn't even mind not getting pepperoni or meatballs on it. We were eating real pizza with real cheese.

Mom asked my brother to help clear the plates. When he took mine, I thought I saw a flicker of sadness. A tiny undercurrent. But then Mom brought ice cream out, and he broke into a dance. Neither of us had eaten real ice cream in over a year. Mom only purchased frozen-juice pops.

After dinner, my stepfather and I pored over the roster that had come in that thick envelope, printed on U.S. Women's National Team letterhead. My name listed among the other elite soccer players from all over the country. The list included the name Alexa Kane from Great Neck, New York, who would end up as my roommate—and a surprising force in my life.

By the time I climbed into bed, I was exhausted but buzzing with nervous energy. Amplified by real, honest-to-God sugar, which my body wasn't used to. I wondered what the girls at the camp would be like. Would I become friends with them?

I wasn't good at friend stuff. Especially girl-related friend stuff. I played on an all-boys team. My friends from elementary school ditched me in middle school, claiming they were fed up with my soccer schedule. I wasn't bullied or anything—I was more of a nonentity. Skated around the edges. I didn't really mind. I focused on school and soccer, with the emphasis on soccer. And I finally got the letter I'd dreamed about.

National camp was the feeder that led to the feeder that led to the feeder to the World Cup and the Olympics. And I wanted that more than anything. I closed my eyes and tried to sleep, something that usually came easily for me. But I just kept tossing and turning. I climbed out of bed to get a glass of water and stopped at the bottom of the stairs when I heard voices from the kitchen.

My stepfather sounded like he was consoling my brother. "It's not fair," my brother said, his voice quivering. "Will I ever make a national team?"

My stepfather stayed very quiet. What would he tell my brother? For a second, I wished I could give my sweet brother the invitation. And my skills. I hated to hear him sad.

"Son," my stepfather began. "I could lie to you and say you will. But that's not fair to you. You are an extremely talented athlete. You will go far. But Kate has a one in a million gift—it's just different."

He started to cry. "It's not fair," he said again, his voice quivering. I felt crushed for him. My brother was the nicest person in the world. I had no idea he felt that way. And then I chided myself for being insensitive. I should have noticed.

My stepfather continued to expound on all my brother's special qualities and talk about how he'd make an incredible mark on the world. But for a kid to hear that his older sister was a better athlete, that must have been devastating. I quietly tiptoed back up the stairs and returned to bed.

By the morning, my ten-year-old brother showed no signs of resentment. Or sadness. In fact, the opposite. He repeatedly volunteered to help me with drills. He asked me all sorts of questions about the camp: Where would I sleep? How would the training work? On and on. He never showed me his pain. And he continued to be my biggest fan. Thinking about that always made my heart swell. I was so lucky with my mom and stepfather and brother. In those moments, I felt blessed that my biological father hadn't stuck around.

The day before my flight, my stepfather sat me down for a serious talk. I thought maybe it would be about my brother and how I should take his feelings into account. Or maybe it would be the typical pre-match speech: *Do your best. Be a good sport, etc., etc.* Boy, was I wrong.

"Kate, your mom and I have always taught you to be kind and considerate." He rubbed his beard. His thoughtful eyes looked agitated. "Now, I have to tell you something different."

"Don't be kind and considerate?" I laughed.

"Sort of. Yes." He went on to explain that every girl going to Arizona would be looking at me and the other players as competition. "You will be fighting for the same spots."

I was used to that. But I also had the ability to be magnanimous because, so far, I'd always been the best on every team. Even regional teams.

"You will be up against the top girls in the country," he continued. "And they will be at your level. Or better." The word *better* made him wince. To my stepfather I would always be the best. Even when I wasn't.

He reminded me that the camp consisted of two age groups. My age, thirteen years old, and the fourteen-year-olds. "Many of the older girls are familiar with these camps. And at your age, a year can make a big difference in strength and experience."

I tried to hide the anxiety creeping up my spine.

"I'm not telling you this to make you nervous," he said, intuitively knowing what I'd be feeling. "I'm telling you because you need to put on mental armor. Don't get attached. Be cordial but guarded. I'm sorry to have to teach you this so early in life."

He genuinely looked distraught. My stepdad, a gym teacher at the local high school near our home in Berkeley, always preached team spirit, kindness, family. He looked physically ill as he articulated the opposite of everything he stood for. But my stepfather put my brother and me before everything and everyone. Always.

The whole flight to Arizona, I thought about what my stepfather had told me—playing it over and over in my brain. I strategized my approach. I'd be nice to everyone because it was important the other girls liked me—otherwise, they might not pass to me. I couldn't be too cold or too distant. But I could make sure I didn't overshare or bond, which, for me, wouldn't be a problem. Or so I thought. I didn't know yet what a force Alexa Kane would become in my life.

CHAPTER 7

Why is Alexa Kane, someone I haven't seen in decades, lying dead in an ice bath of the training room of the U.S. Women's National Team? Why here? Why now? Why *her*? I move my eyes from Alexa's limp body to Savy. She's waiting for me. Arms folded across her chest, steeled for what's to come.

"It's as much a surprise to me as to you." She preempts my accusation, digging her toe into the floor. "Assuming *you* are surprised, Kate," she adds, lips pulled tight.

I want to remind Savy she has much more to hide than me. But I stop myself. We need to deal with the crime scene, meaning get out of here.

I glance at Alexa's body again. My heart sinks. I can't believe she's dead.

"Guys," Quinn interrupts. "What are you talking about? OMG. Did you know her?"

We both glance at Quinn. For an instant, I forgot about her. I imagine that Sav did too.

"Don't be ridiculous," Savy says, dismissing Quinn, her southern drawl back.

Quinn seems too distracted to question her coach. "I've never seen a dead body before," Quinn says, tone low. "I don't feel so good . . ." She bows her head, her body convulsing. She chokes and turns, heaving onto the floor.

I gag at the smell, holding back the bile surfacing in my mouth. We need to call the police.

While I'm not a cop, I come from a long line of law enforcement on my biological father's side. Although, until very recently, Liam Murphy remained a practical stranger. Liam abandoned my brother, mother, and me for his job. I still remember the fight between my mom and Liam. I was six, and we were in his hospital room. The doctors had just removed a bullet from his side. My mom gave him an ultimatum—his family or the force. Liam chose the force, and Mom moved my brother and me across the country. As if that weren't bad enough, Liam made almost no effort to see us on his designated weekends and holidays, blowing us off nine times out of ten.

But when I reconnected with Liam this past autumn, I sensed a change in him. And a nagging feeling his decision to stay on the force was more complicated than I imagined. Or maybe I'm just desperate to believe Liam's a good guy. That's what my brother would tell me, if I had shared the fact that I'm back in touch with dear ole dad.

I dial Liam.

"Hi, Kate." I hear a smile in his raspy voice. "Great live shot! I loved how you held that coach's feet to the fire—"

I glance at Sav. "Thanks. I called because there's an emergency—" I quickly explain the situation.

"An ambulance and police are on their way." He's all business now. "Get out of that room, then call me back."

I make a motion to Savy and Quinn that we need to leave.

"Excuse me," Savy snipes. "Who put you in charge?"

"Give it a rest," I respond. "We need to leave this room. Don't touch anything," I say, looking at Quinn as she picks up a garbage can and leans over, puking into it. "Anything *else*," I say to Quinn. We need to leave before we spread more unwanted DNA, making it harder for the forensic team to uncover evidence.

Quinn puts the can down and wipes her mouth with her sleeve. I scan the space, taking in the physical therapy tables; the second ice bath, next to the one with Alexa's body; and the shelves of supplies—lotions, Ace bandages, latex gloves. I walk to the shelf and carefully remove a pair of gloves and pull them on.

"Where are the trainers?" I ask, realizing they usually come into this room right after the game. Savy says she told them to give the team a little time to celebrate before showing up. That strikes me as odd, given that players don't like to put off treatment. But it does mean fewer people messed with the scene. I wonder what brought Savy and Quinn into this room. It will be my first question to them once we leave.

"Go straight into the office," I instruct them. "Do not tell anyone. We don't want to alarm people. The stadium still has a lot of fans in the stands—" I don't finish my thought. My fear that hearing about a murder could cause a panic among the crowd.

The two women fall into line; Quinn's whole body still shakes. I reach my gloved hand to the doorknob, take a breath, and turn the handle. I'm careful not to touch any other part of the door, so the police can dust for prints. I blink against the bright light as Quinn and Savy walk past me and into the locker room.

The loud music hurts my skin, like hands pawing at me. I want to scream for the women to stop celebrating. The juxtaposition of the revelry with the horror on the other side of the door feels disconcerting. How can they be so disrespectful? I feel shell shocked. The players laugh and dance and drink like they don't have a care in the world. I can't square their euphoria with Alexa's dead body behind the training-room door. It's as if my brain can't hold the two realms in one space. But there's nothing to do. They don't know.

I appraise the players as we walk across the room. Taking in the long ponytails bouncing, the wide smiles . . . the appearance of jubilee. Is someone faking? Or celebrating more than the victory, but also a successful murder? Assuming it was a murder. Given the location and the wound on her head, how could it not be?

But how? Security is at an all-time high. Only a very limited number of people could get to the locker room. Or an extremely clever criminal mastermind.

Hazel sidles up and rolls her eyes. "More Quinn drama? Coach must have really laid into her."

"What do you mean?" I turn to study Hazel. Does she know? Could she be involved?

"Quinn looks like she's seen a ghost . . . Coach must have really ripped her a new one. Right?" Hazel clearly wants to revel in a Quinn beatdown. Does she think Quinn's screams were because Savy scolded her?

"It wasn't like that," I reply to Hazel, disappointed she's acting as petty as Quinn. I quicken my pace, motioning to Quinn and Savy to move faster. Someone shakes a bottle of seltzer, then sprays it around the room. At least they've moved away from alcohol. The liquid soaks my top. Two girls pull Quinn toward them to dance.

"Oh my God, you guys—"

"Quinn," Savy scolds. Quinn drops her head and falls back in line. The girls shrug and return to the rumba, heads back, laughing.

"Kate." Bill grabs my arm as I'm about to step inside Savy's office. "We've got to do some more interviews." He tries to hand me the microphone while telling me Charlie's already called, asking for our footage.

I'd like to tell Bill what's going on. But someone might overhear.

"Give me one minute," I say, explaining to Bill I need to speak with Savy.

Bill puts his hand against the door to Savy's office, keeping me from closing it. He leans down, the smell of cigarettes strong on his breath. "Kate, Charlie won't be happy . . ." He scrunches his eyes, worry flickering across his face. Not for himself but for me. This assignment signals a second chance for me. But Charlie will understand once he hears about the murder. He has to.

"I appreciate your concern." I lean closer to him. "Truly. Trust me when I say, there's no other option."

Bill steps back, sensing I won't relent. "One minute," I mouth and shut the door as he shakes his head.

I lock the door and close the blinds to block the window to the locker room.

The two women sit: Savy at her small desk, Quinn in one of the chairs facing it. The office has an impostor feel—the women soccer posters not quite hiding the permanent NYCFC paraphernalia on the walls. I scan the posters, mostly action shots—one features Hazel, holding a ball in front of the goal, her skin glistening. The other shows Quinn striking a ball while somehow managing to wink at the camera.

I look from the poster to Quinn, slouched in the chair. This could be the first time I've seen Quinn still. Sitting in the chair, she looks, dare I say, vulnerable? With light eyes; straight, fine brown hair; and freckles sprinkled across her cheeks. She must sense me staring. "What?"

I take out my phone and call Liam back.

"The medics and police should be there any minute," he says. "We need to get everyone out of the locker room."

"But we can't cause panic." I remind him of all the fans still in the stadium. "What if we go to the media cafeteria—it's upstairs, but will be away from the crowds." I explain how we could move the players through the tunnel to the elevator and then go to the cafeteria. "We should avoid most people that way."

"What about reporters? Besides you?" he asks, and I can picture his blue eyes, my eyes, puzzling out the scenario.

"You're right, we need to avoid having reporters spot us. What if security tells all the reporters they need to get to the press room? The media is expecting to hear from the players soon, anyway. And that would clear the area."

There's silence on the other end. The music from the locker room seeps into the office, along with laughter. "What happens when no players show up for the press conference? Won't the media get suspicious?"

"We are used to hurry up and wait situations." I think about all the times I waited and waited for a press conference to start. "It's unusual when things start on time. But the police will have to give some kind of statement. It's just a matter of clearing most of the stadium of fans first."

"Good point," he tells me, and even though I'm a forty-three-year-old grown-ass woman, I can't help feeling a little proud about the compliment.

"I'm about half an hour away. And Kate," he says, voice more of a whisper. "Keep an eye out. There might be a murderer still at the stadium."

"Believe me, the thought crossed my mind." I hang up and turn my attention to Savy and Quinn. Time for answers: "Why were you two in the training room?" I ask.

"I don't know what's so surprising about a coach and a player being in their team's training room, Kate. You act like we killed her."

"You don't think the first question the police will ask is why you were in the room?" I'm tired of Savy's obfuscation. "Do you have something to hide?" I look from one woman to the other. Quinn starts quivering. Again.

"Whatever." Savy shrugs. "Go ahead, Quinn, tell her."

"But what if she reports it?" Quinn's voice squeaks.

"Off the record, Kate," Savy states.

"Agreed." I lower myself into the other chair across from Savy, next to Quinn, who is fidgeting with her hair, twirling the ends around her index finger. Over and over again.

"I *tweaked* my knee during the game." Quinn bites her lower lip. "I thought I should get some ibuprofen and an ice pack." She rubs her knee, as if to prove a point. Her whole demeanor collapses. Tears sprout from her eyes. Not for the body of a dead woman she doesn't know. But because she's worried about her career and whether she'll play the next game. If there's a next game.

"You went to check on her?" I ask Sav.

"She was limping pretty badly," Savy says. "I might need to play someone else."

"It's nothing." Quinn jumps up and starts hopping from one leg to the other. "I'm fine. Really. It's just a little ache."

Savy shakes her head, in no mood for Quinn dramatics.

"I almost didn't see the body at all. But when Coach came in, I bumped against the ice tub . . . and her arm."

My mind returns to the image of Alexa and her lifeless body. So many years have passed since we spoke. Decades. I always thought I'd have a chance to explain.

Bill knocks. I unlock the door and pull him inside.

"What's going on?" Bill studies us. I debate telling him the truth. What if he feels obliged to tell Charlie? Still, we are a team. He'd trust me.

Savy glares at me, but I ignore her, turning my attention to Bill. "There's been an incident. I can't go into detail. But it's bad. And if we report it, or even share the information at this moment, we could cause a panic."

Bill looks wary. Then scared. "Are we in danger? Is there a bomb or a gunman?"

"Oh my God," Quinn declares. "No! It's a dead body. Someone's dead in the ice bath."

"Is this a joke?" Bill looks at me, his grizzled brow furrowed.

"It's not," I respond.

"Shit," Bill says, slumping against the wall.

"Shit," I respond and fill him in on the details.

Bill convinces me that we must loop Charlie in and promises me Charlie wouldn't be stupid enough to do something to incite a panic. I don't completely agree, but I acquiesce. Bill goes to the corner to call Charlie as the music in the locker room snaps off.

"Stay calm, please." A woman's voice rises over murmurs. "We are with the NYPD and—"

Savy gets up and pushes past me and out the door. Quinn and I follow. "Settle down," Savy says, stepping up on the bench. The women look from the two police officers to her.

"Are we in danger?" one of the players says. Murmurs rise. Girls start gripping their phones.

"Everyone, put your phones down," the police officer orders. "DO NOT COMMUNICATE with anyone." She tells her partner to collect everyone's devices.

Hazel starts protesting. Other teammates join in.

"Do something," I hiss at Savy, and for the first time ever, she seems at a loss.

I jump up onto the bench next to her. "Everyone, quiet," I yell. "You need to be quiet if you want to know what's going on."

Quinn elbows one of the women to stop talking.

"You are not in danger." I say the words slowly. "But there has been an incident. The concern now is that we don't alarm the fans in the stadium and cause a panic. Please hand over your phones."

There's more grumbling, but the players comply.

After the phones are collected, the officers tell everyone that we are moving locations and to please line up. Nervous looks pass between the women, but they do as they're told.

We emerge from the locker room into the tunnel that just an hour ago felt like sacred ground. Now the concrete walls feel oppressive and tainted. We march to the elevator as sirens sound in the distance. Getting louder. And closer. The echo of a bullhorn reaches us: "Yankee Stadium is closing. Please *slowly* make your way toward the exits."

"They're lying," some of the younger girls whisper.

"I think I heard shots," another girl squeals.

"Silence," the female officer yells.

I walk up to the girls whispering and tell them they don't have to worry.

Their eyes fill with disbelief. Of course I'd say something like that.

We continue as footsteps grow louder. Seconds pass, and then the sounds escalate—breaking into a riotous gallop echoing from the concourse below. Screams from outside reverberate in the hallway. I have the sinking feeling it's no longer a question of *if* someone will be injured, or worse, but how many.

CHAPTER 8

The police rush us into the media cafeteria as pounding footsteps get closer. The female police officer shuts the door and plants her back against it. Outside the door, people keep yelling, "Run. Hurry."

The young officer whispers with her partner and then calls for quiet. "You have nothing to worry about," she says.

"Bullshit." Hazel holds up her phone, which she clearly hid from the authorities. "Someone posted on social media that a crazed man is running around Yankee Stadium threatening people with a knife."

Two players start whimpering.

"Don't believe everything you read," the female officer says. "That is not true."

"It's right here," Hazel responds.

The police officer steps over to Hazel and asks if she can look at her phone. Hazel reluctantly hands it over.

"The person who posted this has a fake profile," the police officer says. "When police ran this account, they found it was set up less than an hour ago from a burner phone."

"Then why the panic?" Hazel says, as if that proves something.

"People tend to believe whatever they see on social media," the officer snaps, clearly exasperated. "It happens more than you'd think."

My mind flashes to the pipe bomb that went off during the 1996 Olympics in Atlanta, Georgia. I vividly recall the incident and the aftermath. I saw it unfold on television, watching with my parents. We listened as the media reported one person had died and hundreds had been injured at Centennial Olympic Park.

I also recall the rush to judgment and false information disseminated through the media. At first, the security guard, Richard Jewell, was hailed a hero for noticing the backpack with the bomb and trying to clear the area. Then, he became the prime suspect. The media cited *unnamed FBI sources.* He was labeled a domestic terrorist. His life ruined even though he turned out to be innocent. And that was before social media.

Outside the door I hear footsteps. Fast. Running.

The female officer walks over to me. "You're Kate Green, right?"

"Yes," I say over the increased volume of movement in the concourse, just on the other side of the door.

"Your father specifically radioed to assure you there is nothing to worry about. To assure everyone." She motions at the panic rising among the players.

"It's like a bad game of telephone," I say.

"You're telling me." She shakes her head.

"Has the post been taken down?" I ask.

"A few minutes ago. It was only up for twenty minutes or so, but it's hard to stop a runaway train. Add the conspiracy theories circulating around it, and well, it's a tragic mess."

"Do the police think someone started a panic on purpose?" I ask, wondering if Alexa's murderer intentionally wanted to cause a distraction. It's smart and diabolical. "Can they trace the burner phone?" I ask.

"I hope so." She shrugs.

Hazel switches on the television, and we stare at the screen. The footage is even worse than what I imagined. The images depict out-and-out chaos among the stadium crowd.

The players start to yell:

"I knew it."

"We have to leave!"

"We're going to die."

"Quiet!" Hazel orders, and the murmurs die down.

The anchor stares into the camera lens. "The NYPD insists that a false statement on social media caused the panic at Yankee Stadium. They urge calm."

Too little, too late. Or, maybe, just too late. And no one running is watching television at the moment.

As if to punctuate that horrible fact, Hazel switches the station and we all gape at images of fans hurtling across the grass toward gates by the outfield and spilling onto the street. Gates that I've never witnessed open to the public. Until now.

Through the television and echoing in the hallway, feet continue to pound against pavement. Louder. Faster. Car alarms ring in the background. The footage switches to the lower concourse, where the bodies are more tightly packed together. The pushing and shoving appears more aggressive. The video shakes, and I imagine the camera operator must have gotten jostled.

"Oh no," I hear myself gasp as the young girl with the shiny blonde hair and delicate limbs—the one who asked for my autograph—smashes against the ground. On screen, bodies rush over the young girl. Then a flash of an adult's hand reaches down to help, probably the camera operator's, and a woman scoops over to collect the girl. But the young girl looks battered and bloody, hanging limp in her mother's arms. I turn away from the video, feeling sick.

The anchorwoman, clearly shaken, mumbles something about how awful the scene is as she tells viewers the mayor will speak any minute now.

Hazel mutes the television; noiseless images of the stampede continue to flash across the screen. I look away and scan the familiar cafeteria, with its coffee vending machine, and stacked plates and empty chafing dishes behind a serving counter.

"Turn on the volume," Savy says as the mayor appears on screen.

Marsha Compton approaches a podium and lowers the microphone. She stares into the television camera, her deep-set brown eyes behind thick tortoiseshell glasses. She's *New York strong*, as she will often remind her constituents. She might be even stronger than that; this is the lady who testified against her own father—also mayor back in the day—in a corruption case that spanned departments from city hall to the NYPD to Gracie Mansion.

"We believe most of the fans are now out of Yankee Stadium," Mayor Compton begins in a *silky mixed with serious* tone. "For those few remaining, there is no reason to panic. Stop running. Calm down. You are not in danger. Let me repeat that—you are NOT in danger!" She stares directly into the camera.

I see a few bodies relax, but other players mumble, "Bullshit."

"I will share everything with you. Because knowledge is power. And you, my fellow New Yorkers, and the rest of the world, deserve the truth. Reports of a man threatening people with a knife are false."

She pauses, running a hand through her short gray hair. "Police did appear on the scene at Yankee Stadium because of an unrelated incident. We are presently trying to determine whether foul play was involved."

I hear the girls start to whisper again.

"Is someone hurt? Dead?"

"Is that why we were moved?"

"We will move forward as if this were foul play"—the mayor pushes the bridge of her glasses up on her nose—"because the safety of our city and of our Olympic guests is the number one priority. We will not cower to intimidation. We will ensure the Olympics proceeds on schedule and safely."

I exchange a look with the female police officer, who gives me a weary shrug.

"I have already established a task force to get to the bottom of the situation," the mayor says as the camera zooms out to show the people she's speaking about. Bill and I exchange a look, because standing next to the mayor is my father.

"Did you know?" Bill steps toward me.

I shake my head. "Liam was on his way here, last time we spoke."

"Hope he handles things differently this time." Bill grunts. My protective camera operator, rightly or wrongly, blames my father for the danger I got into last autumn. Bill believes if Liam had listened to my theories, I wouldn't have set out to investigate on my own. Bill's reasoning is a bit circuitous, considering I made the decision to pursue a killer and put myself in danger. But I love Bill for having my back.

"I don't believe them for a second." Hazel moves to the door. "We need to leave." Others join her, and the two officers have no choice but to move away.

Hazel tries to open the door. "It's locked?" She tries again. Then starts banging.

"For God's sake, girls. Calm down!" Quinn yells.

"Why aren't we being evacuated?" Hazel shrieks at the officer.

Quinn climbs onto a chair so everyone can see her. "Bitches—I said calm down!" Quinn puts her hands on her hips. Everyone quiets down. Even Hazel.

Quinn continues. "It's nothing to worry about. They just found a dead woman in the ice bath in our training room."

"Did Quinn say, they 'just' found a body . . . ," I mutter under my breath.

"But it's working . . . ," Savy says, having moved next to me. She motions to the girls, who appear more curious than anxious.

"I can't believe this happened. It's the worst thing you could ever imagine," Quinn says, forgetting that we just witnessed a stampede in the halls of Yankee Stadium, where people were definitely injured and possibly killed. "I went into the training room for a minute. Grab an ice pack. That kind of thing. And there floating in the ice bath was a woman . . . I didn't recognize her. It was awful. I'll never unsee that. She fucking drowned. I think she was old . . . like coach's age."

Sav shakes her head and laughs. A short burst, which seems to release the tension she was holding. She laughs again. So do I. We're in our early forties, and that's old to these women? I would be amused if the situation weren't colored by murder.

The players crowd around Quinn, asking questions as a throng of police unlocks the door and pushes inside. "We will need to question everyone here," a large burly officer says. "Starting with Kate Green." Everyone turns to me, and I feel the color drain from my face.

CHAPTER 9

"Watch your step." The officer escorting me points to the sea of broken bottles shattered into amber and green shards. The stench of beer and fire hang heavy in the air. *Fire. From where?*

Police are everywhere. Blocking aisles. In and out of doors. Bathrooms. Concession kitchens.

"Follow my footsteps," the officer tells me, crisscrossing through the field of glass. We pass overturned popcorn wagons and hot dog carts; buns and kernels sink into puddles of soda.

"How many people were hurt?" I ask, breathing through my mouth to try and avoid the vile stench.

The officer looks over his shoulder. "Don't know yet." He turns front. "But it's bad."

My mind flashes back to the young girl with the blonde ponytail. *Please let her be okay.*

We pass the elevator, and I see a large craterlike dent in the door. "They tried to get out any way possible," the officer says. "Crying shame."

At the stairs I learn the cause of the burning odor. The garbage cans simmer with smoke, recently doused. "People threw lit cigarettes in," the officer says. "It's like a zombie apocalypse hit this place."

It does look like the postapocalyptic scene from *The Walking Dead* when Rick Grimes wakes up alone in his hospital room.

"Where are we going?" I ask, acutely aware I'm being separated from the group. Do they think I'm involved? Do they know my connection with Alexa? Do they know Savy's? Where is Savy? I crane my neck to look behind me but only see glass and slosh and garbage. No Savy. No players. No Bill.

We take the stairs to field level, where the locker rooms reside. The officer tells me to stay close and not to touch anything. What does he think I'm going to do—reach for soggy hot dogs?

"This way." He turns left in the tunnel and walks me past the US women's locker room, the spot where it all began. I slow down to study the activity. At least a dozen forensic officers are working the scene. I survey the area, my eyes stopping on cinder blocks directly across from the locker room door. It looks like a tomato exploded on the surface, but I know it's blood. Why else would the forensic team be taking so many swabs? Is that where Alexa got the gash on her head?

"Let's go," barks the officer. He leads me around a bend and down a tunnel toward the field. I glimpse the grass, torn up and muddy. I can't figure out why he'd want to bring me on the field, but then he stops at a plaque that reads **STORAGE UNIT**.

I'm going into a storage unit? He registers the surprise on my face and tells me that agents set up a little conference room inside. I square my shoulders, wondering how much to share about my history with Alexa. I really want Liam to be the first person I tell that bit of information. After what happened last autumn, my trust in cops is—as my teenage twins would say—*mid*.

He opens the door. I step onto a lime-green turf floor; netting runs along the concrete walls. I see immediately why it's a storage space; batting machines are stacked along one wall, next to bins bulging with balls, batting helmets, and bats in front.

"Mae, we're here."

"It's Special Agent Flynn," the woman corrects the cop, who doesn't seem to give a crap. She waves me over. "Special Agent Mae Flynn."

She reaches out her hand. "Please sit." She indicates the chair across from her.

She clasps her fingers together and leans across the table. "I hope you don't expect any special treatment because of your father."

"It's been a long day. Let's get to it," I respond.

"Good girl, Kate," she says, unbuttoning her suit jacket.

"You can call me Ms. Green," I say and notice a flash of amusement cross her eyes.

"Please start at the beginning," she says. I share everything I can remember. When I finish, she suggests a short break and gets up to make a call. The other officer brings me a water bottle. I can't believe how thirsty I am and gulp the contents down in a few sips. I feel hot and itchy in the room, which smells of sweat and rubber.

Special Agent Flynn returns to the table. "Are you ready to resume?" She picks her pen back up and taps it on the notepad.

"I guess so," I respond, exhaustion starting to take hold of my body.

"Did you notice when Quinn went into the trainer's room?"

"The game ended at five p.m." I play back the timeline in my head.

"Four fifty-eight," Flynn corrects.

I ignore her interruption and continue. "My camera operator rushed to capture the celebration, and I went to track down Quinn for an interview."

She reviews her notes and tells me my live interview with Quinn aired from 5:03 p.m. to 5:05 p.m. "Where did Quinn go next?"

She seems very intent on Quinn, although I guess she needs to account for the whereabouts of everyone who saw the body. I let out a breath and try to remember. The game feels like it took place a decade ago. "I remember some of Quinn's teammates came over, and they all started hugging and congratulating one another. The next time I saw Quinn was when she was on the sidelines."

"Anything strike you about that?"

"Actually, yes." I tell her how Quinn taunted the goalie from Argentina. "What happened to Argentina's team during the stampede?"

"They remained in the visitors' locker room."

Because their locker room didn't have a dead body in the ice bath.

"Did you go straight to the tunnel?" She wipes her mouth with the back of her hand, smudging her red lipstick. The bun at the back of her head looks loose, with escaped strands of black hair brushing against her cheek.

"No." I explain how I signed a few autographs. And then got harassed by an obnoxious spectator. "Do you have an update on the girl with the ponytail who got knocked down in the stampede?"

She blinks at me in surprise.

"We saw it on television," I explain. "She's the girl I signed an autograph for."

A flash of pity crosses her face, but she tells me she has no updates on those injured and killed.

I suck in a breath. *Killed.* The girl can't be more than three or four years younger than my twins, Nikki and Jackson.

"We need to get back to the timeline." She sounds almost apologetic. "After you signed autographs, you went directly to the locker room?"

"Yes, but the security guard stationed outside the locker room door took his time letting us in."

She glances at her notes and tells me that according to the video they've already reviewed, Bill and I entered the tunnel at 5:20 p.m.

"If you have all this information, why do you need me?" I can't help feeling like she's wasting my time. And hers.

"We don't have anything else until you called Detective Murphy at five thirty-eight p.m." She taps her pen against the notepad. "Tell me, Ms. Green—why did you call your father instead of dialing 911?"

"I didn't . . . it didn't even occur." I stop myself. *Think, Kate. Think before you answer.* "I guess I thought the quickest way to get the police's attention was to call my father."

"You don't have faith in 911 operators?" *That's a loaded question.* "It delayed dispatch of an ambulance." She pinches her lips.

"There was no need for an ambulance. I checked for a pulse."

Special Agent Flynn leans back in her chair and stretches her arms over her head. She then asks me when I last saw Quinn and Savy in the locker room. "Is it possible one of them—or both—attacked the woman?"

I've been wondering the same thing. Quinn and Savy arrived after some of the other players. They must have been among the last to enter the locker room. I saw a few players dump Gatorade over Savy's head about five minutes before Bill and I went into the tunnel. And, come to think of it, Quinn arrived after I did. She made a big show of smashing her gum over the poster of the Argentinian team. Could they have done something during halftime, perhaps?

"Do you have a time of death yet?"

"I ask the questions . . ."

"Hello," a familiar raspy voice calls into the room. I turn to see the welcome face of Liam Murphy. And bless his heart, my father is carrying two Starbucks coffees. *Please let one of those be for me.*

My father bends his broad body down and puts a steaming coffee in front of me. "How you drink hot coffee in this heat is beyond me." He shakes his head, which looks like a modern artist took a turn with his features, everything slightly ajar, like his nose, which was broken at least three times. Even so, my father is a good-looking guy—in a rugged kind of way.

"How you doing, Mae?" He gives her his standard half smile, about as enthusiastic as he gets with that expression.

"She likes to be called Special Agent Flynn." I can't help myself.

"Give me the other cup," she says to him. "If I wasn't so desperate for caffeine, I'd kick you to the curb." She lifts the lid and peeks inside. "Caramel latte?"

"With oat milk." He winks at me and then pulls up a chair between Mae and me.

"Murphy!" She frowns at him.

"Don't bust my ass, Mae. I'm the NYPD's liaison with the task force assigned to this case, along with your boss at the FBI, I might add."

She lets out an audible sigh, and I almost feel bad for her. Almost.

"Kate, do you remember who arrived in the locker room first, Coach Baker or Quinn?"

I tell them it was the coach and that Quinn arrived after I did. "My cameraman was shooting video. And everyone was snapping selfies. You should be able to piece together a timeline."

"Murphy, you want to track that down?"

"Kate's camera guy isn't my biggest fan. Have one of your crew do that."

"Fine." She sighs and tells me I can leave.

"All right, Kate." My father stands up. "Let's get you out of here and bring in the next witness."

I rise and follow Liam out the door into the tunnel. I stop short as two officers approach with Savy. Her hair is still stained with blue Gatorade. She walks right past me, her shoulder bumping mine. I turn my head, and she locks eyes with me—her message clear. *Keep your mouth shut.*

CHAPTER 10
THEN

Day 1 Identification Camp Schedule:
12:30 p.m.—Lunch, Dining Hall, Building C
1:45 p.m.—Bus to Fields
2:00 p.m.—Drills
4:00 p.m.—Rest
5:30 p.m.—Dinner
7:15 p.m.—Bus to Fields
7:30 p.m.—Scrimmages
10:30 p.m.—Tomorrow's Teams Posted
11:15 p.m.—Lights Out

Alexa Kane flew into our room with giggles and smiles as she introduced herself as my roommate. Her words came quickly, mixed with an accent I later learned was typical Long Island, New York.

"Do you watch television? I'm obsessed with *90210!* That and the Yankees. I never miss a game." She raised a brow toward me, red hair cascading over strong shoulders. She flopped down on the bed next to mine, resting her chin on her hands, her legs kicking freely back and forth. She flicked on the television. "Maybe we can watch it tonight?

Oh, look, they have cable! Have you seen a lot?" As quickly as she'd jumped onto the bed, she flew off and rummaged through her bright-pink backpack, which still had tags on it.

She pulled out a Walkman that split into two outlets and told me how she'd brought headphones for both of us. "You like music, right?" Before I'd even had a chance to answer, she changed the subject back to television and begged me to share my favorite shows. "What's your absolute, can't live without, fave?"

"I don't really have one," I said, explaining that my parents limit my television. "Sometimes we all watch a movie together on the weekend."

"Are they strict about other things?" she said. "We need to tell each other everything. We are going to be best friends."

My stepfather's words rang in my brain. *Put on mental armor. Don't get attached. Be cordial but guarded.*

"They don't let me eat junk food," I told her, deciding that a discussion about desserts wasn't deep.

"You aren't allowed *any* junk food?" she said, her eyes going wide. "You can surely have ice cream. My mom considers ice cream a health food because it has milk in it. She's always trying to get me to drink more milk. But I hate the taste." She put her hands around her throat, rolled onto her back, and made a gagging sound.

"When I got the invite to national camp, we had ice cream to celebrate. But usually it's frozen-juice pops."

"Gross." She laughed. I did too.

"See, I told you we'd become besties." She proceeded to ask me question after question. About my family. My team back home. I answered. But was mindful not to overshare. Still, it was intoxicating to have a person my age who seemed so set on befriending me. She was less guarded about herself and shared all sorts of things. She told me she had a younger sister. That her dad played baseball in college and was thrilled when he realized how good she was at soccer. Alexa told me she and her dad were die-hard Yankee fans. But her mom and sister hated all sports. She explained the people in her town were uber rich.

And snobby. But her family didn't have that kind of money. They lived in the house her mom grew up in, and her dad was an accountant at a small firm.

She was in the middle of describing a girl in her grade who'd already had a nose job when someone knocked on our door. It was one of the assistant coaches, telling us we needed to head down to lunch.

We made our way across the campus to building C and found the dining room reserved for us. A woman at the door checked our names off on a clipboard and told us to grab food and take a seat. We stepped inside to a sea of girls dressed the same. Like our counterparts, we wore white polo shirts with the U.S. Soccer logo and black sweats. Wearing the same uniform was one of many rules we needed to follow during those days.

Alexa and I filled our trays with food and then looked around for a space to sit. I started toward the back, where it seemed like girls our age were settling. "This way, Kate." Alexa motioned for me to follow her and walked over to a table with four girls and many empty seats. They looked older, and I guessed they were the fourteen-year-olds my stepfather had mentioned.

Alexa started to lower herself into a chair, when a girl with ashen hair and a southern accent ordered her to stop. "This table is reserved for veterans." The girl lifted her chin and scowled. "Go sit with the newbies in the back, baby."

The three other girls laughed. I watched as Alexa hesitated. "Come on." I pulled her away, not giving her a chance to respond.

"We have every right to sit there," she grumbled, her face flushed.

"Maybe, but let's not make waves our first meal," I said.

"Fine." She followed me, but I could tell she was annoyed. I found us a table with other *newbies*. Alexa was friendly to everyone, introduced herself, and me, and asked all sorts of questions. "Where are you from? What's your favorite television show? What position are you?"

What position do you play was both a smart and loaded question. I'm a left winger. Alexa was a right winger. We wouldn't be in direct competition with one another, but sometimes wingers were swapped around. So, it's not like rooming with a goalie.

"Girls." The head coach stood at the front of the room. "I'm Coach Randall." Everyone looked over at the woman who held our futures in her hands. "Girls, I'm not going to lie." She glanced around the room, and I squirmed when her eyes scanned our table. "This will be the most cutthroat process you've ever experienced. We do that on purpose. If you can handle the pressure here, you can handle anything."

Later in the afternoon, we went to the fields to train. Coach Randall broke us into groups, where we ran through different drills while lines of assistant coaches took notes from the sidelines. I felt like a racehorse strutting about for others to assess. *Pick me. Pick me.* It was stressful and dehumanizing. But the worst part came after. Coach called us into a huddle and told us to take a knee.

"You will scrimmage tonight," she said. Already tall, she towered over us as we knelt. "Then we will separate you into two groups. The A group. And the B group. And every night, we will cut more and more players from the A group, until it's just eighteen of you on the roster. Questions?"

One brave girl raised a hand. The coach pointed at her. "I'm wondering if you can move from the B group to the A group?"

"You can. But it's not common," Coach said. "Okay. Go back to your rooms and rest."

Rest? How could we possibly rest after hearing that information? Alexa and I returned to our room. She seemed totally at ease and suggested we watch a show. I opted to *try* and nap. But sleep never came. I peeked at Alexa listening to her Walkman, bopping her head to the beat, and envied her ease.

Dinner was a buffet of pasta. The idea was to carb load. Digest. Compete. Alexa and I grabbed trays and got in line. The same girl with the southern accent pushed in front of us. "Veterans first, newbies," she said, hands on her hips, her southern accent thick. "Shoo." She made a motion with the back of her hand, as if we were annoying flies that needed to be scattered away.

"That's ridiculous." Alexa held her ground.

The southern girl had four inches on us and pressed her index finger into Alexa's chest. "You want me to tell Coach you're being disruptive, newbie?" she said.

Alexa bit her lower lip, debating what to do. It was her first standoff with Savannah Baker. But far from the last. Or the worst. After dinner, I sat next to Alexa on the bus to the fields. This Arizona heat was like nothing I'd experienced before. Dry. Choking. I couldn't take a deep breath.

"What's wrong?" Alexa asked. "You look queasy."

"I'm having trouble breathing," I admitted. Trying to bring air into my lungs.

Alexa placed her hand on my back and told me to slow my intake. "In . . ." She counted to ten. "Hold it . . . out. Slowly." She had me repeat the mindfulness breaths the whole way to the field. "Better?" she asked as the bus stopped.

I inhaled, filling my lungs, and smiled at her. "Yes."

We walked to the field together and waited in line for our pinnies. Alexa smiled as they handed her number 27. "Nice," I whispered. The second digit referred to our positions. The first digit indicated where the coaches saw you compared to the rest of the girls in your position. The coach handed me mine, and I looked down at the number 41.

"Don't read too much into it," Alexa said, bumping me with her hip in a playful act. "You'll prove yourself. I watched you. You are great. The fastest one out here."

As we walked to the benches, I squeezed my eyes shut against the tears burning against my lids. *I will not cry.* Alexa dropped her backpack, sat down, and pulled out her cleats.

"Don't get comfortable," the southern girl and her minions called to all the newbies. "You girls need to fill the water bottles, pump up the balls, and carry over the goals."

I had no problem with that. Seniority came with benefits, and I certainly had moments when I *instructed* younger players to complete the same jobs. Everything would have been fine if it had stopped there. But it didn't.

With our tasks finished, Alexa and I sat down once again to lace up our cleats. But Savy came for Alexa. And, by extension, me. She stood above us, her body already making the change to woman while we remained underdeveloped.

"On the ground, babies. The bench is for the good players." She shooed us with the back of her hand. I immediately slid onto the ground, not happy that we had already become targets of one of the senior players. Especially because the coaches saw me as fourth in line for my position. Alexa, though, didn't move.

"I said, on the ground, baby." Savy glanced over her shoulder to make sure no coaches were around, then lifted her foot, placed it on Alexa's hip, and pushed her off the bench. Alexa fell onto the ground, bum first.

Alexa's face turned crimson. I watched her fight back tears as she stood.

"What's wrong with you?" she yelled.

"What you gonna do, baby?" Savy sneered, her southern accent strong. "Throw a fit in front of the coaches?" Savy moved her head in the direction of the gate where the coaches had just appeared.

Alexa hesitated. A smirk broke out across Savannah's face as she looked Alexa up and down, her eyes stopping on the hot-pink-and-gold cleats that I knew Alexa had saved up to buy. *I even babysat extra hours for the snobby mom down the street,* she had told me.

Savannah pointed at the cleats and laughed. "Those are so last year."

Alexa could no longer hold in the tears and turned her back to Savy as she began to cry, dampness dotting her cheeks. I put my arm around her shoulder.

Savannah made some kind of harrumph sound and strode onto the field.

"You'll show her during the match." I patted Alexa's back. "Channel your anger into your game."

She nodded and told me I was a great friend. "I knew we'd be besties," she mumbled. But I proved to be anything but a bestie. Because a bestie would have had her back when she really needed it. Not just when it was easy.

Coach called us over and reminded us that after tonight, we'd be divided into an A group and a B group. As if we could have forgotten that bit of information. A newbie bolted from the field, hand over mouth, and ran to the garbage can. We heard her throwing up.

"There's always one." Savy snorted. I found Alexa's eyes. We were just glad that wasn't us.

The coach gave Savy and her three friends captain bands and divided us into teams. "Warm up, and then we'll start the scrimmages in twenty minutes."

I joined a group of girls in a rondo, my stepfather's favorite drill. *It's like monkey in the middle with a soccer ball,* he'd say and then make monkey sounds to get me to laugh. It felt comforting to think of him. Calming. Alexa jogged to the end of the field and joined players taking shots on goal. Her strikes looked weak, and I worried Savy had really messed with her head.

Neither of us started. Savy went in as the right winger along with a squad composed of older girls. I sat next to Alexa on the bench, our thighs touching. The presence of her body helped keep my nerves in check.

Most of the girls were excellent. But it was easy to spot the superstars. One had cleaner shots. Another shielded the ball from every opponent. A third had insane dribbling skills. The only mediocre player on the pitch was Savannah, and the coach pulled her after fifteen minutes. "Number 27—you're in," Coach shouted to Alexa. I squeezed her arm and wished her luck.

Out of habit, Alexa put her hand out to high-five Savy—something every player does when they go in for another teammate. Savy jogged past Alexa, kicked a water bottle on the sidelines, and then slumped onto the bench, head in hands.

She was the only captain pulled from the field. I felt no sympathy for her—karma could be a bitch. And Savy deserved to get pulled. She sensed me staring, looked up and glowered in my direction. I pretended to stare past her at the line of coaches on the edges of each field. About six to a pitch, with clipboards, watching and scribbling.

After halftime, I swapped spots with the left winger. As soon as the whistle blew, my whole body tensed, and I made a terrible pass that went to the opponent. I literally thought I would die.

After a few minutes, I overcame the jitters and started to play my game. *It's just soccer. Just a soccer field.* I beat the defender in a few one v ones and even scored a goal. Unlike team play, no one jumped on me to celebrate. I did get a nod from a few veterans, though, and a *good job* from Coach.

The bus took us back to the dorms, and we were instructed to check back in an hour to see which roster we'd made—A team or B team. Sixty minutes. Our fates decided in such a short time. And yet the wait was excruciatingly long and painful.

Most of us returned to the dining room early. I steered Alexa to a table in the back where other newbies were gathered. She didn't fight me on it. No one spoke. We just stared at the clock on the wall, watching the seconds tick by. *Please let me get this. Please let me get this,* I kept repeating in my mind. I'd never wanted something so badly while being completely convinced it wouldn't happen. My mind replayed every moment on the pitch. *I started poorly. Would that count? I did score. That's good, right? Or should I have passed inside? Were my touches crisp? There was that one that could have been cleaner.* The only thing I felt confident about was my speed. Many girls were fast. But I was the fastest.

I told Alexa I needed to go for a walk. Up front, Savy's friends chatted at their table. Savy sat by herself on the floor in the corner of the room. She looked gaunt. If she weren't so nasty, I might have approached her. Even said something encouraging. Instead, I started a wide circle around her in an effort to avoid a confrontation.

"Hey, newbie—" she called. I considered ignoring her. But my body stopped, and my head turned. "This is a long journey. You and your friend better stay out of my way. You hear?"

As pathetic as it was, I nodded.

The coaches filed into the room, and we all stood. "Wait until the list is posted before gathering around," the head coach said and walked down the aisle to the whiteboard. She secured the list with a magnet. Turned and made her way out of the room. The second she exited, we raced to the front. Like bees to their hive. Alexa elbowed her way to the front, able to get closer than me. I saw two of Savy's friends high-five each other. A few girls rushed away, tears falling down their cheeks.

Alexa turned her head and smiled at me. I couldn't hear her words, but it looked like she was saying we'd both made it. I elbowed my way through and scanned the list. I found *Kate Green* under Team A.

"We did it." She hugged me. Out of the corner of my eye, I glimpsed Savy crying and craned my neck to study the list again. Savannah Baker was on Team B.

I found out from some of the other girls that Savy was considered one of the best wingers in this age group. Until today. But everyone has bad days. I knew Alexa and I would need to watch our backs.

We had forty-five minutes until lights out, and Alexa said we should get some candy from the vending machine and watch television. I promised to meet her in our room after I called my stepdad from the lobby pay phone. When I got off the call, one of Savy's friends approached. Her name was Shira, and she was the best goalie I'd ever seen.

"Hey, newbie." She beckoned me over. "Tonight is your lucky night." She looked around at the core group of fourteen-year-olds. "We invite one newbie a night to join us," Shira said. "Today you're the lucky one."

I wanted to ask if Alexa could join, but she'd said *one* newbie. I felt torn. I'd told Alexa I would hang out with her. But I'd only known Alexa for a day. I didn't owe her anything. This week was about making the national team. I needed to be selfish. And bonding with the older girls could help me on the field tomorrow. If they knew me, they might be more likely to pass to me or include me in plays. Not to mention, if they knew me, maybe they wouldn't bully me. And, by extension, Alexa. Therefore, I convinced myself, I was doing Alexa a favor by hanging out with them.

They had ordered pizzas and were sitting in a corner of the hotel lobby, away from the other girls scattered about. They made room for me and shared their food. Most of the conversation was about Savy.

"Can you believe how bad she was?" one girl said.

"Do you think she'll make it back onto the A team?" Shira asked while downing a third slice of pizza.

"Not a chance," another girl said. "She was awful today. No coming back from that performance. She must really be upset. Is she up in your room?"

"You know Savy, she was more angry than sad. Storming around. Complaining it wasn't her fault," Shira said. "She threw her cleat at the television and broke the screen."

The girls laughed, finding joy in Savy's demise.

"Kate," Shira said, and it was the first time any of these girls called me something other than *newbie*. "We really aren't all that bad." She smirked, and the other girls broke into giggles. I couldn't tell if they were being nice or mocking me.

By the time I returned to my room, it was dark. Alexa appeared to be asleep. I got ready for bed. When I started to get under the covers, I saw Alexa had left a note saying she hoped I'd had a good night. She had also left a chocolate bar. I felt like the biggest jerk.

As I lay under the covers, I again rationalized my actions. Even worked myself up into feeling angry with Alexa. I'd only known her for a day. This was about soccer. Playing for the national team! And the older girls were the national team. I couldn't give that up. Still, an inkling of regret seeped into my being as I fell asleep.

The next day, Alexa acted like nothing had happened. I still felt guilty, but that quickly dissipated as my mind returned to the task at hand—showing that I deserved to remain in A group. The tension in the dining room was palpable. Now the girls didn't sit based only on age but also by group. Alexa and I found a few of the other thirteen-year-olds who'd made A group and sat quietly with them, eating our oatmeal.

I searched the tables for Savy but didn't see her anywhere.

"You looking for the southern player?" the girl next to me asked.

"I was curious where she went," I responded.

"Rumor is she had a tantrum last night in her room—broke a television. They sent her home."

I felt my jaw drop while a smile broke out across Alexa's lips. "Serves her right," she mumbled.

That day was pretty much like the first, except we had to meet with a host of trainers who subjected us to all kinds of demoralizing measurements.

"Shoes off, line up," they told us. I waited behind Alexa to get on the scale. "Next," the trainer said, and I stepped on, watching the dial move to show 105 pounds.

"Hmmm." He wrote on his clipboard. "You could use a little bulk on you," he said and then dismissed me with a nod to get measured. Not only did they check my height, but my arm span, and the length of my torso and legs. "That was mortifying," I said to Alexa as I pulled my sweats over my shorts and sports bra.

"Price of fame." She laughed.

On the bus to the scrimmage, I practiced Alexa's mindful breathing and felt calmer when we arrived at the field.

Alexa and I played on the same team and both did well. I was confident we would make the next cut. Once again, she pushed forward to see the list and confirmed we were among the twenty-five girls who remained in A group. Seventy-five moved to B group. One more cut and we'd be on the national team roster and heading to Italy. If only it had been that easy.

CHAPTER 11

"There's something I need to tell you," I say to Liam as Savy disappears into the storage room.

"Can it wait until tomorrow?" He rubs the scar on his cheek—a permanent reminder of the night he was shot and stabbed, and his partner killed. My mind travels back to that night. I remember waiting in the hospital with my mom and brother, and all the police officers crowded around us.

"Earth to Kate," Liam says, tilting his head. "Are you all right?"

"I am. There's just something else—something Special Agent Flynn didn't ask about."

"Yes?"

"I knew the victim. Alexa Kane and I played soccer together as teens."

"That's some coincidence," he says, leaning his back against the Yankee-blue cinder blocks.

"It gets worse. Coach Baker also knew her."

He sighs. "Do you think the murder could be related?"

"There's a history there—but it's also been a long time."

He nods again, encouraging me to continue. It's such an unusual feeling to confide in my father. We've made progress in our relationship over the last ten months. But there are a lot of bridges to rebuild.

"We were friends a long time ago. And, I'm embarrassed to say, I let Alexa down back then." An image of Alexa pops into my brain. Not the girl dead in the ice bath, but the one vibrant and full of life.

"Am I correct to assume you are planning to pursue this?" he says, unable to conceal the annoyance from his voice.

"Yes," I say. "I already let her down once."

Liam and I have been here before. Ten months ago, I pursued an investigation on my own and almost got myself killed. I had been right about the murderer. Although, I hadn't been right about everything.

Liam rubs his scar and stares down at me. "Kate, murder is serious."

"You think I don't know that?" I hear my pitch rise.

"Murphy," one of the officers sticks his head out the door of the storage unit. "Mae needs you."

Liam tells him he'll be there in a minute and turns back to me.

"We need to talk about this more," he says.

"Fine," I reply, "but it won't change my mind. I also have more to tell you about Alexa."

He leans down and gives me his half hug, cheek kiss, and tells me he loves me, then disappears into the storage unit.

———

By the time I reach my house, it's nearly 9:00 p.m. and I'm flat-out exhausted. Nikki and Jackson both pretend to be watching television but jump on me the second I walk in the door. It seems my ten texts home didn't assuage their concerns.

"Are you okay?" Nikki blurts, her soft brown eyes filled with worry.

"What happened?" Jackson asks, pushing his sandy hair from his forehead.

"I think the city went crazy." I feel the horror of the day wash over me like a wave.

"You must be hungry." Jackson leads me into the kitchen as Nikki busies herself at the stove.

"Grilled cheese, extra grease, coming up," Nikki announces a bit too brightly. She started making those for me in autumn when all hell broke loose.

"I feel like I'm the kid and you guys are the parents," I say, plopping onto the sky blue stool at our small butcher-block island.

"You've been through a lot," Jackson replies. The words hang in the air. *We've* been through a lot. I'm the one who almost died, but the kids suffered too. It was traumatic for all of us. Images from autumn flash across my brain, like a bad movie. I had set out to try and prove my then best friend, Yvette Robbins, didn't murder her NBA superstar husband. Then I found myself in the trunk of a car, the driver on their way to kill me.

The pain in my left side is a constant reminder of the physical effects. The spot where the crowbar pierced my spleen. But the emotional effects remain too. For all of us. I shudder at the memory of lying in the car, believing I was about to die and leave my kids without a mother.

"Here you go." Nikki places the food in front of me, and Jackson takes the chardonnay from the fridge and fills a wineglass for me.

"Stop worrying." I take a bite of the gooey sandwich. "But don't stop cooking."

They laugh. Their voices ringing with hysteria.

"What's going on with both of you? I could use a touch of normalcy. Anything mundane or boring to report?"

"Dad's still pushing me to apply early decision to Dartmouth." Nikki sinks her chin into her hands, her golden hair falling around her heart-shaped face.

"You don't seem excited about that prospect."

"I don't really want to go somewhere so isolated. Or cold." Recently I took Nikki to a bunch of smaller liberal arts schools—she seemed particularly taken with the ones in California, where I grew up.

"You apply where you want to. This is your life. Not your father's."

"Good luck with that." Jackson snorts. "Because he's not getting his Ivy League dream from me."

I finish the grilled cheese, and Jackson insists on cleaning up. Nikki excuses herself and goes upstairs. I sip my wine and watch Jackson, who looks nothing like the sallow, scrawny boy who overdosed less than a year ago. His body is solid, healthy, and strong.

"I'm so proud of you," I say.

"What brought that on?" Jackson turns and rolls his eyes, the same blue eyes I see in the mirror every day. My eyes and Liam's eyes.

"Can't a mom just be proud?" I take another sip of the wine as Jackson dries the plate.

I know now that Jackson's overdose was mostly an accident. He eventually fessed up to the fact he wasn't trying to hurt himself. But it was the scariest moment of my life—watching from the hospital hallway as his heart flatlined. Much worse than my odyssey in the car trunk.

"Your coverage has been really good, by the way." Jackson sits down next to me and smiles. "Maybe I should go into journalism." He looks down at his shoes. "Not on air. But something."

"I love that idea!" I smile at him. "A bunch of schools on your list have great media programs."

Once the kids go to bed, I move into the family room, which also serves as my living room, office, and study. We may live in the ultra-ritzy town of Greenwich, Connecticut—where 90 percent of the residents live in mansions, mega mansions, or country estates—but in this town, our humble abode is, well, humble.

Still, I wouldn't have it any other way. I love our quaint historic Victorian house. I desperately wanted something with character and warmth after spending seven years sharing a sleek modern monstrosity with my ex-husband. I hated how stark that glass-and-chrome house felt.

I sit on my Pottery Barn leather couch staring at the wood-paneled walls, wondering whether to turn on the news. Do I really need to see more video of the stampede? All I want to know is whether the girl with the ponytail survived.

I take out my phone and scan the news reports, skipping everything about the mayhem. Instead, looking for updates on the injured. Or worse. A *New York Times* article says two people died in the chaos. I search for details and breathe out a sigh of relief when I learn the victims were men. Then I chide myself for being so heartless. Someone lost loved ones. There's nothing to feel relieved about.

Next, I read about those injured. Fifteen hospitalized, including two children in critical condition. *Please make it.*

What an awful day. I close my eyes against the images spinning inside my head—Alexa's dead body floating in the tin ice tub. Decades later, she's a stranger to me. Now I will never reconnect with her. I will never get to speak with her. Apologize to her. Her poor parents. I never met her father, but I will never forget the day her mother showed up at our home in California. Shame flushes through me as I remember that encounter.

I gulp down the rest of my wine, then go for a refill.

My phone rings, and despite how weary I feel, a smile creeps across my lips.

I pick up. "Hi there."

"Are you all right?" I hear the worry in his baritone voice. "I was stuck on a story and couldn't call. But I've been thinking about you."

I assure David Lopez—my colleague and recently my sort of boyfriend—that I'm fine. "Better, now that you called."

"How are Nikki and Jackson?" he asks.

"They seem all right," I say and tell him about the grilled cheese Nikki prepared.

"They're great kids," he says, and I feel so grateful he keeps them on his radar. "We still on for tomorrow night?" David asks about our regular Thursday-night date. A new tradition since the kids are with their father on Thursdays.

I tell him we are and hang up. Finally, something to look forward to after this horrible, awful day. What else could possibly go wrong? Except everything.

CHAPTER 12

I'm exhausted. But sleep doesn't come. I look around my bedroom, with its slanted low ceilings and white wicker furniture, wondering if I should give up my attempt at slumber. My mind spins with questions. How did Alexa get past security to the tunnel by the locker rooms? Security has been so tight at these events. Did she get access to a press pass? Or a field pass? Only players and a few VIPs would get those. Not only would Alexa need access, but the killer would also need that kind of access.

Outside, I hear a car pull into our cul-de-sac and pass by my window. Voices rise through the air, and I recognize the conversation of our neighbors in the home we fondly refer to as the Puke House. Until a few years ago, the color palette of the five homes on our cul-de-sac matched well. We each painted our homes in blues and greens. We picked historic but subtle shades. Then a young eager family moved in. They went in a brighter direction. Restoring their house to its original pinks and purples. The historical society responded with utter glee, featuring the pastel Victorian on the front page of their magazine and tour brochures. The rest of us were kind of horrified.

I turn on the side lamp, and my eyes immediately move to the corner of the room and the partition I purchased to hide the file cabinet and bulletin board in the small alcove, where I'm storing the notes on my personal investigation into Liam. More specifically, the night he and his partner were shot.

My mom maintained that night was what finally led her to divorce my father. She gave him an ultimatum, us or the force, and he chose the force. A narrative I believed my whole life.

But, the more I dig, the more inconsistencies I find. My gut tells me there's more to the story than my mom or Liam are letting on. And I'm determined to uncover the truth.

———

My phone pings before my morning alarm. News alerts. Tons of them. And three emails from Charlie. I push myself up against my headboard and start with the emails. The first sent at 5:00 a.m.: Mandatory meeting at 11AM. The second at 6:00 a.m.: Mandatory meeting at 11AM. The third at 6:30 a.m.: Let me know you've received this email.

I send a thumbs-up and move on to the headlines.

OLYMPIC GAMES HOST CITY OVERRUN BY CRIME. SPECTATORS TERRIFIED. I search for more information on victims of the stampede and find the number of dead remains at two. Five people still in critical condition, including a teenage girl caught on camera in the stampede. Her name is Virginia Dell, and the picture confirms it's the girl who asked for my autograph.

I continue to swipe—stopping at a color photo of an adult Alexa Kane. She looks so different from how I remember her. Where I once saw a carefree, Ivory-soap kind of teen, a sultry, glamorous starlet stares back. The headlines surprise me: WHO MURDERED NY'S FAVORITE FASHION DIVA? JEWELRY DESIGNER ALEXA KANE KILLED AT YANKEE STADIUM. WHO SNUFFED OUT MANHATTAN'S DIAMOND?

Manhattan's diamond? Fashion diva? I never kept up with Alexa after what happened. And, as someone who only reads news and sports, I missed her meteoric rise into Manhattan's elite. Although, there's some symmetry to it. She did love shows that featured glamorous stories, like

90210 and *Melrose Place*. A new pang of regret hits me. What I'd give now to speak to her.

"I'm sorry, Alexa," I whisper to no one. "I'll try and make it up to you."

I text Liam to see when we can talk.

He responds immediately. In meeting. Will connect soon. Don't do anything before we speak.

I feel irritated by his message, hoping we aren't going to have a repeat of last time. He must realize by now that I'm going to do whatever I can to get to the bottom of this. With that settled in my mind, I rush downstairs, determined to put on a cheery facade for the kids.

"It smells delicious in here." I slide onto the stool, squinting from the sun spilling through the large bay window that reminds me so much of the bright home I grew up in.

"Here you go." Jackson takes the plate from Nikki and places it in front of me.

"Go easy on the syrup." He hands me the bottle of maple syrup.

"Never." I laugh, drowning my food in the rich liquid, partially to see him wrinkle his nose in disgust.

"And coffee." Nikki swings over with a large yellow flower mug of rich coffee in one hand for me and her green concoction in the other. Nikki downs her juice—she's a true believer in health food, dark-green vegetables, and abstaining from caffeine. "Jackson, we need to leave in five." She straightens her tennis skirt as she walks to the sink.

"How's camp going?" I ask Nikki. "Are you still enjoying teaching tennis?"

"It's okay . . ." She shrugs.

"The kids are total brats." Jackson gets up and grabs his backpack. "But at least she doesn't have to deal with the younger ones." He laughs good naturedly. I know he actually enjoys working with the preschoolers at the town's day camp. But Nikki appears distracted.

"Nikki, everything okay?"

"Totally." She puts on a chipper smile. "I did want to ask you something . . ."

I put down my fork and give her my full attention.

"It's about Gran . . ." She swallows. "Liam. Is he involved in the case?" Nikki bites her lip as she waits for my answer.

"He is involved. He's the point person for the NYPD. There's a whole task force," I say, not sure if this information will make her nervous or put her at ease. "Do you want to talk about it?"

"No." She picks up her tennis bag. "Are you going to work today?"

"I'm going into the office. I'm not sure where things stand with the Olympics. But I promise you security will be tight. So don't worry."

"Wasn't security supposed to be tight yesterday?" she snaps.

"It was," I say, not wanting to lie or sugarcoat anything. I wait for her to speak.

Nikki looks out the window at our little stub of a street, still chewing her lip. "We're supposed to stay at Dad's tonight . . . but we don't want you to be alone—" She looks at Jackson.

"We'd be happy to cancel with him," my son chimes in.

"Nothing would make me happier. But I'm fine. Really. And your dad will give me hell if you don't spend some time with him," I say, thinking of how my ex blows every little thing into a big deal.

"Still—" Nikki starts.

"Would it make you feel better to know I have plans with David?" I ask.

"Yes!" Nikki says, tension releasing from her shoulders. "Make sure to text us throughout the day." She smiles.

"Shouldn't I be saying that to you?"

They ignore me and wave goodbye, disappearing down the hall. A moment later the front door closes, and I hear the key turn in the lock. It was just a year ago when they wouldn't have even considered locking the door when they left for the day.

It's close to 8:00 a.m.; I pour a second cup of coffee, take it into my family room, and flip on the television just in time for a morning briefing by the intrepid NYC mayor, who doesn't seem to shy away from press conferences.

Mayor Compton stands at the podium wearing a tailored gray suit slightly darker than her hair. She pushes her glasses higher on her nose and stares into the camera. "The men and women next to me have been working through the night to secure the safety of the city. We are New York strong, and we don't back down to cowards. The Olympics will continue as scheduled."

She again introduces the task force members, then turns to my father.

"Detective Murphy, can you please give a brief update on the case . . . and the promising leads the task force uncovered overnight."

I see my father's lips pull into a slight frown. No one else would notice, but I register the irritation in his expression. She knows better than to publicly reveal information on an open case. Then again, right now she's worrying about appearances and saving face.

She steps aside as Liam walks to the podium, his navy NYPD Task Force jacket brushing against the microphone. He bends the mic up to compensate for the twelve inches he has on the mayor.

"Thank you, Mayor Compton," he says, in a more congenial tone than I expected. "While I can't get into details, I can assure the public we are making good progress."

"Thank you, Liam," Mayor Compton says, and for the briefest second, she touches his arm with her hand. Does Liam have a connection to the mayor? They are both around sixty. It hits me that I know so little about him. Our relationship has been tied up in our past and present. But I never asked him about all the years between. Relationships. Friends.

I make a mental note to ask my father about his association with the mayor. More importantly, I want to know about the promising lead the mayor mentioned. Maybe Savy's and my history with Alexa is just a strange coincidence.

I listen a little longer as a member of the FBI outlines all the safety measures now in place. "We've raised the alert in the city as a precaution. But we believe this was an isolated incident."

The mayor returns to the podium and encourages spectators to attend events today. "Don't let fear win," she says and then opens the floor for questions.

"What about the stampede at Yankee Stadium?" a reporter yells.

The mayor's eyes darken. "I should ask all of you in the press about that. Some of you disseminated an unverified post on air without checking to see if it was accurate. Your misinformation led to deaths and injuries. The attorney general is launching a full investigation into the media's behavior. You are not allowed to yell fire in a crowded movie theater—and you are not allowed to report that a murderer is running around Yankee Stadium yielding a knife when there isn't one. We are taking this breach of public trust very seriously. People will be held accountable."

Good, I think as I head upstairs. The reporters who spread those lies should be held accountable. And I hope they uncover who tweeted the false information. People died.

Standing at my closet, I push the darker colored outfits aside, pulling out a light-gray sleeveless dress with an asymmetrical tiered hem—my version of professional, which leans edgy. Unlike most women in Greenwich, my clothing consists of blacks, browns, and grays—but never, ever pastels. I add a heart locket that the twins got me last year and pull on white sneakers. Camera ready on top, comfortable on bottom. Standing in front of the mirror, I wrap my honey-colored hair into a loose bun, line my eyes with a thick black pencil, glob on mascara, add a little bronzer to my pale skin, and dab a light gloss on my lips. I decide to forgo my heavy television foundation—dropping it in my bag so I can put it on later if I have a report today.

A blast of scorching heat hits me as I open my front door, and I immediately feel sweat prickle on my back. I had planned to take the train but dig for my car keys instead. The idea of waiting on the steamy platform and then walking through the muggy tunnel of Grand Central Terminal doesn't do it for me. I want air-conditioning, air-conditioning, and air-conditioning.

I turn on the news as I pull out of my driveway—the anchor is recapping the mayor's press conference and the comment about a promising lead. "Sources tell WCBS News that the police recovered important video from the scene."

CHAPTER 13
THEN

Note from Head Coach Randall:

Tonight, we make the final cut. Of the 25 girls in A group, 18 will be rostered to compete internationally. All decisions are final. Do not approach coaches with complaints or questions.

I was nervous. So incredibly nervous, on a level I couldn't even comprehend. My legs felt like Jell-O. I couldn't take a deep breath, and I'd already dry heaved into the trash can. I told myself it was only normal—our final scrimmage to show we deserved to make the roster to travel to compete overseas.

But Alexa seemed like Alexa. Bubbly, smiling, calm as she warmed up with the other girls. I finished lacing up my cleats and went to join the rest of them. What do they say, fake it till you make it? I tried my best to portray confidence. Hell, competence would have been enough.

I did all right during the scrimmage, but Alexa shined. I was sure she'd make the final cut and I'd go home in tears. The coach walked in, marched to the front of the room, and secured the names with the magnet. This time, I didn't rush to view the list. I knew I wouldn't be on it.

Alexa was among the girls pushing to get a look. Unlike the previous crush of bodies, only a few dozen pressed forward. I waited for Alexa to come back and give me the bad news. But it took her a while to return. She stood in front of the list for what felt like minutes—studying it.

As she walked toward me, I spotted tears in her eyes. "We didn't make it," she said, plopping down on the seat next to me.

"I knew I wouldn't, but you played so well," I said to her. "Are you sure?"

Her lower lip trembled as she nodded.

Shira, the fourteen-year-old goalie, came over and sat down—I assumed to taunt us. "You girls should be proud of yourselves," she said, and I listened for sarcasm in her tone.

"Give us a break," Alexa mumbled.

"Seriously," Shira said. "I didn't make it last year. Only two thirteen-year-olds made the cut, and they're bigger than both of you. Mark my words, you'll be back next year." She stood and rumpled Alexa's hair, like she was a puppy, before walking off.

My stepfather met me at the airport, where I collapsed into his arms, a puddle of tears. He didn't say anything, just patted my back to comfort me. By the time school started, I had redoubled my efforts to improve at soccer and trained even harder. A few days before Halloween, my mom handed me a card I'd received in the mail. It was from Alexa. The inside showed a gorilla dressed as a soccer player with the words *Happy Halloween* in big black letters. Inside she wrote:

Dear Kate,
I hope you're as fired up as I am. We need to come back next year and show them how good we are. Keep practicing. Your roommate and future *teammate*,
Alexa.

She had written *teammate* in bubble letters and filled them in with tiny red, white, and blue stars.

For New Year's, I sent Alexa a card, telling her my New Year's resolution was to lift more weights and to run twice a day, once in the morning and once at night. I signed the letter like she did, with the same tiny red, white, and blue stars inside bubble letters.

In the spring, I received another card from Alexa, this one written on lined paper. She secured a Yankee sticker to it.

> Hi Kate,
> I hope your training is going great. I know this will be our year. My coach thinks I'll definitely get invited to the next camp. (I'm sure you will too!)

She went on to tell me about her new training routine and then ended with something fun.

> I know you love puzzles. See if you can figure out the message below.

She again signed the card with bubble letters. This time there was a message in the tiny stars. The red, white, and blue was no longer random. It took me a while to figure it out. I could tell the blue stars were arranged in some kind of pattern, but I couldn't make sense of it. I tried turning it sideways, upside down. Then I held it up to a mirror, turning the paper around a second time. When it was upside down and held up to a mirror, I discovered the letters—*LBUF*. It took a second, but I figured out if I changed each letter to the one preceding it, the message spelled *KATE*. Alexa and I had a secret language. I was so excited, I immediately wrote her back and, this time, put her name inside the bubble letters, using the same technique she had.

———

The invitation came the following week:

U.S. Under-14 Women's National Identification Camp will call up one hundred girls for the spring session from April 20 to April 27 in Carlsbad, California. The camp will be used to select a roster to travel to South America to compete in three friendlies the following month. This group of girls will be made up of thirteen- and fourteen-year-olds.

Déjà vu all over again. But this time Alexa and I would be the older girls and a whole new group would be the newbies. Instead of flying by myself, my parents decided to make the trip into a vacation for my brother. They dropped me in Carlsbad before going to Universal and Disney in Los Angeles. I didn't mind at all—my brother deserved that.

Things were different this time around on all fronts.

The most important, in my mind, was that there was no Savy or her entourage. We no longer were the newbies. The nerves remained, but I already knew I'd be able to keep them in check. The difference between good and out-of-control energy. This past year, I hadn't just worked on physical strength but mental toughness.

The next difference was our accommodations, which were way cooler. They put us up at a hotel with a giant swimming pool. No buses needed this time—we could walk to the fields.

I waited for Alexa to arrive, excited to show her how much bigger and stronger I'd become. She barged in, dumped her suitcase on the floor, and hugged me. "We're here! We're here!" We jumped up and down like silly kids. A few younger girls poked their heads in, and we laughed.

That was the end of the frivolity. We were on a serious mission to make the roster. At dinner, I stood behind Alexa at the buffet, where we filled our plates with pasta. I instinctively started to walk toward the tables in the back.

"Wait," Alexa said and moved in a different direction, putting her tray down at a front table. I followed, and we started eating.

A few newbies carried their trays, looking for empty spaces. The hotel dining room was smaller than the one in Arizona. Already, thirteen-year-olds were crammed into tables. I watched the nervous girl with blotchy skin glimpse in our direction.

"You're welcome to sit here." Alexa smiled and encouraged the girl to join. It made me wonder if Savy taunted us because she was mean. Or whether older girls had done the same to her. Kind of like a nasty rite of passage. But Alexa didn't buy into that meanness and extended an olive branch to these girls. It made me admire her even more.

I sometimes look back at our fourteen-year-old national camp and think karma played a role in jettisoning us onto the roster. Not that we didn't shine during the camp to earn spots. We did.

But I also felt the world smiled down on us because Alexa forged a path of kindness. Unfortunately, good behavior doesn't always beget good results. We learned that soon enough when we were thrust back together with Savy.

CHAPTER 14

Midtown feels like a police state. Officers line Sixth Avenue. They wear bulletproof vests, riot helmets, and hold batons. Barricades block my path across Forty-Eighth Street, making me loop a block out of the way to cross on Forty-Ninth. Something hits my thigh, and I turn to see a man with a briefcase.

"Goddamn it," he mumbles as if I stuck my thigh into his briefcase instead of the other way around.

Heavy air hangs thick between the skyscrapers and boiling concrete. The subway vents sizzle, spitting steam onto the street. I wiggle my way to the front of the crowd as a police officer raises a gloved hand to stop us from crossing. Bodies press against my back, and I feel the sweat on my neck. The light turns green, and the officer waves us across. I surge forward, staying a step ahead of the pack, and turn onto Sixth Avenue.

The straps of my dress stick to my shoulders as I approach the sleek silver-and-glass skyscraper that is not just home to TRP Sports, but all the global enterprises of NetWorld Media Corporation, including the company's newspapers, magazines, and news and entertainment channels. Instead of the usual crowd of tourists staring through the glass window into the studio at the side of the building, additional guards direct pedestrians away from the area.

I push through the revolving doors into the vast lobby. I feel unsettled, taking in the added security standing on the perimeter of the marbled entranceway. Nikki's worried face flashes into my brain, with her morning question about my safety. But if things were truly that unsafe, Liam would have tried to get me to stay home. Nikki will be fine. We all will be fine.

I march past the throngs of people heading to the elevator banks and stop at the velvet ropes blocking the down escalator. Two additional security guards flank the regular guy. "Sorry, Ms. Green." He shrugs. "Everyone needs to show their IDs today."

"No worries." I take out my press pass and put it around my neck after the larger guard looks it over.

Additional security officers congregate in front of the TRP entrance at the bottom of the escalator, where they reexamine my press badge and search my purse. I get the all clear and step through the glass doors onto the working floor of TRP Sports—a rectangular room the size of a football field. I take in the familiar chaos—the blaring television screens, the shouting staff, the bodies rushing across the room. What I don't see is extra security, and I welcome the normalcy of these surroundings.

"Meeting in an hour," one of the producers calls to me as I walk toward the correspondents' section. "Although, I imagine you got the same 5:00 a.m. email as everyone else."

"Yes, I did."

I nod hello to the reporter at the desk next to me and slide into my chair, eager for the modest privacy afforded by the fabric dividers of my cubicle. I take a pen from my COFFEE TILL WINE mug, flicking my Yankees bobblehead with my finger. Seeing the figure reminds me of Alexa's role in transforming me into a fan. *If you're my bestie, you are required to support the Yankees. I don't care if you're from California. It's like a religion to me.* She said the last part while putting her hands together like she was praying.

I move my eyes away from the bobblehead and turn on my computer. Security alerts blast across the screen—Homeland Security elevated the threat level; the president will address the nation this afternoon.

I text Liam again: When can we talk?

He responds with a further delay: Be in touch soon. Stuck in task force meetings.

I'm trying to respect his request to talk before I investigate, but I'm not going to wait forever. And by no means does his request imply I can't review information on the internet. With nearly an hour to kill before Charlie's meeting, I want to learn as much about Alexa Kane as possible. I already read all the scandalous headlines. I'm interested in discovering more about her rise as a jewelry designer. I search for articles on her career and find a feature in *Vanity Fair* from a few years ago.

I'm once again struck by the image staring back at me. In the photo, Alexa looks twenty pounds lighter than the teen I knew. Her solid, muscular body has been replaced by waiflike limbs. Sharp angles and chiseled cheekbones highlight a face once round and full. She's gorgeous in a high-fashion way.

The magazine story begins with a description of Alexa's meteoric rise in the fashion industry, which of course, only *seemed* meteoric. *"It took much longer than people realize,"* Kane said as she perched on the edge of a velvet chair, swinging her Prada-clad foot. *"After graduating from the Fashion Institute of Technology, I bounced around from different jobs. I was very discouraged, but I also loved designing jewelry. I was doing the whole hustle—the trunk shows—and in walked Bethany Chang. I mean, the Bethany Chang."* At that point, Alexa's face lit up with childlike enthusiasm. *"She hired me, and we started working together. It was a dream come true."*

Even I know Bethany Chang. My ex insisted on buying me a Bethany Chang yellow diamond engagement ring. It was a bit much for my taste but came in useful when I caught him in our bed with his secretary. I divorced him, sold the ring, and used the money toward a down payment on my house.

I move on to an article in *People* magazine that describes Alexa and Bethany's collaboration, titled "The Dynamic JEWEL-O." Alexa's sprawled across an overstuffed pink sofa, red hair cascading over her shoulders, her bright-green eyes sparkling as she holds her arm up for the photographer to capture stones that mimic the colors of the couch, her eyes, and her hair. Chang lounges on an adjoining tall ruby plush chair, the same color as her chandelier-like pink diamond earrings encrusted with gold.

"Bethany has been more than a friend, she's been a sister, mentor—I owe everything to her," Alexa gushed, with her characteristic enthusiasm. Bethany Chang watched her protégée, the hint of a smile on her red lips. Where Alexa is effervescent, Bethany remains reserved. "I'm especially proud of the new collection we'll be releasing," Bethany added as she grasped the elegant diamond necklace around her throat.

"It's divine," Alexa said, flashing her brilliant smile.

"Something interesting?" David's voice startles me, and I look up. His hazel eyes dance as he flashes a mischievous smile. He leans down, pretending to look at my screen, and whispers in my ear about our date tonight. I feel flushed and order him to behave. He stands up and puts a little space between us. "Is that the woman who was murdered yesterday? Are you covering it?"

"I assume I am," I say to David. "Since it happened during the soccer game. But then again, who knows with Charlie."

"Ain't that the truth." David smiles. "What a tragedy. She was so young. And what a strange place for it to happen."

"I know."

David pulls an empty chair over and sits next to me, his brows furrowed. "I hope they find the person who sent the false post." He shakes his head. "It makes me concerned for our profession. I used to be proud to be a journalist." He sighs. "Now, most of the time, I'm embarrassed." David gives a sad smile and gets up, walking around the desks to his spot diagonally across from me.

I remember last year, David had the opportunity to break a huge story, and said no. The person he wanted to interview insisted on final say before the story aired. He wouldn't agree to those terms. I've always admired David's strong journalistic ethics.

David sends me a link to a *New York Magazine* article titled "War of the Gems." I look at him, and he winks at me from over the dividers. I feel my face flush again and quickly glance around to see if anyone noticed.

I open the article, and a full-page image depicts both women's faces photoshopped atop cartoon drawings of knights from the Middle Ages. Alexa sits on a large horse and clutches a jeweled spear, which she's thrust into the back of the Bethany knight.

The tagline in the article accuses Alexa of stabbing her mentor in the back. So much for subtlety.

"I would have supported Alexa if I had known she wanted to go out on her own," Bethany told this reporter. "But she did everything behind my back, including telling all my clients before I found out that she formed her own company. I took her in, taught her everything I knew. I thought of her as a younger sister. And then she turned on me."

The buzz around Manhattan is that younger influencers have already started canceling orders with Chang and are moving to Kane.

According to the article, at that point in the interview, Bethany became emotional and ran off, not returning for twenty minutes.

The most damning passage comes toward the end from Oscar-winning actress Cassandra Jorden: *"Bethany Chang was once one of the most popular jewelers in the industry. She became a household name similar to Tiffany and Cartier. But she lost her flare. She phones it in where Kane innovates."*

I lean back in my seat and think about what I read. Bethany Chang certainly has every reason to be angry at Alexa Kane. But even more reason to be angry with the actress. I wonder again about the lead my father mentioned on television. I glance back at the "War of the Gems" article and wonder if it's more likely Alexa's murder is tied to her recent skirmish in the design world. Or could it actually be related to Savy's and my history with her?

David's voice distracts me, and I glance up to see him pinching his lips.

"That's not what I said." His voice travels across the cubicles. He glances over to me, sees me watching, and turns his back. I can't hear anymore, but I observe the tension creeping up his neck. He slams his phone down on his desk, stands without even looking in my direction, and storms off.

Not your business, Kate, I tell myself.

CHAPTER 15

The conference room radiates nerves—thirty of us trapped at a long oval table inside an enclosed glass room. The only "private" space on the floor besides Charlie's office and edit bays. I sit toward the middle. David's across from me and chatting with another one of our colleagues. We came clean about our relationship to Human Resources but aren't sharing with anyone else at work. It's no one's business, we agreed.

About a dozen staff meetings like ours are taking place on different floors at NetWorld Headquarters. We represent the sideline / pre- and postgame staff. And we are among the few units off site and at the games. A large percentage of the coverage is done from the studio due to tightening budgets and upgraded technology.

I study the screens set into the front wall—the first two rows are tuned to our station and all our sister stations. The competitors occupy the bottom row. All TRP's stations are broadcasting the Olympics: TRP Sports—men's soccer, TRP2—women's beach volleyball, TRP Extra—archery. On and on. In contrast, the other stations focus completely on the aftermath of yesterday's stampede at Yankee Stadium and Alexa's murder. One channel shows a reporter in front of the hospital updating the injuries. Another, an interview with Mayor Compton. A third station shares glossy photos of Alexa with Bethany. On the bottom of those screens, the news ticker spews sensational statements: KILLER TERRORIZING NY? TAKE THESE PRECAUTIONS IF YOU ARE A SPECTATOR;

MANHATTAN BOROUGH PRESIDENT DEMANDS GAMES CANCELED. NEW YORKERS FED UP—CALL FOR MAYOR TO RESIGN. The clock shows 11:06 a.m. It's not like Charlie to be late. *Minutes count* is one of his favorite sayings. My phone vibrates with a call from Liam. *Of course he reaches out when I can't pick up.*

"That's all we need," the producer next to me mumbles, and I look up and see Charlie walking toward us with Junior Hutchinson next to him. "You know what it means when a Hutchinson makes an appearance?" he grumbles. "Layoffs. Fucking layoffs. And my youngest just started college."

I don't mention that Junior hinted yesterday at changes. Or that Charlie looked utterly frustrated talking to Wyatt. Maybe Junior's here to calm nerves. Although, I agree, a Hutchinson sighting is never good.

Junior strides through the door, a wide smile on his face. Gone is the boy from yesterday who cowered next to his father. Instead, Junior holds his head high, his shoulders back, and seems comfortable in his own skin.

"His suit probably costs more than I make in a year." The producer shakes his head in disgust. Junior wears a crisp navy suit, red tie, and cuff links that sparkle. He reeks of money. And power, in some ways. But yesterday I watched him get belittled by his father. I wonder which is the real Junior. Or, like many of us, is the answer both? I also tend to regress around Liam.

Junior must sense me studying him; he catches my eyes and winks. I squirm and look toward David, who raises a brow in what I take as sympathy.

Charlie clears his throat and moves to sit at the head of the table, but Junior slides into that seat. "Charlie, before you start, I'd just like to say something." Junior gives a Cheshire cat–like smile and waits for Charlie to take the seat next to him.

"Hello, everyone." Junior's voice rings unnecessarily loud, like he's used to speaking to large crowds. "For those of you who don't know me,

I'm Wyatt Hutchinson Junior. My friends call me Junior. All of you can call me Mr. Hutchinson." He smiles like he's joking, but no one laughs.

Junior moves on. "As most of you know I'm president of content for NetWorld, which means I oversee all the programming and staff. In short, I'm your boss. And your bosses' boss." He winks at Charlie. Another cringeworthy moment.

"Don't worry—no one is getting fired. Today." He laughs. No one else does.

Mr. Hutchinson tells everyone he's here to put people's minds at ease. "We are taking this . . . unfortunate *incident . . .* very seriously."

He outlines new security measures already put in place: extra private guards around the building, private officers available to accompany crews out in the field, an emergency number in case something appears suspicious. "You are the lifeblood of our Olympic coverage, and we do not want anyone to feel unsafe." He nods and looks around the room, attempting eye contact with us. It feels forced and uncomfortable, as if it's something he learned in a class but hasn't mastered: How to Connect with Your Staff. "If anyone has any concerns, please let me know."

David raises his hand, then stands. "Who allowed the false social media post onto our feeds?"

I didn't realize that the fake report ended up on TRP's social networks. David continues, "We had crews there. One of our own people could have been killed." He glances at me, and I feel as if everyone around must realize we are in a relationship.

Junior nods. "I agree with everything you are saying. While the false post was only on our feeds for a short time, it's still a disgrace that we amplified false information. I promise you, whoever is responsible will be dealt with." Junior looks at me. "We never want to put our staff in danger. I am investigating this incident personally. I promise to get to the bottom of it, David. Thank you for bringing it up."

David hesitates before sitting. I can tell he's trying to decipher whether Junior is being sincere.

Junior nods to Charlie to begin and then does the craziest thing. He remains seated.

Charlie stares at Junior. "You're staying?" Charlie says, again showing he doesn't have a political bone in his body. Says what he thinks.

"Would love to see my employees in action." Junior winks at all of us.

"Suit yourself." Charlie grimaces and turns to face us. "All our competition will be focusing on the murder and the stampede. You know why? Because they don't have the Olympics. They didn't shell out billions of dollars for the Olympics. And they're hoping this derails our first foray into the Olympics. It won't. Our focus will be Olympics. Olympics. And more fucking Olympics."

"This is why we keep him around," Junior interrupts.

Again, part joke. All truth. Charlie is good at his job. And has laser focus.

"But isn't murder part of the story?" I cut in. "Especially for women's soccer?"

"Not for us," Charlie says. "You need to focus on tomorrow's match against China."

Junior stands. "Kate." He flashes a broad smile in my direction. "You above everyone know how hard these players worked to get here. Imagine if this happened when you were playing. You wouldn't want the culmination of all you worked for to get sidetracked by some random, albeit unfortunate, crime."

He's not wrong, but his words feel manipulative. I'd rather Charlie just say, *Viewers want to see the games from us. Do your job.* At least I wouldn't feel like I need to shower off a ton of slime.

"In fact, an unforeseen consequence of the murder is that viewership increased overnight," Charlie adds.

Great. So, Alexa's murder and the stampede turned into a plus for TRP.

"And before any of you get on your high horse, complaining that my statement is unfeeling, or politically incorrect, I didn't kill her. I'm just stating facts." Charlie looks at me as if sensing I'd be the most likely to judge him. "So, everyone who has events to cover—it's business as usual." He ticks off the schedule—track and field, gymnastics, on and on.

"One small change for today," Charlie says. "All trainings are closed to the media at the moment. If you were scheduled to cover a training, you got lucky. We don't need reports from you. But take the day to prepare for tomorrow."

That means I don't have a report today—I won't ask twice about a little reprieve.

"One last thing," the assignment editor interrupts. "There was an issue with the server, and some emails from the last few days got clogged up. Keep an eye on your emails—some might pop up a few days late."

Charlie ends the meeting, and I follow the producer toward the front.

"Kate." Junior motions for me to come over. "A minute."

Junior extends his hand and gives a firm handshake. I decide not to overpower another Hutchinson and meet his strength but don't exceed it. Charlie seems confused by my presence.

"Is something wrong?" I ask.

"Not at all." Junior chuckles, and I smell the strong scent of a spiced aftershave. He pats my arm. "We actually have some exciting news, don't we, Charlie?"

"Not that I'm aware of." Charlie gathers his laptop, holding it against his wrinkled Oxford.

"The show," Junior says, as if reminding Charlie of something he forgot. But I can tell this is news to Charlie. And not pleasant news.

"I thought we already had that handled." Charlie glances across the room, where his eyes settle on David.

"Do you need a min—" I move to turn, but Junior puts his hand on my arm to stop me. His fingers are cold. I must appear startled, and he immediately drops his hand.

"No, that won't be necessary." He grins and tells me that I did a great job yesterday. "Your talent hasn't gone unnoticed," Junior says. I smile, feeling a small bubble of pride in my chest. I'm not unaware that the brass blows smoke up our asses. And that they were the ones who suspended me last year. But who doesn't like a compliment? Even from a Hutchinson.

"I don't know if you've heard about the new project in the works?" Junior continues. "*Behind the Game*—a half-hour weekly sports-magazine show."

I tell him I haven't, and he goes on to explain that it will be something they put up against ESPN's *30 for 30*, one of my all-time favorite programs. "Would you be interested in hosting?"

I'm speechless. Would I be interested in hosting a show like that? Hell yeah. I'd love to have a team, dive deep into topics, and not be in the daily grind. Not to mention a gig like that must come with a salary bump.

"I'm very interested," I tell Junior. And Charlie.

"Well, nothing is decided yet." Charlie gives Junior another sideways glance. "We've been in discussions with some other talent." Charlie turns to Junior and tells him he'd like to speak with him. In private.

"As far as I'm concerned, you've got the inside track, though," Junior whispers and follows Charlie out the door.

I'm processing the conversation so deeply that I don't notice David until he's right next to me. His face is red and his eyes distant. "Jesus, Kate . . ." He shakes his head. "Charlie told me I had the inside track."

"You were listening?" I say, stating the obvious because I saw David listening, although he made a show of fumbling with his phone. "I had no idea you were talking to Charlie about the show."

"Well, I have been. For months. You know Junior only offered it to you because he's mad I asked about the false report," David says.

"You think that little about my abilities that I'd only be offered a job to spite you?" I hear my voice shake.

"No, that's not what I meant," he says, but I'm already out the door. As I walk away, I can't help remembering the advice my stepfather gave me when I left for my first Women's National Camp. *Don't get attached—put on mental armor.* Does that go for reporting? My relationship with David? Can we date and work together?

I think I'm capable of it. But I'm a pretty good sport. I'm competitive, but I've also lost enough times in my life to shake it off and move on. This isn't my first rodeo. Is David a good sport too? We should discuss this more tonight. Set some ground rules—otherwise this situation will blow up in our faces. Unless it already has and I just don't know it yet.

CHAPTER 16
THEN

The U.S. Under-16 Women's National Team will compete in an international tournament in Madrid, Spain. The countries participating are the United States, France, England, Canada, Japan, Mexico, and Norway.

Alexa and I sat next to one another on the plane to Madrid. Alexa had never been to Europe. I went to France last year, a trip I'd rather forget. I barely played, and when I did, I was awful. I hoped this trip would be different. Alexa and I together and playing with our age group. It had to be, or I'd likely not make another national team. *This isn't a vacation,* the coaches had told us over and over again.

I sat on the aisle, Alexa in the middle, and a third teammate at the window. The teammate was really chatty. I wanted to catch up with Alexa, but she always made an effort to be nice.

"Are you excited for Madrid?" Alexa asked our teammate.

"Yes." She handed Alexa a magazine. "Did you see this article? Have you ever met her?"

I looked over Alexa's shoulder to see a photo of Savannah Baker gracing the cover of *Soccer Today* magazine. She wore a fierce smile that reached through the page and made my stomach flip. Alexa glanced at me, then read a few lines aloud.

"Savannah Baker is the face of the next generation of women's soccer. She's considered the most talented young player to come up in decades . . ."

I knew that after Savy's spectacular flameout at Alexa's and my first national camp, Savannah had redoubled her training and emerged a leader in her age group. But I hadn't realized she was considered the *most talented young player*. Barf.

"Thanks for sharing." Alexa handed the magazine back.

"Can we catch up now?" I whispered to Alexa, who giggled. Now that we were older, Alexa was fully developed. Tall, strong, her body full. I was still a little behind her, but not much.

Alexa passed me a note with big bubble letters and a secret message in the tiny stars. No one would hear us, but we liked communicating in our secret language. The bubble letters *USA* took up the whole page. This would be a long message. Possibly two words hidden in each letter.

I turned the page upside down and took out my compact mirror, which I'd bought recently since I started to wear makeup. I held the paper up to the mirror and studied the *U*. I found the letters— *DBNFSPO BOE*, which I wrote down and then decoded. "Cameron and—"

I knew from Alexa's last letter that she had gone on a date with a new boy in her high school named Cameron. Last I heard, nothing had come of it. She watched me, and I raised a brow. Alexa shook her head, refusing to tell me anything, and pointed at the paper.

Next, I wrote down the letters I found hidden in the *S*, of *USA*, and figured out the next part of the code: *I kissed*.

"Oh my God," I chirped, and she hushed me, her face flaming beet red. "What was it like?" I whispered, a little jealous because I hadn't done anything except play spin the bottle.

"Amazing." She beamed. The plane shook, and I grabbed the armrest. "Don't worry." She squeezed my hand. "We're fine."

"Is he your boyfriend?" I whispered.

"I think so." She smiled. "He asked me to the junior prom."

We spent the rest of the plane ride talking about what kind of dress she would get and how she would wear her hair. That was the most fun we had that trip. We might as well have been in California or Arizona, because we saw absolutely nothing of Madrid except the glorious photos hanging in our suburban hotel across from a parking lot.

But Alexa and I killed it on the field. They made her captain, and I was a starter. We won each game in our group round and faced Japan in the championship. The final match came down to penalty kicks. Alexa and I both made our shots, and we took the win when Japan's midfielder skyed her PK.

On the plane ride home, all Alexa and I could talk about was the next national camp, a few months away. That would be the camp of camps—where the coaches selected the roster for the U-17 World Cup. For us, the hugest stage we could possibly reach as teens. We vowed to bring our A game. We didn't even think about the fact we'd once again be a year younger than most players. Or, that we'd be back in competition with the treacherous Savannah Baker.

CHAPTER 17

I never wanted a nine-to-five job. The idea of punching a clock makes me ill. Tell me what tasks need completing, and I will get them done. For soccer, I was responsible for my additional fitness, training, nutrition, sleep. TRP provides a similar freedom. If I'm not on assignment, I can sit at my desk or leave—as long as I'm prepared for my story. And no one could be more prepared for tomorrow's match against China than me. Except for, of course, the actual players and coaches.

With a free day in front of me, I dial Liam back.

"We finally connect," he says as if he's called me multiple times instead of the other way around. I hear street noises in the background, cars honking and a siren.

"Where are you?" I ask.

"On my way to the Bronx," he says over the sounds of traffic.

"To track down the promising lead the mayor mentioned on television?" I ask, grabbing my bag from my desk and swinging it over my shoulder. My eyes linger on David, who keeps his gaze focused on his computer screen. Either he's reading something fascinating or he's intentionally avoiding me.

"Guess what," I say into the phone and start toward the exit. "It's your lucky day—today is *bring your daughter to work* day. I have the afternoon off and can meet up with you."

He starts to protest, then swallows his words and shifts gears. He can't put me off any longer.

"I'm assuming I don't have a choice?" he says in his raspy voice.

"You don't," I answer, adding that I owe it to Alexa. "I'll explain in person."

"You're a piece of work." He sighs, but mixed with resignation, I hear a touch of pride. "I'll text you the location." He hangs up.

I arrive at the Yonkers Pawn Shop in the Bronx before Liam. At first glance, the sign reads **PAW SHOP** due to the crooked *n* hanging by a nail. I sit on the bench at the corner and study the narrow store with bars across the windows. Two patrol officers loiter in front, sipping coffee. Definitely too casual for the actual suspect to be inside. A teenager in a bathing suit zips past the officers on a stand-up scooter, pivots around them, then nearly knocks into a three-foot plastic replica of the Statue of Liberty on the sidewalk in front of the neighboring souvenir shop. His scooter wobbles, but he puts his foot down in time to keep from crashing onto concrete.

Liam's navy Chevy pulls under the subway bridge as the 1 train thunders overhead. I walk over while he greets the two patrol officers, patting one on the back. They smile up at him, speaking softly as I approach.

"This is my daughter," Liam says and gives me a little hug and half smile. The officers wait for more information, but he doesn't provide any, and I follow him to the entrance. "Let me do all the talking," he says and opens the door, a bell ringing as we step inside.

This is my first time in a pawn shop. It looks like a hoarder's paradise. Tons of objects stuffed into cases, displayed on shelves, and perched on the dingy rug. I see clocks, vases, jewelry, guitars—a fire-engine red moped.

Another police officer stands in the back next to a bent figure behind a counter. The man appears about eighty and wears a tweed jacket with a bow tie, despite the heat. I feel another bout of sweat across my back just looking at him.

"I saw the news about that jewelry designer getting murdered." He speaks with a strong Bronx accent, his *t*'s sounding more like *d*'s—*da news about dat jewelry designer.* "But I wasn't the one who made the connection to the piece." At this point, the officer holds up a bracelet already inside an evidence bag. I recognize the design—thin rope gold with dozens of gems and diamonds set among the precious metal. The bracelet matches what I saw on Alexa's arm last night. Did she have more on her wrist? One that the murderer removed?

"I paid a pretty penny for this." The man rubs his nose. "It's worth even more, though. The guy selling was in a rush. He settled for ten thousand. It's worth double."

He tells us his daughter came by an hour ago on her way to work. "She's a nurse. She recognized the style and told me it was created by the designer who got murdered yesterday at the stadium." He takes out a handkerchief and dabs his forehead. "A lot of people probably have her stuff, I'd imagine . . . but my daughter insisted I call the police. 'It's too much of a coincidence,' she said. You know daughters—they'll nag you till you listen."

Liam glances at me before telling the man that he did the right thing. "Do you have security footage?" Liam asks.

"I knew you'd ask." He smiles and hands Liam a VHS tape. "You got an old machine that can play this?"

"We do have *one* back at the station." He thanks the owner, and we head out of the store along with the cop from inside. "Haven't been handed a VHS tape in at least a decade." He shakes his head and gives the tape to the officer. "Get this tape to tech and the bracelet to forensics. Maybe we'll get lucky and find something."

Liam watches them drive off. I notice the dark circles under Liam's eyes and ask him when he ate last.

"I can't remember." Liam shrugs as the subway rattles above. I suggest we duck into the pizza place on the corner.

Liam hesitates, glancing at his phone. "I guess I can spare five minutes—"

"You won't be any use to the task force if you pass out from starvation." I pull his arm in the direction of the restaurant. We step inside to a welcome blast of air-conditioning, order slices and root beers, and take a booth in the back.

I settle into the orange vinyl seat as Liam slides across from me, his drink sloshing over the sides and spilling onto his hands. I give him a napkin and ask him to catch me up on the case.

Liam leans back in his seat, watching me.

"I want to help with the investigation," I say to him. "I knew Alexa in a way few people did." My eyes move to my father's eyes. "Besides, I owe her."

"Am I right to assume you will pursue this with or without me?" he asks.

"You are."

He picks up his pizza and takes a bite, appearing to think while chewing. "If we do this, you have to promise to come to me at the slightest hint of danger. I mean it, Kate. No repeats of last time."

"Agreed," I say. What I don't say is that I would have come to him last time if he hadn't dismissed my theories.

"Truth is, I could use your brain," Liam says, picking up his drink and taking a sip. "You're smarter than the whole lot of them on this task force."

I don't know if he means it or is still trying to win me over. Either way, I feel pleased with the compliment. Since Liam and I reconnected, discussing police cases has provided safe ground. I've become a sounding board for Liam during the last months. I enjoy the mental task of puzzling out cases and scenarios. And he's enjoyed the opportunity to bond. And maybe gain some insight or help. But in those situations, Liam didn't share real names or details. Most of what we discussed was framed in hypotheticals. Now is different. An active high-profile case where I knew the victim and was among those to find her.

"Have you spoken with Alexa's parents?" I dive right in. "I believe she also had a younger sister."

"Her father passed away recently. We tried to speak with her mom, but she was really shaken up. We have some officers stationed there. The sister was on her way from the West Coast . . . probably arriving around now." He checks his watch.

"I noticed the forensic team swabbing outside the locker room."

"There were some spots of blood on the cinder blocks," he says, taking a big bite of pizza, cheese dripping down his chin. He puts up a finger as he keeps chewing. Then takes another bite and another. "They match Alexa's blood. There were also fibers and defensive wounds."

"Which means someone assaulted her in the tunnel and then dragged her inside and drowned her?"

"There aren't drag marks."

"So, the person needed to be somewhat strong to lift her," I say, turning over this new information. Alexa was five feet, eight inches, one inch taller than me. "I'm assuming you've examined her phone and computers. Anything interesting?" I ask, nibbling on my slice.

Liam takes a sip of soda and then tells me the tech team hasn't pulled up anything of interest on her computer. "Her phone was in the tub and sustained a lot of damage. The tech team was able to recover most of her messages . . ."

"And?"

"There was one message that came through during halftime. We haven't been able to track down the number."

"That could be the murderer," I think aloud. "Did she disappear around then?"

"It seems that way. But we still have a lot of work to do before we can confirm the timeline." He pushes his empty plate forward and wipes his mouth.

Up front, two teenagers walk in, holding hands and giggling. I wonder if Alexa and Cameron went on dates to get pizza. *Focus, Kate,* I tell myself, thinking about Alexa's Instagram posts from yesterday. She posed yesterday from the gold luxury box, coincidentally next to the platinum box. I was physically so close to her. Did I pass her in the hallway without noticing? The thought makes me shiver.

"Alexa posted a bunch of Instagram photos before the game," I say. "But I didn't see anything once halftime hit."

"Security footage shows Alexa leaving the gold box at halftime. We are getting mixed reports on why she disappeared. One witness said she went to get a bite to eat. Another said she had words with a former colleague."

"Bethany Chang?" I ask.

"You read about the—War of the Gems?"

"Yup."

"Bethany is down at headquarters now, being interviewed by Special Agent Flynn."

"The charmer from yesterday."

Liam ignores my swipe at his coworker, returning to the crime. "Bethany certainly had motive. We're just trying to figure out if she had access. Who knows, maybe she coordinated with the clown who tried to sell the bracelet to the pawn shop."

I wonder about that. Why would a fancy designer have someone steal a bracelet and bring it to a pawn shop? It doesn't make a lot of sense. Unless grabbing the bracelet wasn't part of the plan. I move on to my next question, knowing that any second, I will likely lose Liam to another task force meeting.

"Any word from the coroner?"

The teenagers take their pizza and drinks and sit behind us. The boy takes out his cell phone and holds it up to take a selfie of the two of them.

"We got a preliminary report from the coroner." Liam glances over his shoulder to see what I'm looking at. He leans toward me and whispers, "The cause of death is drowning."

I think about that for a minute. If Alexa drowned, then she was alive when she was dumped into the tub. Did the perpetrator force her into the water and hold her down? Or was she already unconscious? "Can they tell if she was conscious when she was put into the water?"

"As of now, they can't determine that. Not sure if they will ever be able to. I'm talking to the coroner later."

"There's something that I can't figure out," Liam says, and I can tell the great Liam Murphy is about to ask for my help. "Why do you think there were no signs of forced entry? I would have bet money the locker room door would have been bolted. And it's not an easy lock to pick."

"The locker room doors get left open more than you'd think," I say, telling him about a time during a professional soccer game when a stalker hid in the locker room and attacked a teammate of mine. "We were able to pull him away quickly. But he got in."

Liam sounds disbelieving. "Security's been intense."

"That's true." Even before yesterday, cops were swarming all over the stadium, but where the public was. "Security wasn't crazy in the tunnel, though," I say. "It would have been really hard to get into the locker room. But not impossible." I take a bite and think about it a little more. "The plastic," I say.

"What?" He sounds confused. I explain that a work crew must have accessed the locker room at some point to put the protective plastic over the lockers. "It was there after the game," I explain.

"So, you think someone on the crew did this?" he says, trying to connect the dots.

"Not necessarily," I say. "They could have just left the door open, by accident. But that would mean that the killer didn't necessarily plan to dump the body in the bath."

"Or that they had access on their own."

We sit in silence a minute, thinking through all the scenarios.

"I'm surprised you came to the pawn shop yourself," I say. "I'd think you'd have a whole task force of people at your disposal."

"I do," he says. "But I wanted to get my own read on the owner . . . just in case he was covering up something." He looks off a minute. "I can't go to everything. I'm sending a few task force members to the candlelight vigil this evening."

"What vigil?" I take a last bite of pizza and crumple up my paper plate.

"Alexa's family is holding a small vigil outside her high school. They've been trying to keep it out of the media. Don't tell anyone." He gives me a look. "But we're helping coordinate security with the local Great Neck Police Department."

"And you never know who will show up—"

"Correct." He checks his watch. "I really need to go. But first, are you ready to tell me about your connection to Alexa?"

I put my soda down and take a deep breath. "As ready as I'll ever be."

CHAPTER 18
THEN

U.S. Under-17 Women's National Team

> *Dear Kate,*
> *You are invited to the U.S. Under-17 Women's National Camp from August 7 through August 14. We will make our final decision here regarding the roster for the Under-17 World Cup roster.*
>   *This is the highest honor a youth player can achieve.*
> *Good luck.*

I brought Alexa a pink Yankees hat as a gift. Alexa never outgrew her obsession with the Yankees. In fact, she told me that a prerequisite for agreeing to go out with Cameron was that he pass her Yankees quiz. I think she was kidding. Maybe. She actually made me take the quiz. I passed—barely.

"Thanks," she mumbled, tossing the hat to the ground without even a glance. I felt a little hurt; usually she was so excited when I brought her something. Maybe she already had a pink Yankees hat? Now that I thought of it, the present was probably stupid.

"I'm going to head to the gym." Alexa took out leggings and a T-shirt and started toward our bathroom.

"You getting shy?" I laughed because we'd always changed in front of one another.

She didn't answer, just closed the door.

At dinner, we stood in the line together, waiting for our food. Alexa was quieter than usual. "Did something happen with Cameron?" I asked as we took a seat at an empty table.

"Why would you think my mood has to do with a boy?" she snapped. "Sorry, Kate. I didn't mean that. I'm having a bad day."

"It's all right," I said and started to eat my pasta.

"Can I sit here?" A new girl approached our table. The coaches were always rotating in a small number of players.

"Sure." I motioned toward an empty seat. Then Alexa cut me off.

"No." She blocked the spot with her hand. "Newbies in the back."

The girl's eyes filled with tears, but she scurried off. "Alexa? What's going on?" I turned to her, shocked.

"We need to watch out for ourselves this week," she said, stuffing a large bite of spaghetti into her mouth. "This is the World Cup. It's not about being nice. It's about winning."

Alexa's actions surprised me. They resembled Savannah's treatment of us all those years ago. I always thought of Alexa as the anti-Savy.

Maybe Alexa's coach told her something similar to what my stepfather had told me years earlier. Still, her reaction to the girl seemed extreme. I wanted to ask her more, but after the night's scrimmage, she went back to the gym to run on the treadmill, and by the time she returned to our room, I was sound asleep.

On the field, Alexa was incredible. Even better than two months ago in Spain. She had an edge to her play—running every ball down, taking on each defender with a fierceness I'd never seen. Even Savy steered clear of her.

Alexa did everything with verve that week. Although, when we needed to go for our weigh-in, she asked me to tell the trainers she wasn't feeling well.

On the final day, the coach posted the roster. We pushed forward and saw both our names on the list. I was ecstatic. I grabbed Alexa and started to hug her.

"Kate." She pulled away. "Stay calm. We still have a long way to go. We can't let up." She told me she was going back to the gym for a nighttime workout before bed.

"Not even a break to sneak a chocolate bar from the vending machine?" I was sure I could entice her with that.

"No," she said and walked off.

I realized later I had fallen asleep before she returned. At first, when I heard loud knocking, I assumed it was Alexa and she had forgotten her key. But when I opened my eyes, I saw Alexa passed out on the bed next to me, still in her sweats and a T-shirt.

I went to the door, opened it, and before I could focus, felt something slip over my head. "Stay still." Savy's accent was unmistakable. I remembered my stepfather warning me that I might encounter some hazing rituals. *If it's not bad, just go with it. But if it's serious, let the coaches know. Your safety is the priority.* He said they might make us do funny dances. Maybe play truth or dare. I wasn't sure where covering our heads with bags fell on his spectrum. But I decided to go with it for now.

I felt hot breath through the rough material around my head. "Don't speak or else . . . ," a second voice, which I recognized as Shira's, ordered. The bag lifted, and something sticky got pressed against my lips. This was not all right. I started to panic and tried to remember the breathing exercise Alexa had taught me on the bus of our first training camp. Then I realized I couldn't take a breath through my mouth because of the tape. I felt my pulse rise. *Remember, Kate,* I told myself. *You handled the hard stuff—making the roster. You can get through this.*

I reached out my hands, trying to orient myself—looking for a bed or dresser or Alexa.

"Hands down." Savy swatted my arm, and I felt the burn on my skin as someone wrapped rope around my wrists.

"Do not make a noise," she said, then laughed. "Oh, that's right. You can't."

Another girl also giggled; then I heard the sound of a high five.

Shira grabbed my arm and jerked me forward. I could tell it was her by the spearmint gum she always chewed. I stumbled but remained on my feet. In my brain, I was screaming for Alexa. Finding her would calm me. Was I the only one being taken away? Or was she near? What about the other two girls our age who also made the team?

"Step down," Shira ordered, and I placed my foot down and immediately pulled back. We were moving outside. "Go." She bumped me forward, and I stumbled again.

The sound of crickets reached my ears—so much louder than I'd ever heard, heightened by my inability to see. Below the chirping, I was aware of something else. I strained to listen. It sounded like whimpering. "Stop crying, baby," Savy yelled.

If Savy was yelling at someone, I knew at least one other girl was with me. But now, I hoped it wasn't Alexa, because whoever it was seemed to be crying.

A pain shot through my toe. I tried to hop and reach for the pebble or rock stuck on my foot, but Shira pushed me on. I jammed my back into her, but she just shoved me harder. "Don't make this worse on yourself," she said, and I couldn't decide if she was trying to help or hurt me.

I heard a car door open and felt a hand on my back pushing me forward. I stumbled down and groped around, finding a car seat. "Get in," Savy ordered.

That was the first time I became aware of Alexa. She was already in the car—I smelled her strawberry shampoo. Her whole body shook, and I heard her crying through the tape. I reached my hand to hers, hoping to reassure her.

"No touching," a voice from the front ordered, and she swatted my tied wrists. How had they even gotten a car?

Every time they turned, I fell onto Alexa or she fell onto me. She was still shaking and whimpering. We drove for about half an hour, until the road got bumpy. It felt like the car turned onto gravel or dirt. Alexa started shaking harder. I wanted to tell the girls to stop. But I also felt like we must be nearing the end of their trial. Plus, I had tape over my mouth and couldn't speak if I wanted to.

The car stopped, and an arm grabbed me and jerked me from the car. My knee scraped the door. Shira pushed me to the ground.

"Stay on your knees," Savy ordered. The ground was cold and sticky, like we were in mud.

I didn't dare move. Then I heard giggles and a car drive away. My mind immediately went to next steps. Remove the bag, get the tape off.

I wriggled my hands free, then pulled the bag off. I blinked Alexa into focus—curled in a fetal position in the mud, whimpering. I ripped the tape from my mouth and stepped to her. "Alexa." I picked up her head and rested it in my lap. "It's over. We're okay."

I bent my head down to look into her eyes, but she stared passed me, as if she didn't see me at all.

The other two sixteen-year-olds were also here and ran over to me, trying to sooth Alexa. Her body rocked back and forth on my lap. Alexa was scaring us more than Savy had. I scanned the thick woods, not recognizing our surroundings. "Do either of you know where we are?"

"No." They shrugged.

"I hear a car in the distance," I said, listening to our surroundings. "There must be a road down that hill." I pointed behind us, where a light blinked through the dark pine trees. "You guys go try to find someone to call 911. Alexa needs a hospital."

They agreed and ran off. Talk about a trust exercise. Part of me worried they wouldn't come back once they left.

I held Alexa's hand and spoke to her. "Everything's all right. It's over." I didn't believe my own words. I was terrified for her. It's like she had traveled into a different dimension where I couldn't reach her. Like a demonic being had overtaken her body.

I began to distinguish parts of the environment. Behind me the pine trees were thicker and taller than the ones to my left. The mud puddle where Savy and her friends had dumped us was in the middle of a small clearing. Beer bottles and food wrappers littered the ground, suggesting this was a spot people came to hang out. Images of every scary movie I'd ever seen flashed into my brain as I feared each little noise.

A glimmer of light lifted into the trees—the sun rising. The light made me feel a little safer, but it also made me wonder what was taking my teammates so long. How hard would it be to track down a house with a phone? Did something happen to them? Shouldn't medics have already found us?

The sound of tires reached me. I remember relief flooding my body until I caught sight of my teammates. Where were the doctors?

"Oh no." Shira sprinted to Alexa. "It's all right. Everything's all right."

"Stop it," Savy ordered. "Let's get her in the car. She'll be fine."

"We need to get her to a hospital," I screamed as they lifted Alexa from me and placed her into the car. "She needs a doctor!"

Shira walked me toward the car. I was yelling but didn't feel connected to my voice. "Where's the closest hospital?" I yelled. "Where? How far?"

"Quiet. Quiet!" Savy ordered. Shira put her hands on my shoulders and shook me until I stopped speaking.

"We are not taking her to the hospital," Savy said in a matter-of-fact tone.

I looked at Shira, who urged me into the back seat, Alexa leaning on me.

"Savannah, she needs to go to the hospital. Look at her. She's in some kind of trance," I said, my hands stroking Alexa's hair. Savy ignored me, driving on a main road before turning into the hotel lot, and I realized we were already back. They must have taken us on a joyride before dumping us in the park.

"If we were so close, why did it take so long for you to get me and Alexa?" I asked.

"We had to think," Savy said as she motioned to Shira to help carry Alexa out of the car.

"I'll get the coaches," I said, figuring the coaches, at least, would take Alexa to the hospital.

"You will do no such thing," Savy yelled as we walked into the hotel and back to my room, which was somehow open.

They put Alexa on the bed; then Savy turned to me, placing her hands on my shoulders. She was still bigger and stronger than me. "Here's what we will do. You will tell the coaches that Alexa woke up crying. Suggest she had a bad dream. But you will *not* tell them about our little outing. Or that we *borrowed* the trainer's car. Do you understand?"

"She needs a doctor," I say, realizing they must have stolen the car and didn't want to get exposed for that on top of everything else.

"The coaches will get the team doctor. But that's what you'll tell them, unless you don't care about your soccer future." She raised her brow, making her threat clear. If I didn't follow her instructions, she'd find a way to get me kicked off the team.

"Savy, please," I cried. "Please, she needs help."

"And she'll get it as long as you agree." Savy folded her arms across her chest. I looked at Shira, who hesitated and then nodded her agreement.

"Fine," I yelled and started to run from the room, but Savy grabbed me.

"First change out of your muddy pajamas," Savy ordered.

I did as I was told and tore down the hall in search of the head coach. Somehow I mumbled Savy's nonsense and urged them to get the doctor.

I don't remember how long it took for the staff to descend on our room or to break Alexa from her trance. I'm not even sure I was there when she got better. At some point, the coach made me leave and sleep with my teammates.

I do remember waking up in the morning; my first thought was that the incident had been a bad nightmare. Then I realized I was on the couch in a different room. I ran through the hall back to my room, where I found Alexa packing her suitcase.

"Alexa, are you all right?" I rushed over to her and put my hand on her arm.

"Don't!" She pulled away and zipped up her suitcase.

"What are you doing?" I asked, reaching for her again. "Are you all right. I was so worried. What happened? I wanted to take you to the hospital, but Savy, she—"

Alexa turned to me, her green eyes cold. Her voice low and detached. "Don't ever talk to me again, Kate. We are no longer friends." Then she picked up her suitcase, walked past me, and out the door. It was the last time I saw Alexa alive.

CHAPTER 19

Liam must have guessed I would go to the candlelight vigil. It was inevitable once he mentioned it. I feel so much regret where Alexa is concerned. It's not like I didn't think about her—a Yankees game would pop on screen, or I'd pick up a caramel cluster. I'd remember her bright eyes and enthusiastic smile. But something always stopped me. Probably shame.

I arrive in Great Neck early. The main street feels so familiar even though I've never been here. I drive by the movie theater where Alexa had her first date with Cameron, the deli where she'd carbo-load on crispy fries, and the chocolate store where she bought us treats. *You need to try these,* she said the first time she presented me with the small white box stuffed with peanut butter–caramel clusters. *If you only get chocolate once in a while, it must be these.*

Alexa's high school looks just the way she described it—like something out of the *Archie* comic book. *It is a gorgeous school, like a private school,* she told me as she explained how much money her friends' families had. People are already gathered on the lush front lawn, which reminds me of some of the small colleges Nikki and I recently visited. I follow a Mercedes to the back parking lot, watching as two women emerge from the car.

The first wears a loose top over a very pregnant belly with a matching short skirt. The other looks like a toothpick in skinny jeans, with a rhinestone-studded tank top. Louis Vuitton totes swing from their shoulders as they clasp bouquets of roses. I get out of my car and walk behind them, wondering if they were Alexa's classmates. Maybe people she told stories about? *The girl who got a nose job at thirteen?*

The women wind their way to the front of the school, where a makeshift shrine commemorates Alexa. Candles glow from inside cylinder glass jars, casting shadows over photos. Flowers are scattered across the concrete steps at the entrance of the building. They stop in front of a photo of Alexa and a boy I recognize as her first boyfriend—Cameron.

The one wearing the rhinestone top bends down and places her bouquet next to the photo, an Alexa Kane bracelet dangling from her wrist. "Everything about her was so . . . unexpected."

The pregnant woman asks what she means as she, too, bends to place her bouquet down.

"I don't know. She just seemed to have a dark side."

Pregnant lady nods, looking a bit bored as she scans the growing crowd gathering on the lawn.

"I think she had a breakdown senior year," the rhinestone woman whispers to her friend. That gets the other woman's attention.

"Didn't your brother go out with her?" the pregnant woman asks, uncapping a bottle of water and taking a sip.

"Forever. Then her junior year, she just dumped him," rhinestone woman says. I think back to my last time rooming with Alexa. Had she mentioned breaking up with Cameron?

"Was it because of soccer? Wasn't she really good?" Behind us, I hear a man counting into a microphone, "One, two, three. Test, one, two, three."

"She was an amazing soccer player. Alexa got selected to play in the youth World Cup when she was sixteen. And then she quit. It was so weird. Playing on the national team was all she talked about when she'd stay over for dinner."

Guilt floods my insides. Again.

"She went to boarding school her senior year, right?" The pregnant woman is fully engaged in the conversation now.

"I forgot about that. Yeah. Word is her parents sent her away."

Someone waves to the women, and they walk off. My eyes scan the rest of the photos, landing on our World Cup team photo taken just after we got selected. Alexa and I stand in the front, my arm over her shoulder. I'm grinning ear to ear, but she's frowning. At the time, I thought she was trying to mimic Savy, who always gave a death stare in photos, looking tough and intimidating. But Alexa actually looks more sad than anything else.

I wipe a tear from my cheek and walk toward the crowd at the edge of the sidewalk, where candles are being handed out. The crowd has swelled to over one hundred. I get in line in front of a folding table, raising my arm to block the sun, which hangs low in the sky. A woman hands me a Dixie cup with a thin candle placed inside. I take mine and join the group gathering in front of a podium on the lawn.

"Can I light that candle for you?" a sad-eyed man in a baseball cap flicks his lighter, and I hold out my candle. His dry, brittle hands don't match the handsome, forlorn face staring back.

"Cameron." A woman approaches and holds out her Dixie cup. "Can you light mine also?" As he reaches the lighter toward the candle, her neck flushes. "Thanks, Cameron. And if you need me to cover more shifts at the restaurant, I'm your girl." She smiles. Too bright.

"Thanks, Ginny." He walks off. Cameron? Restaurant? I tap the girl's shoulder.

"Hi," I say. "I'm a friend of Alexa's from soccer. Was that *the* Cameron? Her boyfriend?"

The girl studies me from behind wire-rimmed glasses. "Yes, he's so committed and caring. She broke his heart when she ended things."

"In high school?" *That was so long ago.*

She laughs, like I live on another planet. "I don't think he'd still be mourning a high school breakup, silly," she says, in a voice unusually high for an adult. "She broke up with him last week. He was sure this time they'd end up getting married. Between us, he'd even bought her an engagement ring. He showed it to me at the restaurant. He's the owner and chef of Cameron's Place. He's a genius. His food beats any Manhattan restaurant hands down."

"You work with him?" I ask, hoping to encourage her to keep speaking, although she's already the chatty type.

"I'm the weekend hostess. I work Saturday and Sunday nights. I want to work more hours, but I'm also stuck taking care of my mom." She rolls her eyes. "I grew up next door to Alexa. She was my neighbor." Ginny reaches for her hair, patting down the frizz. "How did you know Alexa again?"

"We played soccer together. When we were young."

"You look familiar," she says. "Did you go to school here?"

"We played together on youth national teams. I'm in one of the photos on the stairs," I say, hoping to keep her from making the connection between me and television me. *A reporter's here. Get her out.*

"She used to love soccer—" Ginny says, her mind seeming to travel over a memory. "I couldn't believe how easily she gave it up. When we were little, she always talked about wanting to play in the Olympics." She studies me again. "Did you play in the Olympics?"

"I did."

"Aren't you a reporter?" She folds her arms over her chest and glances around. She's debating whether to call me out. I can feel it.

"I'm not here as a reporter. I'm here as a friend," I say. She's weighing what to do—I need to distract her. "What kind of food do they serve at Cameron's Place?" I give her my biggest *you can trust me* smile.

"OMG—it's the best. Seriously, he's phenomenal. It's American fusion. The dishes look like pieces of art. My favorite is the pistachio-crusted tuna. It's divine." The two women from earlier walk by us, one of their designer totes hitting Ginny in the arm.

Ginny's face flames red. "That's Cameron's sister. She's a bitch." She adjusts her glasses. "I'm sorry. She just made my last years in high school miserable."

"That's awful," I say. "Was she friends with Alexa?"

"She pretended to be nice to Alexa." Ginny leans closer in a conspiratorial way. "But she always talked behind her back. Between us, she told everyone she thought Cameron was way too good for Alexa."

Ginny and I are interrupted by a man at the podium. We walk over and stand in a semicircle with the other people. The service starts with the Kane family's rabbi, who struggles with his own emotions. "I knew Alexa since she was a baby." He chokes back tears as he describes all her accomplishments. As he speaks, I look around at the men and women gathered on the lawn. A man hands a tissue to his wife. A cluster of women stand close together, arms around one another.

My focus returns to the rabbi as he wraps up. "We will remember her most for her verve. So much enthusiasm and energy, that one. Always a giant smile on her face."

Next, the high school chorus sings Eric Clapton's "Tears in Heaven." As the voices carry across the grass, I imagine Alexa perched on a blanket, sitting here with friends while laughing and joking. Or puzzling over math homework, her least favorite subject.

The rabbi announces the final speaker, and I watch Alexa's mother, Harriet Kane, approach the podium. Her eyes red and hollow. Her voice strong and bitter. "Alexa was the light of our family. A beautiful girl. Thank God her father passed—because this would have killed him. This is just beyond comprehension. I'm so angry I could explode." Harriet's whole body quivers. "Alexa was thriving. She began talking about starting a family. Her career was flourishing. And I want to let the authorities know, they better solve this case. Because I, for one, will not rest until the hateful maniac who did this is behind bars."

Scattered murmurs and applause sound from the grass. *You tell them, Harriet. We're with you.* Her anger will morph into despair at some point. But, I imagine, the anger is easier right now. "Alexa was a fighter. Even when things got tough." She looks out at the crowd, her eyes traveling across the bodies. Her gaze falls on me. Does she recognize me after all these years?

The moment passes, and I'm not sure if I imagined it or not. It's been thirty years since Harriet Kane flew across the country to confront me about Alexa. But at this moment, it feels like yesterday.

CHAPTER 20
THEN

Alexa's mother showed up at our house in Berkeley two months after the hazing incident. One week before our team would leave for the World Cup. I was in the yard running through my agility drills when my mom came to the back door and called me inside. "Someone wants to ask you a few questions." She put her hands on my shoulders. "It's about a friend."

I racked my brain, trying to figure out if something had happened at school, and came up with nothing. I didn't recognize the small woman perched on the edge of the living room chair, thin hands twisting together. She removed large round sunglasses when she spotted me and stood up.

"Hello, Kate." She extended her arm. "I'm Harriet Kane—Alexa's mother."

I barely shook her hand before retreating to the couch. Had Alexa told her what happened in the woods? Did she plan to report me? Was I about to get kicked off the team?

I squirmed on the couch across from her. My mom seated on one side of me, my stepfather on the other.

I pulled my legs under me to keep from fidgeting. When I'd come home after the hazing incident, I tried to reach Alexa over the phone.

Each time her mother told me Alexa was busy. I wrote Alexa a letter and hid a cheery secret message inside the bubble letters. She never responded.

I figured if Alexa wanted space, I needed to give it to her. Besides, life got busy. With the World Cup around the corner, I turned my focus to training. I ran in the morning and after school. Worked out at the gym when I wasn't playing with my team.

Then the packet arrived outlining all the details about the World Cup, from travel to training to rooming assignments. I was put with the goalie Shira. I figured Alexa had requested a new roommate. But when I searched the roster, Alexa wasn't listed. I tried calling her again. That time her mother had been more direct, telling me Alexa didn't want to speak with me.

Mrs. Kane dove in, her words tight and pointed. "Why didn't Alexa want to speak with you after the last training camp? Did you do something to her?"

I felt my mom's eyes on me as I shrugged my shoulders.

"What happened, Kate? She used to run to the phone when you called."

"I didn't do anything," I said, so softly she leaned in to hear.

Mrs. Kane lowered her voice to a whisper and tried to smile. "You're not in trouble. I'm just trying to figure things out," she said, attempting a different approach. "Please tell me what happened at that camp."

I just shrugged again.

My mom jumped in to fill the silence: "Kate never said anything about a problem with Alexa." Mom turned to me, eyes questioning. "Did something happen?"

I shook my head but couldn't form words.

Mrs. Kane ignored my mom and kept glaring at me. I felt her eyes, even as I refused to look up. "Kate, are you the reason Alexa quit soccer?"

"No!" My head shot up at the question.

"Are you accusing Kate of doing something?" My stepfather put a protective arm around me. "That's not why you told us you wanted to speak with our daughter."

I saw my brother through the window, riding his bike down the street, and I wished I could blink myself outside with him. Mrs. Kane leaned forward. "I'm sorry I sounded like I was blaming you. I know teens have their drama."

"Mrs. Kane—" my stepfather warned.

"Did anything strange occur at the last training camp?" Mrs. Kane asked.

"Like what?" I pressed my back into the couch as if the cushions could protect me from her glare.

My stepdad turned to me. "Kate, something very serious happened. Alexa tried to hurt herself. She almost died."

"What?" I felt as if someone had punched me. Had I caused Alexa to attempt suicide?

"Did anything strike you as odd?" my stepfather continued.

I remembered Savy's warning that there would be repercussions if we didn't stick to her story that Alexa had woken up screaming in bed. And I had no doubt Savy would deliver on her threat. *Besides,* Savy had said, *we don't really know the cause of her breakdown.*

"The last night of the camp, she started shaking and screaming in her sleep," I said, my voice soft. My parents already knew this part.

Mrs. Kane narrowed her eyes. "Something must have triggered that reaction. That's never happened to Alexa before. What did you girls do to her?" She stands. "You tell me now, Kate Green. My daughter slit her wrists and nearly drowned in her bathtub."

I shrank into my stepfather's arms, sobbing.

"We didn't do anything. I swear." I cried harder.

Mrs. Kane reached to grab my shoulders, but my stepfather jumped up and interceded, pushing Mrs. Kane away from me.

"Kate would never lie." My stepfather pulled her toward the door. "I am sorry about Alexa, but you need to leave."

He opened the door. All the while she kept yelling, "I know you're lying, Kate Green. I know you're lying."

I bolted from the couch and ran to my room, tears pouring down my cheeks as I threw myself onto the floor. I was inconsolable. My parents thought I was upset about Mrs. Kane's accusations and Alexa's suicide attempt. They weren't wrong. But I was mostly disgusted with myself. I wanted to rip my insides out of my body. I vowed that moment never to lie again. But I kept the secret. That one secret.

CHAPTER 21

The service ends with a moment of silence. Dusk settles across the horizon. Harriet Kane stands at the center of a circle of mourners, her small body mostly blocked by taller figures. I feel a fierce desire to walk over and tell her about the hazing. I want to purge myself. Throw myself at her mercy.

The crowd around Harriet starts to thin, and I see a woman next to her who must be Alexa's sister. As if sensing me, Harriet finds my eyes. Behind the red-rimmed lids, a knowing intelligence registers my presence. She steps in my direction. Her daughter seems startled and grabs Harriet's arm. They confer, the daughter looking at me, then shaking her head. Harriet swats her daughter's hand and, once again, moves toward me. I stand ready.

"Mom," the daughter tries again, worry crossing her face. A couple nearby turns to stare, looking from Harriet to me to Harriet. I hear whispers. Someone recognizes me: "Can you believe that reporter had the nerve to show up?" I hold steady as Harriet closes the gap.

I'm prepared to tell Harriet everything. She deserves that. I should have told her when she came to visit all those decades ago.

"I'm surprised to see you," she says, her voice throaty. "Were you in touch with Alexa?"

"No." Regret resurfaces. "But Alexa meant so much to me when we were young. I wanted to pay my respects."

"Thank you for coming," the daughter says and puts her hand on Harriet's arm, urging her in the other direction.

"Stop it." Harriet's words are sharp. "I'm not a child." She keeps her eyes on me, concentrating on my face. "I want to ask you something. And I want you to tell me the *truth*." She draws out the word *truth*.

I nod. I'm ready. Her daughter fidgets while I wait for the inevitable question—*What really happened with you and Alexa and the team all those years ago? Go ahead, Harriet. I'm prepared to share. You deserve the truth.*

"The police told me you were one of the people to find Alexa," Harriet says, staring into my eyes.

The daughter shakes her head. "Please, Mom. This won't help."

"Kate." Harriet reaches her hands up to my face, holding my cheeks in her palms. "I want you to tell me how she looked. Did Alexa seem scared? Did she know what had happened?"

I'm slow to process her words. She was supposed to ask about the past. The hazing incident that propelled Alexa into a spiral. I didn't expect a question about her daughter's corpse. My mind flashes to Alexa in the ice bath, her emerald eyes frozen with terror. Her mouth stuck in a silent scream. I glance toward Alexa's sister.

"Don't you look at her." Harriet squeezes her palms tighter against my cheeks. "Look at me. And tell me the truth."

I take both of Harriet's wrists in mine and gently pull them from my face, my fingers finding her fingers. "She didn't know what happened." I maintain eye contact. "She looked peaceful. Beautiful."

Harriet chokes down a cry and falls into my arms. I wrap her in a hug. She pulls away, her lips quivering. "Thank God. Thank God. Thank you, Kate, for telling me the truth." I wince at her words, but she doesn't notice; her back is to me as her daughter leads her away.

"You lied." Ginny startles me. I had no idea she stood loitering at my side. "I mean there's no way she didn't know what happened. From what the papers said, it doesn't sound like her death was quick."

"I need to get going." I turn.

"Don't forget the family will be sitting shiva for the rest of the week. You have Harriet's address?" I feel like Ginny savors drama—she must rubberneck at car wrecks. Maybe the other women have reason not to like her.

"Here." She thrusts a business-size card with her contact information in my hand. "The Kanes' home is the white ranch next to mine. With red shutters." She waves and walks off. As I watch her go, I wonder whether Ginny was friend or foe to Alexa.

I reach my car as the moon appears in the sky. My spirits lift slightly thinking about my plans tonight with David. We can straighten out the tension from the morning and then enjoy the rest of the evening. During the last months, I've grown fond of our talks. We sit for hours eating pasta at the corner Italian bistro down the block from his apartment. At first, we spoke about work. But our conversations grew deeper. We shared our histories. He opened up about his childhood and the devastating loss of his sister, Maria, who died in a car accident. I told him about my mom's decision to move us across the country after my father was shot. We laughed over the similarities between our ex-spouses, debating which one was shallower.

I'm sure David will realize he overreacted to the news that we are both in consideration for the same promotion. Maybe we can discuss boundaries. We can make a joke of it—may the best woman win. I send him a text that I'll be at his place in an hour and start my car.

I pull out of my spot as my phone pings. I stop and look at my screen, disappointment seeping through me. The text is from David.

Rain check? Really tired. Sorry.

I want to respond, *No! No rain check! How many nights am I free?!* Instead, I put my phone back in my bag and sit there. Maybe David isn't who I think he is. His response feels spiteful. We've spent many nights together when we were both exhausted. What's different about tonight?

Someone honks at me. I wave for them to drive around me. As the car passes, I recognize the driver. It's Curls Hutchinson, who I saw flirting with three women in his family's luxury box at Yankee Stadium. What the hell is a Hutchinson doing at the candlelight vigil? And how did I miss spotting him earlier?

CHAPTER 22

I feel as if I'm breaking a rule by coming home alone. Like the kids will ground me if they find out. Despite the thick humidity in the evening air, I shiver as I walk toward my house. Usually, I leave the entranceway light on; I must have forgotten. I start to put the key into the lock—the door creaks open just from pressure. Did I also forget to lock the door? That's so unlike me.

"Hello," I call, groping for the entranceway light switch with my palm. "Is anyone home?" My heart pounds in my chest. *Calm down.* "Nikki . . . Jackson . . ."

Only the tick-tick of the grandfather clock answers. I grip the car key between my fingers and close the door with my foot, keeping my eyes forward. *The kids probably came home and forgot to lock the door. Or I was in such a rush this morning.* Tell that to my racing pulse.

I snap on the lamp in the family room. Yellow light streaks across the leather couch and thick cushions. Nothing looks displaced. No lurking figures hiding behind furniture.

I creep across the narrow hallway; the floorboards moan from my weight—the familiar sound is not comforting at the moment.

"Hello," I call, holding up my fist with the key through my fingers. I flick the light switch and scan the kitchen.

I take in the pile of unopened mail on the kitchen counter and kicked-off sneakers by the back door. I double-check the lock and confirm it's secured. I'm letting my imagination get the best of me. Deep breath. Still, I do feel safer when the alarm is on—and I've neglected to call the company since it malfunctioned last week. A situation I will rectify first thing tomorrow morning.

Once I've checked all the rooms, I pour myself a large glass of wine and heat up leftover pizza.

My phone rings with a call from Liam. "Hi," I say, swallowing a bite from my second slice. "You caught me having dinner. Leftover pizza."

"I had pizza again too." He sighs, exhaustion in his voice. "I wanted to give you an update on what we found on the pawn shop videotape. We identified the guy in the footage as a security guard from Yankee Stadium."

"Is he the murderer?" I put down my slice and refill my wineglass.

"Doesn't look that way. The idiot security guard says he found the bracelet on the ground in the tunnel behind a trash bin." I hear chatter in the background. Liam explains he's downtown at the task force headquarters.

"Do you believe him?" I ask, taking another sip of wine.

"He's absolutely a piece of shit—but the stadium security footage shows him standing on the field for the whole game. He was still there when you called me from the locker room. It's not clear what he did during the stampede . . . but there's no question he couldn't have killed Alexa."

"I guess it would have been too easy," I muse. "You must be under a lot of pressure—"

He grunts. "You have no idea—" I hear him shifting his weight or moving or something. "Listen, there's something I need to tell you." His voice grows serious. "We had to bring Coach Baker in for questioning. As you probably imagined. I had no choice but to follow up on what you told me."

"I expected that," I say, downing the rest of the wine. "I just hope to keep it out of the press, unless it turns into something. What do you think of her?"

"She's a tough cookie."

"Ain't that the truth," I say.

"She's definitely up there on our list of suspects, but there's still a lot to assess." He asks me to hold on a minute, and I hear him talking to a colleague.

"Kate—" He returns to our conversation. "We found something else. Someone sent a threatening text to Alexa the morning of the game. It said, 'You better back down or else.'"

I let out a deep breath. Maybe Alexa planned to go public about the hazing incident and Savy found out. Savy had so much to lose.

"I imagine it was sent from a burner phone," I say, staring out the kitchen window as a bunny rabbit darts into the shrubs lining the edge of our backyard.

"Yeah. Unfortunately." Liam sighs—I can imagine him shaking his head.

"Did Savy even have the opportunity to kill Alexa?" I ask. All eyes would have been on her. Personally, I never noticed her leave the sidelines.

"That's more difficult to prove," Liam says. "She went into the locker room during halftime, along with all the players. According to witnesses, Savy stayed behind for a few minutes, after everyone else went to the field. That would have been her only opportunity. After the game, she was one of the last people to enter the locker room."

"In that scenario Alexa would have sat dead in the ice bath since halftime." I try to picture it, but even Savy couldn't work that fast. Could she? "Does the timing gel with the footage you're reviewing?"

"Too early to say," Liam replies and asks me to hold on again. I hear more talking in the background. Outside, the rabbit returns and nibbles the grass in the middle of the lawn. I flick off the exterior light to give it some cover.

"Sorry." Liam returns. "Crazy here. I need to go in a minute. But there's one last thing."

"You want a list of all the people involved in the hazing incident?" I say. "In case Savy had an accomplice."

"I do," he says with pride. I agree to email it over when we get off the phone.

"I also want to hear about the candlelight vigil," he says. "But right now I need to run."

"You did know I would go," I reply. "Was I there to do legwork?"

He chuckles. "I was hoping going to the vigil might give you some closure."

The candlelight vigil gave me anything but closure. But there's something sweet about Liam hoping it would help. We say goodbye, and I finish my wine.

Later that evening, I remove the folding partition in my room and step into the little alcove with all my notes from my investigation into the night Liam was shot and his partner killed. I wonder if my kids noticed the decorative screen or wondered whether I was hiding something. The one downside of our small house is the lack of private space. But they rarely come in here, so I think it's unlikely.

I stand in front of the bulletin board and study the two articles I pinned on top. The first is a photocopy from the police blotter of the *New York Post* from thirty-seven years ago—dated January 5.

Two police officers responded to a domestic violence call in Washington Heights, NY. Emergency operators received a call at 11:48 PM from a woman crying that her boyfriend was beating her with a coffeepot. Officer Harley Butler and Officer Liam Murphy arrived on the scene to gunshots. Officer Butler died at the scene from a bullet to his head. Officer Murphy was rushed to New York Presbyterian Hospital, where he remains in critical condition.

I study Harley Butler's photo, remembering my dad's partner, who always told me to call him Uncle Harley. He looks so young, with bushy eyebrows and a thick mustache. He used to wiggle his mustache and tell me a friendly caterpillar lived there.

For my birthday, he got me the book *The Very Hungry Caterpillar* and claimed the author based the caterpillar on the one in his mustache. He even had the caterpillar sign the book.

> Dear Kate,
> I hate when Uncle Harley sneezes.
> Love,
> The Very Hungry Caterpillar

The next day, the story was front-page news and the information reported about the shooting significantly changed. *The NYPD Public Information Officer told a room full of reporters that Officer Butler died when he heroically tried to break up a sophisticated drug ring. Seven gunmen opened fire when the NYPD arrived on scene, killing Officer Butler and severely injuring his partner, Officer Liam Murphy. Murphy, despite his wounds, was able to apprehend one of the suspects, who now faces felony charges, including the murder of a police officer.*

Why did the NYPD's story change so drastically over one day? How did the report go from a 911 call about a domestic violence incident with a coffeepot to a sophisticated drug operation with armed assailants? At first, I thought the discrepancy was a mistake. But then I became suspicious. My efforts to get a copy of the 911 recording were met with roadblocks. The recording "went missing." Then I attempted to locate the transcript. Also missing. It felt too convenient. I reached out to the reporter from the first article. She passed away a decade ago, and her husband had no memory of the incident.

I felt so desperate; I asked my mother. After all this time, I hoped she would open up to me. She's all about honesty and authenticity and healing. Or so she claims.

At first, she evaded. *It was so long ago; I really can't remember that far back.* I tried again when she and my stepfather came to visit last month.

Thinking about the past is painful. I want to enjoy my time with you and my grandkids. I tried a third time—a few weeks ago. Then, she lost her temper and yelled at me to drop it.

Our interactions only made me more determined to keep digging.

Next, I approached Liam. In fact, he's the reason I started doubting the whole story in the first place. When I was in the hospital last fall with my injuries, Liam told me that to safeguard our kids, we sometimes make tough choices. We were discussing my decision to protect my friend's daughter. But I felt weight behind his words—like it was personal. When I recently reminded him of our conversation, he told me I'd misunderstood. But he broke eye contact as he spoke. And breaking eye contact is a Liam Murphy tell.

Over the last few months, I've focused on tracking down the 911 operator. I started with a long list and slowly narrowed it down to one woman, Karen Hall. She doesn't have a social media presence, but I found the person I believe is her daughter.

I return to my bed and take out my laptop. I've emailed every two weeks, and I'm a little past due. I type a new message.

Dear Ms. Hall,

I hope your mother is feeling better. I saw on Facebook she was in the hospital. I'm so sorry to bother you—again. But I really would like to ask your mother a very quick question about her time as a 911 operator. Sincerely, Kate Green.

I stare at the screen, hoping to see a response. Lately, my efforts have felt inept. Roadblock after roadblock. I blink at the computer as three dots flash in the message box, and then a text pops onto the screen.

Dear Ms. Green,

My mother is extremely ill. She probably won't make it through the week. I confess, initially, I didn't tell my mother about your messages because, frankly, I thought you might be a scammer or crackpot. But last night, during a lucid moment, my mother told me about a 911 call she received that has greatly troubled her for decades. She didn't want to die without sharing the truth. I now understand why you have been trying to contact my mother. I will reach out when things settle here. Nancy

CHAPTER 23

My alarm goes off at the ungodly hour of 4:00 a.m. I hit snooze. The alarm goes off again at 4:09 a.m. We play this game until I'm up—dressed and caffeinated by 4:45 a.m., which gives me a half hour before I need to drive to Yankee Stadium for pregame morning live shots. Whoever scheduled today's match at 10:00 a.m. wanted me to suffer.

Too early to eat anything big, I munch on a granola bar as I check my emails. Overnight, I received a big dump from TRP, some dating back a few days. I guess they finally fixed the server problem. Most of the emails are junk, but one gets my attention.

The sender is Alexa@KaneJewelery.com.

The subject line: Help.

I feel my blood run cold.

Dear Kate, I know it's been a long time. Looking back, I believe I'm as much to blame as you are. You don't know the whole story, but I'm ready to share it with the world. In fact, I need to go public, and I want you to conduct the interview. Please call me the second you get this email. Alexa.

Below her signature, she left a cell phone number. I immediately check the date on the message. Alexa sent the email the morning she died. I feel nauseous. If I had seen this message earlier, could I have changed the trajectory of the murder? And what did she mean—*I don't know the whole story?* I start to call Liam, realize the time, then opt to forward him the message with a note to call as soon as he can. I read the email again and then reluctantly sign off my computer. I need to get to Yankee Stadium.

There's something about New York City at the crack of dawn that gets me every time. Not that I often wake up early. Let alone drive to the city at the crack of dawn. But once in a while—for an assignment—I find myself watching the city wake from slumber. The moment after late-night partygoers straggle home and just before the morning workforce stirs. The sun peeks over the horizon. The air cools for a brief moment. And the city seems still. To witness the moment from the field of Yankee Stadium makes it that much more spectacular.

I bet Alexa would have loved to be here right now. If Bill thinks I fangirl over the Yankees, I can only imagine what he would have thought about her.

"Stop gawking." Bill sidles up to me, a cigarette hanging from his lip.

I wave the smoke from my face. "Can you believe how quickly they cleaned this place up? There's no sign of the stampede."

"And yet New York is still a dump." Bill drops his cigarette and uses his toe to stub it out.

"You know I'm going to pick that up and throw it in the garbage, right?"

"Hey—you do you." He shrugs and raises a hand to block the morning rays from his eyes. "Good news about that girl who was injured during the stampede. Her condition has been upgraded."

"I know," I say, not mentioning I have been speaking with her mother and planning a visit over the next few days.

"Kate." Willow, the public relations officer for Savy and the US team, strides toward us. "We need to talk." She gives Bill a curt nod.

"Rules for today." She glances at her clipboard. "First, you can't go beyond the security guards during warm-ups."

"That's not what was agreed on." I interrupt her as I pull up my email from Charlie. An all-night negotiation led to very specific guidelines for today. I read her the list:

1. Unlimited access to the field before the game for video but no interviews.
2. No interview during halftime.
3. Postgame interview with star player and Coach Baker.
4. No access to locker room. Kate asks first two questions at press conference.

"These orders come from Coach Baker, not the Olympic reps." Willow snaps her gum.

I search the field for Savy and spot her by the players warming up. I'm not close enough to read her expression, but she's watching us.

"Come on, Bill," I say and march toward Savy and the players. He lifts his camera onto his shoulder, and I whisper for him to start shooting. Savy storms toward us, her expression full of rage.

"Point the camera toward Coach Baker," I order and hold my microphone up. *You want to battle, Savannah—do it on camera.*

"What do you think you're doing?" She puts her hands on her hips, leaning into her southern accent.

"Hi, Coach Baker." I use my sweetest voice. "Kate, from TRP Sports. We appreciate the agreement that the Olympics worked out with our station last night. And thank you for letting us get the pregame footage."

I stare at her—*go ahead, test me.* For all she knows, this exchange is being broadcast live.

She digs her toe into the ground. A second passes. Another. She forces a smile across her lips. "Well, Kate, we are just so happy that we could work out an arrangement that allows fans to see our players in action while also keeping everyone safe."

She glances at Willow and gives a quick nod. Willow cracks her gum and motions Bill to follow her, leading him past security and closer to the players. He bends down on one knee and starts shooting.

Savy looks at me—she's dying to say something. I see it in her ferocious expression. She opens her mouth to speak, then closes it, glancing at the microphone in my hand. "We'll talk soon," she says, the words benign but the tone menacing.

I decide not to push my luck, and keep my distance from Savy. All the girls wear black armbands in memory of Alexa and the men who died in the stampede. Quinn stands in front of the goal with other offensive players. She steps to shoot, and skies the ball, sending it into the stands.

"Focus, Quinn!" Savy calls. "Again!"

Quinn shoots a second time. It's on goal but soft. Hazel easily stops it. Savy shakes her head and digs her toe into the grass. The other striker, Gayle Adams, a star back in the day, steps up and smashes the ball into the net. Quinn grimaces. Savy calls the attackers over, giving Hazel a quick break. I jog to Hazel as she grabs a water bottle from her backpack. "I'm not talking today." She wipes her face with a towel to rub off the sweat.

"I don't want to ask you a question as a reporter. I'm just . . . curious about something."

"Are you bullshitting me, Kate?" she asks as she takes another sip of water, then squirts the liquid on the back of her neck and over her head.

"I promise, I'm not." I open my hands to show no microphone.

"Better make it quick," she says, motioning toward Willow, rushing in our direction.

"Have you heard anything else about the note found in the backpack of the Argentina goalie? Did they turn it over to the police?"

"Turns out I was wrong about the whole thing." Hazel looks down. "A private security firm checked the note for fingerprints. One of her own teammates put it in her bag." She shakes her head. "Honestly, Kate, I can't stand the nastiness. I just want to play the game like when you and Savy played." Hazel holds such a glorified view of the past. I wonder what she'd think if she learned the truth.

"Kate, you know the rules!" Willow puts her hands on her hips.

"You're in trouble now." Hazel chuckles and jogs toward the goal.

An hour before the game—Bill and I find shade in the Yankees dugout. I pour Bill a cup of black coffee from my thermos and then another for me.

He picks up the to-go coffee cup I brought along this morning. It's the one he gave me for Secret Santa a few years ago with a fun saying: GOOD LUCK FINDING A BETTER COWORKER THAN ME.

"We must be the only people drinking hot coffee today." He takes a swig.

"There aren't many of our breed left." I laugh, then sip from another Secret Santa mug: BUT FIRST—COFFEE.

The sprinklers turn on, irrigating the field.

"They may have cleaned the place up." Bill stares at the half-empty stands. "Looks like a lot of people will be watching the match from home."

"It sure does," I say, thinking about Charlie's assertion yesterday that the murder was good for ratings.

"You have any food in that bag of yours?" Bill asks. I take out a granola bar and hand it to him. "And this is why you're my favorite reporter."

"I thought it was my scintillating personality and the fact I clean up your cigarette butts."

"Kate Green." I turn to see Junior Hutchinson standing at the edge of the dugout. I shoot up and walk onto the grass, feeling self-conscious that Junior caught Bill and me taking a break, even though we've been working our asses off.

"Nice perk." Junior motions to the dugout. "How many people get to relax in the Yankees dugout?" He leans on the word *relax*.

"Quick coffee break before the match," I respond. "We've been here since 5:45 a.m."

"I wasn't judging," he says, crossing his arms in a very judgy way. "Dad is over there reviewing security measures again. He's very worked up. As you can imagine."

I glance over Junior's shoulder and see Wyatt Hutchinson engaged in a conversation with a man dressed in a suit with a gun tucked under his jacket.

"Dad insisted we make a very public display of being here—to show how sincerely we believe in the security put in place." He raises his voice over the subway rumbling in the distance.

Junior looks over his shoulder, then starts fidgeting with the pass around his neck.

"Perk of owning the station that's broadcasting the Olympics." He picks up his all-access pass like it's a piece of jewelry. A reminder he's a billionaire who can flick me or anyone else away like a fly. "Have you thought more about the documentary show? I think you'd be fantastic for it."

My mind returns to David and his outrageous reaction when he learned I was in the running for the position. I can't control it if David is a bad sport. If David proves a man with a fragile ego—then I don't want to be in a relationship with him anyway.

"I have thought about the job," I say to Junior. "I'm very interested."

"Great. Like I said—as far as I'm concerned—you have the inner track. Well, nice to see you."

"Junior—I have a question for you—"

He smiles. "I like that you called me Junior. No Mr. Hutchinson for Kate Green. Yes, it comes with a salary bump."

"That's good, but no, my question is about your brother. I think I saw your brother last night at the candlelight vigil for Alexa Kane."

He looks confused.

"The woman murdered here two days ago. I thought I saw your brother at the vigil for her last night in Great Neck," I explain.

"The girl was from Great Neck?" he asks, and I nod. Across the field, I see the referees gathering on the sideline.

"That's where we grew up," Junior says. "We didn't know a lot of the local kids, though—parents sent us to private school. But I guess Curls could have known her from town." He puts his hand on my arm. "I really need to go. Pops doesn't like to be kept waiting."

I watch Junior walk away and wonder if Curls is at the stadium. I'd sure love to find out the extent of his relationship with Alexa.

CHAPTER 24

"We need you live, now," Charlie barks into the phone.

"Did something happen?" I grab the microphone from Bill, looking around the field. Everything appears normal.

"Yes, something happened! We lost the feed to volleyball and need to fill! You ready?"

Bill pats down my flyaway hairs, then hands me a powder puff.

"Okay, Kate," a voice whispers in my ear. "David is in the studio." She tells me the main anchor is sick and will be out for a while. "David's going to talk pregame with you. Okay?"

I nod and listen as she counts down in my ear. I hear David introduce me, and I assume I'm in a double box right now. "Our own Olympic star is covering the USA women's team for us and joins me now. Hi, Kate . . ."

"Hi, David," I say. "It's a very different scene today than two days ago. You can see all the extra security on the field behind me and up in the stands. In fact, only about half the fans are here compared to Wednesday."

"What reason did people give for not coming?" David asks, and I muster all my discipline not to yell into the camera that he's asking an idiotic question. *I haven't spoken to the people NOT here. How would I know?*

Still, it takes more than a stupid question to throw me off balance. "David, I think the better question is how the fans *here* are acting—they are more subdued . . ." I continue to describe the atmosphere.

"And how did the players seem during warm-ups?"

"They seemed focused. Most of the players looked good during warm-ups. I spoke to a few off camera, and they told me they're ready for this match."

"Do you believe them?" David asks, and again I fight to keep my anger in check. Did he really just ask me if I think the players are *lying*? Could you imagine the headlines if I answered in the negative?

TRP REPORTER KATE GREEN ACCUSES OLYMPIC SOCCER PLAYERS OF LYING.

"I believe they possess enough discipline to focus on their game. They're *professionals*—" I draw out the word *professionals*.

"Kate. Sorry to cut you off. Our volleyball feed is back up—" David says, returning viewers to the volleyball game.

"Well, that was interesting." Bill takes the microphone from me.

"That's one way to describe it. Do you think he intentionally tried to sabotage me?" I hate to even ask.

"They were loaded questions." Bill puts the microphone in his bag. "But he also might be nervous. He hasn't anchored much."

"Yeah. I hope it's the latter."

The match against China gets off to a shaky start. Quinn looks like she'll score but takes too long. A defender clears the ball. A few minutes later, Quinn misses an easy tap-in. Savy pulls Quinn and replaces her with the veteran Gayle Adams. The energy on the field quickly changes, with Gayle scoring a beautiful shot from far away. Everyone, except Quinn, runs to embrace Gayle.

As the whistle marks halftime, the USA team looks confident as they head to the lockers. Over the loudspeaker, a deep voice announces a "celebration of Olympic soccer sponsors."

"I'm heading inside for a break," Bill says. "Coming?"

"Nah, I'm going to hang out here," I say, interested to see if a particular sponsor decided to make an appearance. The announcer calls names as CEOs march onto the field—there are execs from airlines and athletic wear and sports drinks companies and the one I was curious about: Bethany Chang Jewelry.

I watch the woman from the "War of the Gems" stride onto the field in a sleeveless black jumpsuit, belted with a gold chain. She's smaller than she appears in the photos. It's hard to imagine this lean figure being capable of hoisting Alexa up to dump in the ice bath. But adrenaline can explain a lot. So can the help of an accomplice.

The camera pans over the group, providing close-ups of their faces. Bethany gives a coy smile, her red lips perfectly outlined.

"We'd like to thank our sponsors for their support," the announcer says. "Everyone give a warm round of applause to these fine men and women." Tepid claps follow as the sponsors leave the field.

The USA comes out fired up in the second half, with Gayle scoring another goal to lead the team to a 2–0 victory over China. Once again, Quinn remains on the bench as the girls come together to celebrate the win. The United States Women's National Team will head to the semifinals after an incredible showing, despite heartbreaking circumstances.

Bill and I jog toward the celebration for the first of our agreed upon interviews. Willow pulls Gayle toward us. Unlike Quinn, she shakes my hand, offering a shy smile.

"Congratulations on a great game," I say into the microphone. "Two goals. How does it feel to lead the team to such an important victory?"

She giggles. "It was really a team effort. Everyone helped make this win possible." She brushes some loose strands of hair away from her eyes.

"It must feel good, though, to have come off the bench and scored two goals—"

"I'm just happy to do my part." She smiles.

I switch gears. "How hard was it for all of you to focus today after the murder and stampede two days ago?"

"I'd be lying if I said things were normal," she responds. "But Coach Baker and the rest of the staff really made us feel safe and kept us focused on our jobs. We have a lot of fans who count on us. And we didn't want to let them down. At the same time, what happened to Alexa Kane was a tragedy. We are praying for her family as well as the families of those hurt and killed in the stampede."

I thank Gayle for her time and watch her jog off.

"What a nice change from Quinn," Bill says, taking the microphone from me.

"But you know Charlie would rather have the outrageous answers," I respond. The crazier, the better the ratings.

Next up, Savy. Bill and I watch as Willow goes to get Savy from across the field. I see them locked in a discussion, Savy shaking her head.

"Do you have the coach yet?" the producer asks through my earpiece.

"She's jogging toward us but—" I don't get to finish my sentence, as the producer informs me they are coming to us live. I hear David introducing me from the anchor desk. "Kate Green has the women's head coach now. Kate."

"Thanks, David—" I turn as Savy approaches, glances at me, and then jogs away. Off camera, Willow shrugs in defeat.

I turn to the camera. "Looks like Coach Baker needs to get into the locker room." I smile. "It's been a lot for everyone these past few days. We'll catch up with her soon. But what a win for the United States—the team heads to the semifinals, where they will face the incredibly strong German team."

"Thanks, Kate," David says. "We have the head coach of the men's soccer team standing by . . ." And then the studio feed dies. *Of course you do.* I hand Bill my microphone as my phone rings.

"Kate. What the hell?!"

"I don't know, Charlie. Maybe she needed to run to the bathroom . . ."

"This isn't good. You're on the story because you're *friends* with her," he yells. "This better not happen at the semis." He hangs up on me.

"Don't sweat it," Bill says. "He's under a lot of stress. Something's brewing—the Hutchinsons have been on the floor a little too much for comfort."

"You think Charlie's job is in trouble?"

"I think all our jobs are up for grabs . . ."

You're safe, Junior said. But whoever trusts a Hutchinson?

The press room is packed. Bodies crammed onto folding seats, pushed against walls. I circle around the riser where the camera operators' tripods sit and push my way to the front row.

Willow grabs my arm. "I don't know what you did to piss off Coach Baker, but she made me give away your reserved seat in the front," Willow tells me as she chews her gum. "And—she forbade me from letting you ask any questions, let alone the first one."

Of course she did. Spiteful to the last.

"Are you going to listen to her? Or the billions of dollars TRP paid for the Olympics."

"I'm not crossing Savy—if TRP asks, I'll tell them you're persona non grata. It's probably better for you not to broach the subject. Maybe she'll cool down by the semis."

Savy be damned. She's not going to bully me a second time.

I position myself by the front, kneeling in a way that I'm camouflaged by the crowd so Willow can't see me from her spot across the room.

The door opens, and Savy walks in, followed by Gayle and the whole team. Gayle and Savy sit in the first two seats; the rest of the team stands behind them. One seat remains empty. Quinn saunters into the room, head down, and I wonder if the seat is for her. But why—she hardly played. If anything, Hazel, as captain, should take it. Quinn gazes at the empty seat, then steps back to join the line of women standing. Head down, she shifts her weight, picking at her fingernails. A buzz of speculation circulates like an electric current—hypothesizing who we are waiting for. No one guesses correctly. To everyone's surprise, in walks the mayor of New York City—Marsha Compton.

"Before we get to questions about the game"—Willow speaks into the microphone that's passed around to reporters when they ask questions—"we are privileged to have a special visitor with us. Mayor Compton, why don't you start."

Mayor Compton sits in the metal chair and moves the microphone in front of her. She's prettier in person, her face softer than on television. Her eyes flash with intelligence.

"I wanted to come myself today to say how much I admire this team. Their fortitude and perseverance are examples of what make our city strong." She clasps her hands together and turns to the women behind her. "No one will keep us down and by playing . . ." She takes a dramatic pause. "And *winning*, you have stood tall in the shadow of tragedy." The mayor smiles to the crowd. "Coach Baker, you are to be commended and I won't take more of your time." She passes the microphone down to Savy.

"Thank you, Mayor Compton." Savy flashes a smile. "I'm going to keep it quick—I'm very proud of how well everyone played today, and I'm proud of how my players persevered in the shadow of tragedy. Willow—" Savy finds her public relations officer. "Let's start the questions with ESPN."

I figured Savy would pick my fiercest competitor for her first question. I'm ready. Willow passes the microphone over, asking everyone to send it to the reporter on the aisle in front of me.

"Excuse me." I take the microphone from him. "Coach Baker must have forgotten that TRP gets the first two questions."

To his credit, my competitor doesn't fight me. He certainly wouldn't want me to big-foot him at a game ESPN was broadcasting.

"Coach Baker. Congratulations on the win." I smile sweetly. "I'm curious what went into your decision to pull Quinn so early in the game, and do you expect to start Gayle in the semis?"

Out of the corner of my eye, I see Quinn flinch. For a second, I feel bad about the question. But even if I weren't feuding with Savy, I'd ask this question. But maybe it wouldn't have been my *first* question.

"Well." She draws out her southern accent, forcing a smile. "As you know from personal experience, Kate, everyone needs a turn on the bench."

Willow skulks around the edge of the room, working her way toward me.

"True, Coach Baker, I absolutely know what it's like to ride the bench. It is not fun." My colleagues chuckle. "But no one cares about what happened with me decades ago. Fans want to know what went into your decision today."

Savy narrows her eyes—will she attack me and risk a scandal? Lesser soccer spats have landed national coaches in hot water. She smiles. She'll wait for another day. "It's a good question, Kate." She leans forward, southern charm oozing from every pore. "And you're right—no one cares what happened with us decades ago." She pauses to make sure I understand her meaning. "I'm lucky to have two excellent strikers on the roster. Quinn didn't seem herself on the pitch, so I pulled her and put Gayle in. As for the semifinals, no decisions have been made."

As the conference wraps up, I make my way into the hall, hoping for a quick word with the mayor. Seeing her sparked a memory about her father. I was six and at the hospital when my mom was pushing my father in his wheelchair. Mayor *Tony* Compton stood in the lobby to greet us, along with the media. While everyone watched the mayor speak, my eyes stayed on my dad and his refusal to make eye contact with the mayor as he declared Liam a hero.

"Madam Mayor," I call over the security guards blocking me. "Can I have a quick word? Off the record." I put up my hands to show her I don't have a microphone. She's about to keep walking, then looks at me again, before motioning her security guard to let me through.

"I'm Kate—" I say.

"I know who you are, Kate. I've followed your career for years."

"Are you a sports fan?" I ask.

"Truthfully, no. But on camera I love the Yankees, Mets, and all New York's wonderful teams." She leans a little closer, looking up at me. "I'm a fan of your father. We go way back. He's also the best damn cop I've ever met. I'm lucky he agreed to a role on the task force."

Her bluntness surprises me. But if she's going to be direct, then I should too. "I wanted to ask you about *your* father," I say and watch her body stiffen. "I have this memory of your father at the hospital after my dad was shot and—"

"Kate." She straightens her shoulders. "Let me stop you there. I have nothing to say about that period in time." She stares into my eyes. "You should drop it," she whispers, then walks away, flanked by her security detail.

CHAPTER 25

The exchange with the mayor shakes me. First, Mayor Compton acts all friendly. Then she completely cuts me down. What about my question sparked such a strong reaction? I get the history between her and her father is sticky. But I've watched interviews where she openly discussed her feelings regarding him. It wasn't that I asked about *her* father. It was that I asked about her father's connection with *my* father.

I can picture Mayor Tony Compton in the hospital lobby the day Liam got released. Heavy rain blanketed the city, but Mom still made me wear a dress. She also pulled my hair into pigtails so tight my head hurt.

Mayor Compton pinched my cheeks with his thick, sweaty fingers and then announced to all the media, *Officer Liam Murphy is a hero and represents the best of us. On behalf of the city, we personally thank you.*

Mayor Compton reached his hand to shake Liam's hand. The mayor grinned down at my father. But my father kept his eyes on the ground. Something was going on below the surface. And it made my father so uncomfortable he refused to look the mayor in the eye. Did Liam already know this mayor was corrupt? Or was it something else?

"There you are." Bill approaches as members of the media exit the press room. "Charlie needs me across town." He swings the tripod over his shoulder. "Want a ride into the city?"

"I'm good. I think I'm going to grab a bite first," I say.

"The coffee and granola bars weren't enough of a meal?" He laughs and heads off.

I'm absolutely famished and sick of pizza. I decide to stop at the Hard Rock Cafe connected to Yankee Stadium. The idea of a juicy burger and fries makes me giddy. My mouth waters just thinking about the first bite. Not to mention the much-deserved glass of wine.

For 3:00 p.m., the restaurant is crowded, but I'm able to get a seat at the round bar in the center of the action. I order a BBQ-bacon cheeseburger and fries. The burger tastes divine. I feel myself relax as I sip my chardonnay. The soft buzz of conversation washes over me, mixed with familiar '80s music my stepdad liked to blast when Mom wasn't around. I finish off the burger and start in on the fries.

My mind returns to Mayor Marsha Compton. Does she regret pushing so hard for the Olympics to be held in New York City? Over the last few days, all the headlines in the press have maligned her. MAYOR COMPTON BRINGS CHAOS AND DEATH TO THE CITY. Something the right and left media outlets actually agree on.

When the election rolls around this November, I don't see how Mayor Compton endures the hit. Her opponents are already relentlessly hammering her in the press every chance they get. "Excuse me." A man in a suit comes over and waves for the bartender. "We need more drinks. The waitress seems to have disappeared."

"Shift change," the bartender says and promises to send someone right over. "Next round on us, for your trouble."

"That's awfully generous of you," I comment.

"You know who's at the table, right?" He tops off my wine and whispers, "The big sponsors. I'd never hear the end of it if we pissed them off."

I turn around to study the group more carefully. About a dozen men and one woman sit at a long table. Only the back of the woman's head is visible, but there's no question it's Bethany Chang. What I'd give to speak with her.

Bruce Springsteen comes on. I continue drinking and watching them, pretending to be mesmerized by the television screen just above their table.

"You know how much money they represent?" The bartender has no doubts where my eyes are actually focused.

I shake my head.

"Billions. At least."

I watch a waitress approach the table to take orders and hear one of the men make a comment about wanting the best whiskey. Bethany shakes her head, placing her hand over her partially full martini glass.

The waitress is quick about bringing the drinks. And the men are even quicker to down the liquor. Bethany seems a bit bored, her foot tapping against the floor. She stands, and I signal to the bartender for the check, but she walks toward the back instead of leaving.

"Be right back," I say as he places the check down. I hop off my stool and follow Bethany into the bathroom. She's at the sink, outlining her lips with a lip pencil.

"Did you follow me?" she asks without looking away from her reflection.

"As a matter of fact, I did."

"I'm not talking to reporters." She puts the pencil away and pulls out the lipstick.

I tell her I'm not here as a reporter. "I was a friend of Alexa Kane's," I say. "We played soccer together."

She smiles into the mirror and starts putting the lipstick on her upper lip. "And you want to talk to me because you read all the headlines about big bad Bethany, who's so angry at Alexa for starting her own company?"

"Something like that." I try to meet her eyes through the reflection.

She finally turns to face me. "You're wasting your time. The whole feud was largely manufactured. I knew Alexa would go out on her own at some point. When the media created the narrative of our feud—we, as Alexa liked to say, *leaned in* to it, because it brought attention to both of us and actually boosted sales."

"What do they say—all publicity is good publicity?" I ask. "Was your fight with Cassandra Jorden for publicity too?" I continue, remembering the vicious words the actress said in one of the articles.

Bethany blanches, the first sign of her losing composure. "No, that's real. She's vindictive and unstable." Bethany snaps her purse shut and walks past me. "And if you want to quote me on that—feel free."

I laugh at her comment about Cassandra. But should I believe there was no tension between her and Alexa? Did they really lean in to that narrative for sales? I wonder what story Bethany told the police when they spoke to her yesterday. I make a mental note to ask Liam next time I talk with him.

CHAPTER 26

As I step out of the restaurant into the blazing afternoon heat, I get a text from David. I'm sorry for acting like a bad sport. Can I make it up to you tonight? Dinner at our favorite restaurant? Three heart emojis. I debate what to do as I walk to the far lot, where only a few cars remain. The parking attendant waves from his beach chair, Bon Jovi blasting from a large speaker next to him.

On the one hand—David's text is sweet, and we really do need to talk about navigating a relationship while working at the same station. Also, this morning Nikki and Jackson got asked to fill in as chaperones for a camp overnight, so it turns out I'm free this evening. On the other hand—David acted like a jerk today with his pointed questions on air. I hear Nikki in my brain: *Give him a chance.*

I reply telling David I'll meet him at seven. It's 4:30 p.m. now, and without even thinking, I know where I'm heading. Over the last few months, it's a place I keep finding myself drawn toward. My car takes me to Washington Heights and the building where Liam was shot, and Harley died.

Standing outside the row of well-cared-for brownstones, it's hard to imagine such a violent crime took place here. But back then, the crack epidemic overtook this neighborhood and many others in the city.

The brownstone where the shooting occurred looks nothing like the old newspaper photos. Where a grand curved stone staircase leads to double doors of glass and wood, crumbling concrete steps led to a wooden door with planks hammered across rotted sections.

A freckled woman with a large floppy gardening hat emerges from the basement apartment. She turns on the hose and fills a watering can as she waves at me. "Back again, I see." She takes the stairs two at a time to reach me. The exact stairs where Liam fell after the gunshot pierced his abdomen.

"I'm sorry to just show up—again."

"Don't be sorry," she says, walking over to the first terra-cotta pot and tilting the watering can over the dry soil.

"Your flowers look lovely," I say, admiring the bright-red geraniums.

"I'm actually glad you're here." She moves to the second planter, full of rosemary, thyme, and sage. I recognize the herbs from my mom's small garden in the front of our house.

"Remember I told you we bought the apartment from an attorney?" she says, pushing the rim of her hat up to see me.

I nod, recalling my frustration. I wanted to track down the original owners, but they seemed to have vanished into thin air. According to court records, the couple who lived in the basement witnessed the shooting. But their names were redacted from all the documents, and I couldn't uncover any paper trail.

A BMW turns onto the street and parks in front of us. Two girls in tutus run from the car and up the steps of the brownstone to our right, the mom racing behind them.

"A woman in her sixties came by last week and claimed she lived here when the shooting occurred."

"Really?" I'm shocked by her words.

She returns to watering the herbs as she explains her initial skepticism. "Then she showed me a picture of herself standing in front of that grill by the window." She stops watering and points to a stain in the stone that's shaped like a lima bean. "The marking was exactly the same."

"Do you think she'd talk with me?" I ask, aware of holding my breath.

"I know she will." She tells me to wait as she disappears inside her apartment. The jingle of an ice cream truck plays—a boy and a girl skip past me to the corner, joined by another group from across the block. "Ice cream." She emerges from inside. "That jingle brings back memories." She smiles to herself, then holds out a piece of folded lined paper. "Her name is Theresa." She hands it to me. "She said to give her a call."

Back in my car, I hold the paper in my hand as if it's a fragile bird that could fly away. After months of halted attempts to uncover information on Liam's shooting, I have not one, but two real leads. First, the 911 operator's daughter, who promised to meet with me soon. Now, Theresa, who might be the woman who witnessed the shooting.

I savor the feeling of hope—before taking out my phone to call. I punch in the numbers and wait.

"Hello?" A woman with a hint of an Irish accent picks up.

"Hi, Theresa? This is Kate Green, you—"

"Yes, hold a second, please." Her tone turns formal. "Hal—it's the exterminator. I'll take it in the other room." I hear footsteps, followed by the closing of a door. "Sorry about that." Her voice now a whisper. "My husband doesn't know I'm considering speaking with you. He doesn't want me to."

Through my windshield I see the two kids returning from the ice cream truck holding cones filled with soft serve swirls. Chocolate ice cream covers the boy's face and hands. The girl eats neatly, controlling any spills. They remind me of my kids when they were young. Nikki so precise while she tackled her ice cream, where Jackson wore more of the dessert on his hands and face than he ever managed to swallow.

"I don't mean to put you in a bad spot," I say. "But I'd love to ask you a few questions—"

The ice cream truck drives past me, the jingle getting louder before petering out as the van turns on another street.

"I want to talk to you, I do." She sounds unsure, despite her words. "It's just—"

"Please, it would mean so much to me. Just a few minutes? I'll meet you anywhere." I hear how desperate I sound.

"Ummm—I usually go out for a morning walk in Central Park."

"I can meet you there," I say.

"Okay, let's plan on . . . 9:00 a.m. by the castle?"

"Sure."

"Coming, Hal," I hear her yell as she ends the call.

A quick internet search shows one castle in Central Park, the Belvedere Castle at Seventy-Ninth Street, in the middle of the park— not a bad walk from David's, assuming I stay the night. Meanwhile, I have just enough time to make it to our 7:00 p.m. dinner.

I open the door to the neighborhood Italian restaurant and soak in the aroma of cheese and marinara sauce. My stomach rumbles despite the hamburger I ate recently.

"Hi, Kate." The bartender waves from behind the high-gloss wooden bar covered in glowing candles. "David's already here."

"Thanks." I step past two women clinking oversize wineglasses and approach our usual table in back.

"I'm so happy to see you." David wraps me in a hug. I stand stiff— not able to return his affection. "You look beautiful." His hazel eyes glint with sadness.

"I look sweaty and tired." I sit down as the hostess brings me a glass of chardonnay and David his favorite cabernet.

He sighs. "I owe you a few apologies." He looks down at his hands. "I asked stupid questions on air today. I haven't anchored in such a long time, I was nervous."

A busboy places warm bread and whipped butter on the table. I wait till he leaves before responding. "It's hard to believe *nerves* inspired such pointed questions." As the words fly out of my mouth, anger bubbles inside me. I pushed my fury down earlier today because

I needed to maintain my focus. But now that we're talking, I realize how enraged I am.

What reason did people give for not coming? Did I believe the players when they said they're focused on the game?

"How are you two lovebirds?" Our regular waitress approaches with a notepad. We both freeze, like we've been caught misbehaving. "Want your usuals?"

David answers yes for both of us.

"Okay, cards on the table," David says. "I think part of me did try to trip you up today. I really want that job anchoring the new show. Charlie told me I had it." He leans back in his chair and closes his eyes. "I'm ashamed of what I did to you today." He opens his eyes and gazes at me. I don't respond, and he reaches for my hand, then holds it in both of his. "I should be angry at Charlie. And Mr. Hutchinson." He pronounces *Mr.* with derision. "This industry gets to me. Pokes at my insecurities. And that's not your fault. It's not a good excuse. But it's the truth. And I'm sorry."

I pull my hand away but feel myself soften. "That must have been hard to admit," I say. "And I get it. The business is difficult. But how are we going to navigate a relationship if you get so competitive? I mean, you tried to sabotage me."

"I will do better," he says, offering a weak smile.

I pick up my wine and take a big gulp, letting the liquid ease the edges of my anger, and wonder whether David can do better. Is David the competitive person I saw today or the sweet man across from me now? Was his behavior today a mistake? Or a warning sign? Nikki's voice pops into my head again, scolding me for being hard on the men I date. *Give people a chance,* she says.

It's not like I'm getting engaged to David. We're hanging out. Having fun. When he's not trying to torpedo my career, he's sweet. And sexy. It's been a long time since I've let my guard down with a man after being burned by my ex-husband.

I raise my glass. "To giving it a try." His face morphs into a smile, eyes dancing as he clinks glasses with me.

I finish off a second glass of wine as David orders my favorite chocolate dessert and two glasses of sherry. We plunge our spoons into the gooey flourless cake and laugh about the silly haircut one of our colleagues got.

David takes my hand in the elevator of his apartment building, and I snuggle close to him. Inside his loft, he offers me another drink. I decline, wrapping my arms around his neck and pushing my body close. He reaches his hands to my cheeks and tilts my face up—his lips finding mine as we stumble to his bed.

———

I wake up with a jolt, scanning the high ceilings with exposed pipes and the brick walls of David's apartment. I hear the shower and smell rich coffee. I wrap the sheet around me and shuffle to the kitchen, where a fresh pot of coffee waits with a ceramic mug next to it. I smile, pour myself a cup, and take out my phone, where there's a message from Virginia Dell's mother.

> Virginia loved your flowers. She's been moved from the ICU to her own room. She can't believe you are going to visit. The doctors say maybe by the end of the week.

I text back to give her a kiss from me, then pour myself more coffee.

A loud buzz catches my attention, but I'm not sure where it's coming from. David's phone sits quiet on the counter. The sound rings again. And again. I get up and follow the vibrations to a drawer by David's stove. Pulling the drawer open, I see a second phone and pick it up. The caller ID shows Julie.

"You got the coffee." He smiles, drying his hair with a towel, another towel wrapped around his waist.

"You have a second phone?" I ask, puzzled by the discovery.

He steps over, takes it from my hand, and looks at the caller ID, wrinkling his brow. "For family." He puts the device back in the drawer.

"Who is Julie?" I ask.

"A very annoying but lovely wrinkled aunt of mine." He leans in for a kiss, then tells me he's anchoring again today and will need to rush out soon. I kiss him back, then scoot into the bedroom to get dressed.

Twenty minutes later, David and I leave his apartment together, hand in hand.

"Mr. Lopez." The doorman calls David over to his desk. I watch them conferring in whispers. The doorman points outside.

"What was that about?" I ask David when he joins me outside.

"Just an issue with UPS."

I lean toward him to give him a kiss goodbye, but he just squeezes my hand and rushes off. "Sorry, I just realized how late I am."

CHAPTER 27

I feel the sweat on the back of my neck even as I stand in the shade under the awning of David's Upper West Side apartment. David disappears around the corner, and I remain in my spot, stunned by his abrupt shift in behavior. I'm getting whiplash from his Jekyll and Hyde mood swings.

"Out of the way." A man bumps against me and rushes past. Maybe I was in his way—*but take a step to the left, buddy.* I study his clipped steps and clenched fists. He's on edge. Everyone in New York feels like that.

Increased tension in every crevice of the tristate area, from the platforms of the subways to the outskirts of the suburbs to the steaming concrete sidewalks.

And now, after the murder and the stampede—I feel the resentment rise yet another degree among city dwellers. Angry at the continuous interruptions to their routines, resentful of the swelling crowds on the sidewalks. The intensifying traffic. And now the exponential increase in the presence of the police. Add to that the knowledge that a murderer remains on the loose—one smart enough to kill and evade detection within a crowded and secured Yankee Stadium.

I'm angry too. That Alexa is dead, along with two spectators from the stampede. I'm angry the sweet teenager Virginia Dell remains in the hospital. That Savy is back at her games, retaliating against me for telling the police the truth about our history with Alexa. The Hutchinsons and this looming sense of doom hanging over TRP's staff, mixed with the hint I might get a promotion. Mayor Compton and her agendas. And David. Especially David. With his mixed messages and secret nonpackages.

I push against the revolving door and swing back into the lobby. The young doorman looks at me from under his blue-and-gold hardtop hat. "Can I help you?"

Now that I'm standing in front of him, I'm not sure what to say. *Were you and David really discussing a problem with a package? Because whatever you said to David really triggered a mood shift.* But even if David did lie—why would an employee from *his* building tell me?

"I thought maybe I could swing by later to pick up the package David needed," I start to ramble. While I try not to lie, I can certainly throw out a hypothetical to catch someone else in a falsehood.

"I'm not sure what you mean—" The poor boy looks confused.

"Never mind." I got my answer and experience a deep sense of sadness that I ended up being right. Maybe I'm one of those people not meant for relationships.

My phone vibrates with a message from Liam. Quick lunch and catchup? Noon?

I don't need David, I think, leaving the building. Instead of worrying about a guy who seems bent on letting me down, I will focus on Alexa—the girl I let down. The girl I owe my attention. But first, I need to meet with Theresa. I have just enough time to grab a coffee and walk to the designated spot in Central Park.

Standing at the entrance to the castle, I can't imagine how I will find this woman. I don't know what she looks like, and dozens of women are passing by. My heart jumps as a smiling lady strolls in my direction, her hand lifted. I take a step toward her, but she walks past me, stopping to give a man a hug.

It's 9:15 a.m., and I'm thinking Theresa changed her mind about talking. I finish my coffee and toss the cup in the trash, then notice a woman in a flowered dress coming up to me.

"Kate," she says, and I hear a lilt of Irish in her voice.

"Theresa?" I ask, and she nods, suggesting we sit on a bench in the shade.

"You look just like him." She studies my face, her expression far away. Is she remembering that night?

A skateboarder rolls past, music blasting from his phone. Theresa startles and does a visual sweep of the area before turning back to me. "Do you mind if we walk?" She turns away from the benches, and I follow her along one of the paved paths in Central Park.

"Do you think someone is watching us?" I ask, feeling jumpy now myself.

"You can never be too careful," she responds, telling me her husband would be furious if he knew we were talking. We pass a souvlaki truck with an impressive line despite the early hour. "Hal and I just moved back to the area after being away thirty-seven years," she tells me.

Thirty-seven years can't be a coincidence. Liam's shooting was thirty-seven years ago. "Did you move after the shooting?" I ask her.

She nods but doesn't expand. She tells me they returned to Manhattan because their daughter had a baby. "We want to be involved in our granddaughter's life."

Her phone rings, and she picks up. "I'm just out for a walk, Hal. I'll be back soon." She hangs up and informs me she needs to head home.

"You haven't told me anything," I say, alarmed at her near departure.

"It's just, I'm scared someone will see us." She looks around again.

I do the same, noting all the people in the park, but not spotting anyone watching us. "Who would care that we're talking?"

She looks at me, her eyes incredulous.

"Please." I hear the desperation in my voice. "Tell me what you know about that night, and I'll never bother you again."

"Tell me what *you* know," she says, motioning that I follow her down a path that seems less busy.

I tell her that I know Officer Harley walked up the steps to the door on the first floor.

"Yes, Hal and I were poor then and lucky to find anything, even a basement apartment in a drug-infested neighborhood. We were young and thought we were invincible."

I continue, recounting what I learned from the papers. That Harley broke down the rotting door, which was easy because it was basically plywood. The shot to his head came quickly, before he even stepped over the threshold, and he fell back like a log, jettisoned onto the sidewalk, probably dead before he landed.

A jogger appears next to us, and Theresa startles. I wait until he's out of sight. "Liam raised his gun and shot three times, according to the police report. He hit one man in the leg before a bullet hit Liam in his side."

"You call your father by his first name?" She studies me.

"My father," I continue, "managed to pull himself over the banister and out of the line of fire, landing on the pavement by the stairs leading down to the basement apartment. And then he was able to apprehend one of the men."

We reach a lake and sit on an empty bench facing the water.

"Correct," she says. "What you don't know from the papers is that your father saved my life. I was peering through the window when one of the drug sellers spotted me; he lifted his gun to shoot when your father knocked him over. The man's gun went flying, but he pulled a knife and cut your father in the face. Officer Murphy was bleeding from his cheek and his abdomen, but he managed to wrangle the man and handcuff him."

She turns from me and gazes out at the lake, where a family of ducks swims near the shore. I hear music in the distance, something soft and soulful. Her phone rings, but she doesn't answer.

"As soon as the man was subdued"—she turns back to me—"your father collapsed. Like his effort sapped him of life. I ran out and put pressure on his wounds until the ambulance came."

"There wasn't any mention of you in the police reports," I say as she nods knowingly.

"I need to go." She takes my hands. "But I wanted you to know your father is a hero." She leans toward me like she's about to kiss my cheek; instead she whispers in my ear. "Stop digging into this. There are dangerous people who want the incident to remain buried."

She glances around again and darts off, her flowered dress bouncing around her legs as she disappears up the path. Was she in witness protection? Is that why all traces of her were erased?

I walk back to my car, getting ready to drive downtown to meet Liam for lunch. Part of me wants to ask him about Theresa, but he's going to blow me off if I do. I need more ammunition. I need the 911 operator's daughter. I've almost messaged her a dozen times. But I understand her request for space while her mom is sick.

My phone rings as I reach my car. I don't recognize the number. Maybe the daughter sensed me thinking about her? "Hello?"

"Kate! It's Ginny from the vigil. Hope you're good!"

I hold the phone between my ear and chin as I fumble to open the car door. The leather interior scorches, and I pull back my arm in pain.

"Kate," the voice on the other end yells into my ear, bringing me back to the call.

"One second." I turn the ignition and blast the air conditioner, which blows hot. The air changes from boiling to warm as I pull the door shut. "Ginny?"

"You know, Alexa's neighbor. We hung out at the vigil." This girl is a strange bird. *Hope you're good. Hung out.*

"Mrs. Kane came over early this morning," Ginny gushes. "She asked if I knew how to get in touch with you. I guess she remembers us talking at the vigil. Anyway—lucky I took your number down."

"I don't remember giving my number to you," I say as I pull onto Columbus Avenue and drive toward Police Plaza.

"Of course you did, silly. Anyhoo—Mrs. Kane said, and I quote, 'Tell Kate it's incredibly important she come to the shiva.' You can't come today. It's shabbat. But you can come tomorrow. Mrs. Kane said there's something she needs to give you. Okay. I texted you the address.

And you have to tell me what it is because she wouldn't. What do you think it could be? Maybe it's—"

"Ginny!" I say, louder than I mean. "What time is the shiva tomorrow?"

"It starts at 11:00 a.m. and goes until sundown but—"

"Tell Mrs. Kane I'll be there." I hang up before Ginny can continue speaking. She must have tracked my phone number down another way. I know I didn't share my information. But if Mrs. Kane wants me to come over, I will go.

Liam is already seated in the back of the diner. I wave and turn my body to squeeze past the long line of customers waiting for takeout. Someone calls my name. I turn to face Special Agent Mae Flynn holding two paper cups filled with coffee. She looks just as worn as when she questioned me in the storage unit on the day of Alexa's murder. "Kate." She steps in front of me.

"Hello." I greet her and try to move past. But she blocks me. "Do you need something?" I ask.

"You should have told me what happened with you, Alexa, and the coach," she begins.

"I told Liam," I respond.

"Your father doesn't have the perspective others do. You had a motive to want to keep Alexa from talking."

"That's ridiculous." I step closer to her, tired of contending with games. "Even if I had a motive, which I don't, I didn't have opportunity. You know it. I know it. Liam knows it. The whole damn task force probably knows it. So, unless there's something else, get the hell out of my way."

Her lips turn into a tight smile, like she wanted to poke the Kate bear. Was she testing me to see if I have a temper?

"Mae breaking your balls?" Liam stands and reaches over to give me his signature half hug. My cheek brushes against his NYPD T-shirt, which smells like detergent.

"Yes. She suggested I might be the killer." I slide into the seat across from him.

"She doesn't really believe that. She's just seeing if you're holding on to any other information—hoping to shake something lose."

"Like what?" I make a mental note to add Special Agent Flynn to my list of jerks playing games.

"She's just frustrated by the case." He sighs. "We all are."

"I thought you had a lead." I take the large laminated menu from the waitress. "The air conditioner feels weak," I mutter.

"Too many people for too small a space." He puts his menu down on the table. "We do have a lead—order, and then I'll tell you about it."

Despite the time, I study the breakfast-all-day items, opting for chocolate, raspberry, blueberry pancakes. Liam gets the same, minus the blueberries and raspberries.

"You could add a little fruit," I scold.

"Guess you didn't completely inherit my love for junk food." He gives his half smile.

"I came close." I laugh.

"I wonder if that's genetic or environmental?" he quips as the waiter brings him an iced coffee with milk and me a hot coffee.

"Or it could be the ultimate rebellion, given Mom's insanity when it comes to health food."

Liam's powder blue eyes gloss over at the mention of my mom. Does he still love her? Does he regret his decision to leave? Or, maybe, it really wasn't a decision but something he had to do. I think again about the message from the daughter of the 911 operator. *She didn't want to die without sharing the truth. I now understand why you have been trying to contact my mother.*

Liam looks at me as he drinks his iced coffee. "Are you all right?"

"I should be asking you that, you look . . . tired." I take in the dark-gray circles under his eyes and the tension in his broad shoulders.

Liam grimaces and leans close. "You can't imagine all the crap going on. All the politics. This isn't just a murder investigation. It's an international disaster and a public relations nightmare." He sighs. The waitress places a plate of steaming pancakes in front of me, with bacon and hash browns. The smell of grease calms me.

"Since when do you care about public relations?" I ask while pouring maple syrup over my pancakes and bacon.

"I don't. But the mayor does. The new task force does. And I'm up to my waist in everyone else's shit." He takes a large forkful of a pancake and swallows. "That's enough whining from your old man."

"Let's talk out where things stand," I suggest. "First things first, what did you think about the email I forwarded you from Alexa?"

"That email was flagged by our tech department about the same time you forwarded it," he says as an officer walks by and nods at Liam. He waits for the woman to pass before turning back to me. "Do you think Alexa was talking about the hazing incident?"

"I think so—what else could it have been?"

"Why talk to you?" he says.

"Because I could confirm her story? Or because, despite what happened between us, she trusted me."

"She must have had a lot of reporter friends," he says, referring to her status in the fashion world.

"Maybe they weren't really friends," I suggest.

He nods and moves on to tell me the police made headway in a few places.

He tells me the luxury box where Alexa spent the first half of the game was purchased by Bethany Chang Jewelry. "Which initially seemed strange, considering their public feud, but—"

"But Chang told the police that the feud was more for show?" I say, raising my voice over the chatter from the table next to us.

"Yes." He leans forward. "How did you know?" he asks, a bit of pride in his voice.

"I ran into her," I say.

"The question is whether we believe her. Bethany's lawyered up, so we didn't get much else out of her." He puts up his finger while answering his phone, which looks like a miniature in his palm. He nods as he listens, his eyes narrowing.

"Something important?" I ask as he hangs up.

"Maybe." He doesn't expand. "What I was going to tell you is that the tech team went back over the stadium video and discovered some interesting things about the actress Cassandra Jorden. She also watched the first half of the match from the box with Alexa and Bethany. Second, she had a blowout argument with Bethany just before halftime. It was caught on video. Another person in the box turned it in a few hours ago. And guess who Cassandra left with at halftime?"

I put my fork down. "Alexa?"

"That's right!" Liam seems excited, at least as much as he gets with that emotion. "The last video we found shows Cassandra and Alexa walking on stadium level. Cassandra leaves Alexa to go into the women's room, and Alexa continues toward the tunnel that leads to the locker room."

"Was there a camera at the tunnel?" I ask, too engrossed in this information to continue eating.

"Get this—the recorder stopped a minute before halftime. A supposed malfunction."

"That's convenient," I say, trying to picture the scenario. The field-level concourse gets pretty crowded during halftime. The two women walk together, Cassandra goes to the bathroom, and then Alexa walks to the tunnel entrance. How does she get in?

"At any point, did the video show Alexa with a pass to get access to the tunnel?"

Liam's eyes glisten. Like he hoped I'd ask that question. He nods. "When?"

"The tech team has been sifting through all the social media footage with Alexa and found a frame where she places a press pass over her neck. It happens just after she parts ways with Cassandra."

"Now you've solved access." I take a sip of my coffee. "Did the pass have the name of an organization on it?" I ask, thinking about how my credentials list my name and station.

Liam shakes his head. "We're lucky we could enlarge the frame enough to see the pass."

"Can you tell if it's real or fake?"

"We're trying—it's possible we won't be able to determine that." He scrapes the last bits of his food onto his fork, then swallows one big bite.

"What did the security guards stationed at the tunnel entrance say?"

"They weren't helpful. One swears he spotted Alexa Kane. The other swears she never walked by."

I dip a piece of bacon into my maple syrup and nibble it. We sit in silence a few minutes, thinking. The waitress comes and clears Liam's plate. I'm still making my way through my food.

"There's more," Liam says, wiping his mouth with the napkin. "Thanks to your information on Cameron, the boyfriend, he's made our list of possible suspects." Liam tells me he needs to get going. He signals for the check.

"Did you interview Cameron?" I ask.

"Cameron lawyered up immediately, too, which felt odd." Liam shrugs. "All we wanted was an alibi. He finally gave one, with his lawyer at his side, and it's shaky."

I follow Liam out of the diner, putting my hand over my eyes to block the blazing sun. "What was his shaky alibi?"

"He says he was in the office of his restaurant, but no one can confirm it."

Liam bends down to give me a half hug and starts across the street.

"Wait." I run after him. "What about the list I gave you of girls involved in the hazing incident?"

"One player from your list was at the game." He steps back as a bus whizzes past.

"What's her name?"

"Shira Appleton." He checks his phone. "I really need to go." He waves, and jogs across the street.

Shira, I think, remembering the goalie from our youth national camp years. She was part of Savy's inner circle. I always thought of her as Savy's henchman.

CHAPTER 28

I search Shira's Facebook page and find she lives on New York's Upper East Side. I send a friend request and get an instantaneous response.

Hi Kate! it says. I'm glad you reached out.

Can we talk? I reply.

She says yes and suggests a coffee shop near her apartment. I drive back uptown, which takes me an hour and a half with all the city traffic. But I have nothing else to do.

"You look the same." Shira sits across from me at a wooden table by the window of the French bakery and coffee spot she picked. "Don't worry." She laughs when I hesitate. "I know I've changed." She motions to her soft, curved body draped in a designer dress.

"You seem happy." I laugh.

She smiles and lifts her bone china coffee cup.

"Do you miss soccer?" I ask, the question always on my mind when I run into former players.

"I don't. But I stopped a lot earlier than you." She puts her coffee down. "I dropped out after my sophomore season in college."

"What happened?" I ask, assuming her reason must be connected to an injury or something like that.

"I got sick of it." She notes my surprise. "We sacrificed so much to play, Kate. I wanted to experience other things. College. Parties. Boys." She laughs.

A woman walks in, holding a young boy's hand. I hear him squeal with delight as she orders him a chocolate croissant. Shira tells me the chocolate croissants from here are still her youngest son's favorite. We swap stories about our kids and commiserate over the college-application process. It dawns on me how much I like Shira and could imagine, if things had been different, that we might have been not just teammates but friends.

She finishes her scone and wipes her mouth with her napkin. "You know the police talked to me about Alexa's murder," she says. A man passes close, and Shira pauses, waiting for him to move on. "I'm assuming that's why you reached out. You want to talk about Alexa."

"Yes," I say.

"The police actually asked if I colluded with Savy to keep Alexa quiet." She laughs as if that's the funniest thing in the world. "And they asked if I had an alibi for the time period the murder took place. Luckily, I had three other families with me at the game, not to mention my kids and their friends, who vouched for my whereabouts."

I remember even as Savy's soldier, Shira showed Alexa and me moments of kindness. But never in front of Savy. I guess we were all scared. Behind me, the coffee grinder whirs as the barista fills a bag of beans. I wait for the noise to die down and ask Shira if she ever spoke to Alexa. Or Savy.

The fragrance of the freshly ground coffee floats my way, and I breathe in the acrid smell.

"I reached out to Alexa ten years ago to apologize. I felt so guilty about my part in the hazing incident." Her eyes cloud over, and she looks out the window, struggling for words. "I have two girls about the same age that you and Alexa were. I feel gutted anytime I think of something like that happening to them." She turns back to me and reaches for my hands. "I owe you an apology too."

I squeeze Shira's hands and tell her she's forgiven. "The truth is—I feel awful about my role. I should have told the coaches." I look away. "Or insisted we take Alexa to the hospital. Something."

We both sit lost in thought. Shira excuses herself to get some water from the help-yourself jug at the counter and starts chatting with the barista.

When she returns, she tells me she was surprised Alexa agreed to meet with her. "She forgave me and said not to worry about it."

"That was gracious," I say, wishing I also reached out. "Have you spoken to Savy?" I watch her lips tighten.

"No. I'm so angry at myself for following her. But I'm furious at Savy for her meanness. How she cultivated her present image as the golden girl of soccer." Shira shakes her head. "Well, it's beyond me. How do you stand to interview her?"

"It's not easy," I say, and we both laugh.

A waiter comes over to clear our dishes, and Shira tells me she needs to get her son from soccer camp. I walk with her onto the sidewalk, and she wraps me in a bear hug. "One last thing. If I ever decide to go public about—" She hesitates. "About it. I'd like to tell my story to you, Kate."

"If that's what you decide—I'm here for you." We hug again, and Shira walks off as I wonder if she ever mentioned the thought of going public to anyone else.

CHAPTER 29

As I pull into my driveway, my phone rings with a call from Liam. "One second," I say over the drilling of a utility crew working on power lines. I run up my walkway and into the house. "Sorry, people are working outside."

"I could hear." Liam laughs and tells me he has important information to share about Alexa. I sit down on my couch, waiting for him to continue. "Our tech team took another look at Alexa's phone records. Get this—" I presume he keeps talking, but I can't hear him. The call drops. My cell signal has been especially spotty this week. I walk into the kitchen and dial from there. Busy signal. I stab at the redial as I move to the dining room.

"Hi—" He sounds surprised. "I'm heading into another meeting."

"I didn't hear what you said. The call cut out."

Liam's speaking to someone on the other end. There's a lot of talking and movement. "One second," he whispers. "Are you still there, Kate?"

I tell him I am, and he continues.

"Did you hear what I said about Alexa's call?" he asks.

"No—only that you wanted to tell me something."

The drilling outside gets louder, vibrating to the back of the house. "Kate—can you hear me?"

"Yes!"

"Alexa's phone records show she called TRP about half an hour after she sent you the email."

"She tried to reach me by phone?" After thirty years, she reached out twice in one day—the day she was murdered. I feel sick. "I never got a voicemail," I tell Liam. "Although we had problems with the email server. Could that have impacted voicemail?"

"We're looking into it. The call lasted two minutes," Liam says. "We assume she got put on hold, maybe bounced around or something."

Alexa needed me, and I didn't even know.

"Kate, this isn't your fault," Liam says. "We don't even know definitively she was trying to reach you. We can't trace the call beyond the main switchboard, but—"

"It's the only thing that makes sense."

"I need to run. The mayor is requesting my presence." He hangs up. The *mayor.* A reminder I need to figure out the relationship between Liam and Mayor Compton.

I sit back on the couch and rub my temples. I feel like the drill outside took up residence inside my head. My brain actually hurts.

I change into shorts and a tank and go outside for a much-needed run. I sprint past the drilling and turn the corner, where a more preferable sound greets me—laughter from a mother and son shooting hoops in their driveway.

I breathe in the floral scents of summer, tilting my face upward to catch the afternoon sun, imagining the rays melting the threads of discourse fighting for attention in my brain. *One thread at a time,* I tell myself. First—Alexa and the new information I received from Liam.

After all these years, decades, what triggered Alexa to reach out to me not once, but twice within an hour? On the day she was murdered. I keep returning to the idea that Alexa wanted to go public with the hazing incident—yet I feel as if I'm missing an important piece of the puzzle.

I turn toward the park as I think about the phone call. After I didn't respond to the email, she picked up the phone to call me. A half hour later.

"Excuse me!" a woman walking two apricot labradoodles yells as I veer onto the sidewalk, inches from bumping into her.

"I'm so sorry," I apologize. She shakes her head and walks past without acknowledging my comment. *Focus, Kate.* I turn onto the path leading down to the Long Island Sound and allow a second strand into my brain—Bethany and that actress, Cassandra. Could their drama somehow be linked to Alexa's murder? I just don't see a motive. Even if Bethany lied to me at the Hard Rock Cafe, Bethany couldn't go around killing her competitors. And the fight in the box wasn't between Alexa and Bethany or Alexa and Cassandra. It was between Bethany and Cassandra. So, murdering Alexa doesn't make sense.

My mind moves to the press pass—video shows Alexa putting it on just as she separated from Cassandra. Could the actress have provided her with the pass? Even if she could, why would she?

I glance out at the Long Island Sound, boats dotting the water. Although I can't see her home, Alexa lived across this body of water. She smelled the same salt air I'm smelling right now. I wonder what Mrs. Kane has for me. I'm surprised she'd bother with me at all.

My thoughts start to jumble. I practice Alexa's mindfulness breathing, something I hadn't thought about in decades. *Breathe in. Hold. Breathe out slowly. Repeat.*

I turn away from the water and jog up the hill to the park exit. Above, clouds cover the sun, providing a momentary reprieve from the oppressive heat. Stopping at a light, I wait for the pedestrian walk signal to appear. A car speeds by me, inches from hitting me. So close, I feel a rush of air. Adrenaline pumps through my veins as I realize how close I came to becoming roadkill.

"What the hell!" I hear myself scream.

"Are you okay?" A woman comes over and directs me back onto the sidewalk. "You're shaking." She puts her hand on my back as I bend my head down, hands on my knees. "Maybe we should call the police."

I straighten my body. "Did you see the driver? Or catch the make of the car?"

"It looked like a woman—hair in a ponytail. But I couldn't make out any features. The car was a light-blue Honda."

"I don't think we have enough for the police," I say, wishing I'd caught part of a license plate. "Probably some idiot on their phone."

I thank the woman for her help and walk the rest of the way back to my house. The peace I momentarily found, completely sucked from me. David calls as I turn onto my block. I debate picking up, but right now I could use a friendly voice, even if I'm presently annoyed with that person.

"Hi," David says. "Someone's daughter might have told me you are alone tonight." He explains that Nikki called him to let him know she and her brother were spending a few days in the Hamptons with their father, a last-minute trip they got sucked into. "I could almost see her wink through the phone." He laughs.

"I can't believe Nikki." I don't know whether to feel embarrassed, loved, or both.

"Are you all right?" David immediately picks up on my tone. I tell him what happened with the car, and he says he's coming over. No discussion. I don't argue. I would like the company.

I have just enough time to shower and dry my hair before the bell rings. David stands in the doorway, holding a bag of food from my favorite local Mexican restaurant in one hand and a UPS package in another.

"I come bearing gifts." He leans over and gives me a kiss.

"I love gifts." I laugh, feeling the tension ease from my shoulders as we walk into the kitchen. "I know what's in the food bag, but I'm intrigued by the package." I stare at the UPS box—it's about the size of a paperback but double the thickness. Is that what David was inquiring about this morning? I feel ashamed thinking he tried to hide something from me.

"Not until after dinner." He smiles as I put out plates and fill two glasses with wine.

"A man of mystery." I sit next to him as he serves me the chicken enchilada smothered in cheese and pico de gallo sauce. I scoop guacamole on my plate and take a big bite. He laughs at my food enthusiasm and dips his fork into a taco salad. Outside the window, the couple from the Puke House walks down the block hand in hand, leaning toward one another.

I look at David and wonder about our future. Could I see myself in a long-term relationship with him? Maybe.

"Are you finished?" he asks, staring at my completely empty plate.

"Very funny." I pick up his plate and mine and bring them to the sink, refilling our wineglasses when I return.

He turns his stool to me and presents me with the package. "I wanted to give this to you last night. But it arrived late." He hands me the box. "Open it."

I rip off the brown paper and find a small box wrapped with red ribbon. "What's this?" I feel a little breathless. David's never gotten me a gift before. And the package I'm holding appears to be a jewelry box.

"Open it." He smiles, enjoying himself. I untie the ribbon and lift the lid.

"This is gorgeous." I stare at a silver cuffed bracelet with my name engraved across the front. I put it on my wrist—very me, not too showy. "What's this for?" I reach my arms around his neck to kiss him.

"Just because," he says and pulls me toward him, urgency in his embrace. We stumble up the stairs like teenagers and fall onto my bed, wrapped in one another's arms.

———

I wake up to the smell of something sweet. David's side of the bed is empty, but I hear movement downstairs. I pull on my sweats and tiptoe down the stairs to the kitchen, where a decadent breakfast awaits.

"You pulled out all the stops." I sit at the counter, and David pours coffee.

He brings over two plates with french toast, topped with strawberries and powdered sugar, then slides into the seat next to me.

"Where'd you get the ingredients?" I ask, pretty certain I only had some eggs and flour in the house.

"Maybe I brought them with me"—he elbows me playfully—"hoping we'd have a sleepover."

"Ahhh." I smile. "A bit presumptuous, aren't we?"

I finish my food and pick up our plates. "Why don't you take the first shower, and I'll clean up."

"You sure?" he asks. "Can I tempt you back upstairs?" He nibbles on my ear, and I put the plates down, ready to follow him as his phone beeps.

"It's all right," I say. "You should check it."

He looks at his phone, then looks at me. "Care to guess?"

"Charlie."

He nods and tells me Charlie wants him to fill in again on the anchor desk. "Guess I will go take that shower after all." He leans over and kisses me. "Alone." He makes a little sad face and heads up the stairs. I listen to his steps. A comforting sound in the morning and something I could possibly get used to.

David reappears in the kitchen as I'm pouring myself a third cup of coffee. The grandfather clock marks 8:00 a.m. as I walk him outside onto the porch. I still have a few hours before I need to drive to Great Neck to see Mrs. Kane.

A blue car peels away from the curb outside my door. I catch a glimpse of a woman with a ponytail, the same description as the person who nearly ran me over yesterday.

"Oh no—" David yells, and I assume he's wondering the same thing, until I see he's staring at my car. I look from him to my beloved convertible and see the word *BITCH* scratched into the door.

"What the hell." I walk to the vehicle and take in the violent cuts in the black paint. I feel myself shiver despite the muggy morning air.

"They also slashed your tires." David puts a protective arm around my shoulder. "Who would do this?"

My mind considers the possibilities. Does Savy have a new soldier that she sent to scare me? It hardly seems her style, but I can't rule it out. Then my mind falls on yesterday and Theresa's warning. She told me not to dig into Liam's past. Is the woman in the blue car trying to send me a message?

The sound of kids laughing reaches us, and I see the neighbor's grandkids on the outdoor swing set. I turn to David, remembering he needs to be on air soon. "You're going to be late."

"I can call Charlie and tell him what happened," David says, which makes me feel all warm and fuzzy inside, despite the wreckage to my car. The teacher who lives across the street walks in our direction, a yoga mat under her arm.

"Oh my," she exclaims. "What happened, Kate?" She tells me she's on her way to a class but could wait with me while I call the police.

"Actually, David, could I borrow your car today?" I turn to my neighbor. "Would you drop David at the train station?" They agree to my suggestion, with the promise I call the police immediately.

CHAPTER 30

It's been a while since the desk sergeant from the Greenwich Police stopped by my house. Diane, whose last name I can't remember, stares at the scratches on my car, shaking her unruly red curls.

"What is it with you and vandalism?" She bends down and runs a gloved finger over the scratches.

"To be fair, the last one was mostly meant for my ex," I say, reminding her that last Halloween's vandals got their houses mixed up.

She ignores me and motions to her partner, telling him to take pictures and dust for prints.

"Can you think of anyone who would do this?" she asks.

"I can think of several people—too many, in fact." I give her a quick overview of the past week.

"I see you're making friends," she says in one of her typical sarcastic snipes. A lawn-mowing truck turns onto our block and pulls in front of the house across from mine. A crew climbs out, with a heavy-duty mower.

"There is something else, probably stupid—but."

Across the street, the mower whirs to action, loud and powerful.

"Tell me." She steps closer, yelling over the noise.

"Well, I got heckled during the group round at Yankee Stadium. A man was very aggressive and made a threat. There should be a police report. He was led out in handcuffs by the NYPD." *I'll get you for this,* he screamed at me.

"We'll make a call." She puts her hand on my arm and looks into my eyes. "Seriously, are you all right?"

I shrug, not wanting to lie.

Once they leave, I jump into the shower and get dressed. In an effort at transparency, I also send Liam a message about the vandalism before locking my door and getting into David's car. Liam phones before I even turn on the engine.

"Are you all right?" His voice sounds worried. "Did you fix your alarm system?" he asks. I remain silent. "Jesus, Kate!" I hear his anger bubble over. Even though he's right, it makes me feel defensive. I'm too old to be scolded.

"I'll call someone and get it taken care of today," I respond.

"Let me deal with it," he says, asking which company I use. I reluctantly give him the information, knowing he will likely be more effective at getting their attention. But also feeling angry at that fact.

I try to ask him for an update—but he hangs up before I finish my sentence. Punishment?

I drive back to Great Neck, pass the high school where the candlelight vigil was held, and continue toward Kings Point. Alexa had described this area as the *fanciest* part of town. Although, she also noted, her home was a holdover from the 1950s, before the mega mansions replaced the ranches. A simple green rectangular sign with white letters marks the entrance to the village. I roll down the windows to breathe in the smell of saltwater wafting off the Long Island Sound. I remember Alexa telling me how much she loved that smell.

An enclave of white brick mansions sits on lush green lawns. Variations on a theme—some with grand columns, others with ornate balconies. The car in front of me slows; the GPS takes me left and up a slope, where an estate outshines all others. The main building looks like a stone castle and rests on a hill with a rolling lawn to the water. The property is dotted with three gingerbread-like cabanas, along with gardens, a pool, and a tennis court. Unlike the mansions in Greenwich,

Connecticut, which lie hidden behind gates and bushes, this estate is visible to all who drive past.

A car behind me honks; I stop gawking and turn right onto a shady street. Alexa's house looks just how she described it—a white ranch with red shutters. I park David's vehicle behind the long row of cars and step outside.

A slight breeze rustles the leaves of long-established trees. Did Alexa climb on these branches? Play kick the can on this pavement? I close my eyes and hear her voice—telling me how her dad set up a goal in the middle of the road and directed traffic around her so she could practice free kicks. *The whole neighborhood was very supportive.* She giggled. *I think my dad bought everyone bourbon as a thank-you.*

"Hey, silly." Ginny's unmistakable voice rings from behind, and I see her bounding across the overgrown lawn of the ranch next to Alexa's. Unlike the Kane house, Ginny's home looks in dire need of a paint job. "Did you figure out what Mrs. Kane has for you?"

She strides next to me as I walk past the cars parked on the street. "Oh, look." She points to a yellow van with **CAMERON'S PLACE** written along the side. "I bet Cameron's dropping off food. He's so thoughtful that way." Her cheeks flush.

"Let me know if you spot him," I say, thinking how I'd like to talk with Cameron about Alexa.

She gives me a sideways look, but for once doesn't comment. We climb the concrete steps to the entrance of the house. A handwritten sign tells visitors to come inside and not ring the bell. I step into the dark hallway, mirrors covered with cloth.

"This is a good turnout for a shiva." Ginny assesses the crowd of people milling about. I cringe at her words as I try to spot Mrs. Kane.

She's in the living room, seated on a brushed-gold couch with thin cushions. She's in conversation with the rabbi I recognize from the vigil.

"You can't interrupt her when she's with the rabbi." Ginny pulls me toward the dining room, where bakery boxes sit open on top of a lace tablecloth.

"Are these from Cameron's Place?" I ask, taking in all the food laid across the table.

"These are." She points to a platter of chocolate éclairs. "A lot of the other stuff is from the grocery store." She scoffs.

Ginny scans the crowd, spotting a woman in a catering uniform. Her face drops. "Cameron sent her." She points to the girl. "He's probably busy at the restaurant. It's so sweet that he's sending all this food to Mrs. Kane," she says again.

I nod and reach for an éclair.

"Isn't it good?" Ginny chirps. She may be annoying, but she knows her pastries.

I take another bite. "Delicious."

"Oh no." Ginny's shoulders sag as she stares at the front door, where the pregnant woman and her toothpick-thin friend, Cameron's sister, stand. They see Ginny and walk toward us.

"Aren't you just everywhere, Ginny?" Cameron's sister says.

"Just trying to be helpful."

The other girl giggles as they move into the kitchen. "Ignore them," Ginny says as if they were rude to me and not her. "Ohhh—it looks like Mrs. Kane is free. Don't forget, you promised to tell me what she says."

"I didn't promise that, Ginny. I'm going to respect her privacy. Thanks for pointing out the éclair. It was fantastic." She beams, and I walk in the direction of Mrs. Kane.

Mrs. Kane looks childlike in a loose oversize black dress. Her gray hair hangs in curls framing her weathered face. She stands up and walks toward me. No greeting. No handshake, just a nod and a whisper to follow.

We return to the dining room, wind through the kitchen, and step down a hall, away from the cluster of people. She opens the last door on the left and beckons me inside. "This was Alexa's room."

My feet refuse to move—like they know once inside, I'll be over-wrought with emotions. Mrs. Kane puts her hand on my back and nudges me over the threshold. I recognize everything even though I never saw it. Alexa described all of it. She told me about the Mia Hamm poster over her bed, the pink carpet she hated but didn't have the heart to tell her mom, who was so excited about it. The trophies on her bookshelf. I take a step closer and see a framed picture of the two of us from our first camp.

"She really cared about you." Mrs. Kane's words come as an accusation. *You should have been a better friend* is what she means. She tells me to sit on the bed as she slides into the chair at Alexa's desk.

I lower myself onto the edge of Alexa's striped comforter, watching Mrs. Kane as she lifts a delicate jewelry box into her hands. A lullaby plays while the ballerina on top twirls. Her eyes water. And then, as if she doesn't want me to witness her pain, she thrusts the box back onto the table and wipes her hands on her dress.

"We need to talk." Her voice is harsh.

"I know," I sigh. "When you came to our house in California—" I start, forcing myself to maintain eye contact. "I lied to you about national camp. Something did happen to Alexa—"

I expect Mrs. Kane to yell. Or something. Anything. But she makes no response. Just stares at me with the same angry eyes.

"The truth is the older girls kidnapped us, threw bags over our heads, taped our mouths shut, and dumped us in the woods."

Mrs. Kane continues to watch me—still without a change in her expression. I hear voices from the crowd outside the door. A hum of conversation that grows louder, then softer.

"Alexa freaked out—she was shaking and screaming. I wanted to take her to the hospital but—" I stop myself. I'm too old to blame Savy or the older girls. Even at sixteen, I should have done the right thing. "I should have brought her to the hospital."

From outside, the beeping of a truck backing up rings into the room. Through the window I spot a delivery truck.

I look back at Mrs. Kane. "I'm sorry."

She watches me with so much anger I feel physically assaulted by her eyes. But I deserve it. Finally, she looks away and picks up a black-and-white composition book from Alexa's desk.

"I know all about it," she says over the rumbling from the street. "I found this diary yesterday. Alexa wrote about the incident." Mrs. Kane stands and walks to the bookshelf with the trophies. "Soccer gave her so much joy. If you had told me the truth, I could have helped her find her way back to the sport."

Mrs. Kane's shoulders quiver. I stay still, knowing my efforts at sympathy would only increase her pain. She turns to face me. "You did such a disservice to me and Alexa by keeping the hazing from me. You could have helped me help Alexa recover from part of what was haunting her."

Someone knocks.

"Please leave us alone," Mrs. Kane says.

The doorknob turns, and Ginny pokes her head inside. "Mrs. Kane. Do you want me to get you a plate of food?"

"No!" Mrs. Kane walks to the door. "I would like privacy." She pushes against the door, nearly catching Ginny's head. We both wait until we hear her footsteps recede.

"You said *part* of Alexa's distress." I address Mrs. Kane as she returns to her seat. "Was there something else?"

"Alexa did say you were smart," she snaps, as if that's a bad thing. Two men unload what appears to be a dresser and start walking toward the house across the street. "I can't figure out the last entries in the diary," Mrs. Kane says. "Alexa's writing in puzzles. I remember she once said you and she had a secret code."

Our bubble letters.

"I want you to figure out what she wrote." Mrs. Kane stands and extends the notebook toward me. I put my hand on it and almost feel Mrs. Kane's anger through the pages between us.

"Kate." She stares up at me. "Promise me that this time you will tell me the truth. No matter what—"

I stare into her eyes and promise, then grip the notebook close to my body.

CHAPTER 31

I glance at Alexa's diary on the passenger seat of my car. A simple marbled composition notebook: her name scrawled across the front with hot-pink marker. Glittery stickers in the shapes of hearts, soccer balls, and stars decorate the cover. I'm both desperate and terrified to crack it open and travel back in time.

A knock on the window startles me, and I see Ginny's eyes staring at the journal. I quickly push the book into my tote bag before rolling down my window. "You're leaving without saying goodbye." She puts her hands on her hips.

"This wasn't a social call, Ginny. And I need to go."

"You promised you would tell me what Mrs. Kane said." She leans her arm onto my window so I can't roll it back up.

"I never promised that. In fact, I told you I wouldn't break Mrs. Kane's trust. Thank you for calling me on her behalf, but I need to leave."

"Kate—you promised." She refuses to move. The heat from outside leaches into the car.

"I need to go, Ginny." I start my engine to prove my point.

"What did Mrs. Kane give you?" She stares through the car at the spot where the notebook sat moments ago. "I saw you put something in your bag."

I glance down at the notebook safely tucked away and wonder if Alexa wrote something about Ginny. Does Ginny have a secret she wants to keep buried?

"I need to go. Please step back." I put the gear in drive to show her how serious I am.

Her eyes go angry, and then she giggles. "Fine, we'll discuss it another time." She backs up and waves. "Bye, Katie Kate."

I roll the window up, trying to erect a barrier against her. I can't decide if she's a benign annoyance or a dangerous psychopath. She's watching me from the street, so I drive down the hill and stop at the corner to get out of her line of sight. I wonder if Cameron's sister and her pregnant friend have good reasons to dislike Ginny. Maybe Ginny is the mean girl in their triangle and not the other way around.

Do I tell Liam to check Ginny out, or am I being paranoid? At the moment, I'm a bit irritated with him. But I promised to let him know if I thought anything was dangerous, and I'm not going to let some petty disagreement stand in the way of that promise.

I text Liam Ginny's name and address and tell him a little history: She has a big crush on Alexa's ex. Maybe jealousy?

While I wait for his response, I glance out again at the large Gatsby-like estate on the water. From this angle, I see a private dock with a yacht. Alexa told me Kings Point was home to some famous comedians. I wonder if one of them lives in that mansion.

Liam texts back, Thanks. Sorry about before. I was just worried.

I smile and put Cameron's Place into my GPS, glad Liam owned up to his overprotectiveness. Maybe we're both maturing.

I don't know what I expected Cameron's Place to look like, but it wasn't this. Maybe the fact that Ginny works as the weekend hostess made me think the restaurant would be loud and unappealing. But it's the opposite. I feel like I stepped into a time machine back to the '20s.

"Welcome." A young hostess greets me.

"I love the interior," I say, and puke internally, because I've never thought or uttered a sentence like that before.

"The owner is really into art deco," she replies, then asks if I have a reservation. I shake my head, scanning the tables full of patrons eating and laughing.

"It's okay. There's room in the back."

I follow her across the marble floor and into a second area, where she seats me in a semicircular booth. She hands me a heavy menu and disappears. I lean back in the plush black leather seat, feeling my shoulders relax.

Everything on the menu looks good—and I'm famished. The waitstaff bustles about; one person brings a basket of rolls. Another refills my water glass. They wear black jackets and bow ties and look like they popped out of an old-time movie.

"Can I take your order?" One of the many workers approaches, this one with black, gelled hair tufted in the front. The music in the background turns to Frank Sinatra, and the elderly couple at the next table smiles and clinks glasses.

The waiter clears his throat.

"I'm between the steak and the branzino," I reply.

"The steak." He seems relieved to find I speak. "The chimichurri sauce is sublime." He writes the order down. "Anything else?"

"Actually, yes." I give him a big smile. "I need to speak with Cameron when he has a moment."

"Is there a problem?" he asks, his eyes darting around the table as if worried a knife is in the wrong place or a glass moved.

"Not at all. We have a mutual friend," I add. "It's actually kind of important."

"Very well." He gives a slight bow and walks toward the computer screen, where I see him type in the order. *Go find Cameron*, I think, hoping my thoughts propel him in search of his boss. He disappears around a bend, and I decide to believe my mind meld worked.

The composition notebook peeks from the corner of my bag, which I laid next to me. I pull it out, keeping it below the table, and run my hand over the cover—feeling the spots where the black-and-white outercoat wore through to cardboard.

How many times did Alexa hold this very book? I open to the first page and straighten the wavy warped pages—tears springing into my eyes. Alexa wrote her name in bubble letters, with *Women's National Team* under it. No doubt a secret message hides within the tiny red and blue stars that fill the bubbles. The low ambient lighting is too dim for me to try and decipher a message. That will need to wait until later.

My eyes move to the first entry, written in Alexa's familiar loopy handwriting, with her fancy *y*'s and curly *r*'s.

> Dear Diary,
> I'm so excited you are one of my Hanukkah presents. My sister didn't think a notebook was such a good present. She was really hoping for a bike. Good luck with that. But, in addition to getting you, I got a large pack of bright markers in really cool colors.

For the word *colors*, Alexa used a different colored marker to punctuate her point.

> And my parents added a sticker pack of soccer balls and hearts. My dad said it's good to write down your thoughts. Keep an accounting. Ugh, another dumb dad joke. He's an accountant—keep an accounting. Vomit. Vomit. Anyway, nice to meet you diary, I promise to tell you everything.

Alexa wrote the way she spoke. It takes me by surprise, and yet it makes so much sense. I close my eyes and can almost hear her gushing about the present and laughing at her father's joke. This is harder than I imagined. *Come on, Kate. You owe Mrs. Kane.* I refocus myself and move on to the second entry.

> Dear Diary,
> Soccer, soccer, soccer. I've finally found my calling. I've always been good at it, but I just got invited to a

select showcase of all the top girls on Long Island. My dad said it's a first step toward the National Team. As if. I'm sooooooo excited to go. And I really love the girls on my soccer team. I feel in synch with them.

"Interesting reading?"

I blink and realize Cameron is standing at the table, his sad eyes watching me. I shut the notebook, shove it back in my tote, and turn my attention to him.

"The waiter said you needed to speak with me?" he says.

"Could you sit for a minute?" I ask.

He hesitates, then slides across from me, staying on the very edge of the seat, as if he believes he might need to sprint away at a second's notice. "You look familiar. Do I know you?"

Now that Cameron's here, I'm not sure how or where to begin. I want to ask him why Alexa said no to his marriage proposal. But I can't start there.

"You might know *of* me," I say. "I was Alexa's roommate from the women's national soccer camps, when we were teens."

He puts his hands on the table and starts rubbing the knuckle of his left index finger with his right hand. "Kathy?"

"Kate," I correct him.

He smiles to himself. "I remember. She used to drag me to the chocolate store to buy you candy."

"That's me." Forever famous for what I wasn't allowed to eat.

"You were at the vigil, but I didn't put it together. She spoke about you." His eyes remain neutral, so I can't tell if she told him the bad things too.

Glass breaks behind us, and we turn to see the older woman yelp as red wine seeps across the white tablecloth. She covers her face and mutters how sorry she is.

Cameron jumps up and is at her table in a millisecond. "Don't worry about it," he says in a congenial tone. "Happens all the time." He dabs the spill with a cloth napkin. Within seconds, tuxedoed men and women converge, resetting the table. "Please get this lovely lady a new glass of wine on us," Cameron says, and I see her relax. Alexa always said Cameron was kind.

He walks back to my table but doesn't sit. "I really need to get back to work. It was nice to meet you."

"Wait. I actually need to talk to you." I hear my words come quickly. "About what happened to Alexa."

He stares at me, as if debating what to do. "Give me half an hour. In the meantime, enjoy lunch. On me."

"That's not necessary," I call, but he's already halfway down the aisle. A burst of laughter comes from the entrance to this room, and I spot Cameron's sister with her friend.

"Here you go, ma'am." The waiter places the piping hot steak in front of me, smothered in green sauce that smells rich and spicy.

"Thank you," I say, as the hostess leads Cameron's sister to a table at the far end of the room. I want to ask her about Ginny and Alexa. After I eat. I cut into the steak and take a bite. Delicious.

I'm halfway through my meal when someone clears their throat. I look up and spot Cameron's sister has come to me.

"Can I sit?" she asks and takes a seat before I reply. Up close, I see how much she resembles her brother. But where his features are soft and vulnerable, hers appear hard.

"Who are you?" she says, pinching her brows together.

Her bluntness surprises me. "Who are you?" I respond.

"I'm Paula Nolan. My brother owns this restaurant," she says as if that explains her presence at my table. Like she's the queen of the palace.

"It's a very nice restaurant." I smile and take another bite of my steak.

The couple next to us signals for the check. The complimentary red wine gone from the glass. A smile returned to the woman's face.

"I'm here out of concern." Paula softens her voice. "Sorry. I should have explained. You want to be careful of your new friend, Ginny."

"We're not friends," I say, watching the man from the other table put his hand out to help his wife. They walk away, arm in arm.

"Come on." Paula gives an exaggerated sigh, jangling her bracelets as she speaks. "I saw you together. Ginny is trouble."

I put down my fork and knife and stare at her. Whatever Paula's agenda, she very likely has important information. "My name is Kate Green. I'm not friends with Ginny. I just met her. I was friends with Alexa Kane. We were teammates as teens."

"Oh." Her whole demeanor changes, and she looks embarrassed. "It's awful what happened to her."

"Were you close?" I ask, adding that I know Alexa dated her brother. Now she seems hesitant to speak. "I mean—we weren't close. I'd see her at the house." She looks down at her hands and starts fidgeting with her fingers—the same nervous habit as her brother. For a woman who came on both barrels blazing, she's uncomfortably quiet.

"Was Ginny close to her?"

She laughs. At least I found the right question. "Ginny's had a crush on Cameron since she was a kid. So, no, she wasn't Alexa's biggest fan. But Alexa was too nice to realize it." She stands up. "Sorry to have bothered you. I'm embarrassed that I came on so strong." To her credit, she looks contrite.

"Wait." I reach out and grab her arm. "Why does Ginny worry you so much?"

"She may seem harmless, but she's not. I've seen how she manipulates my brother, who, like Alexa, is too nice for his own good."

I watch her walk away and again wonder about Ginny. Could she be involved? I'm anxious to see what Liam uncovers about her.

I finish my lunch and signal for the check. "Lunch is on Cameron," the waiter reiterates. I leave a generous tip and go in search of Cameron, who never returned to continue our conversation.

The kitchen is in the back of the restaurant. I walk in that direction, stopping in the hallway. The metal doors swing open, and I glimpse the active kitchen, with cooks working at stainless steel tables. Another waiter rushes through, and this time, I spot Cameron, wearing a chef's hat, hovering near a cook stirring something over the stove.

Now or never—I push through the doors and into the kitchen, immediately met by a man in an apron, with two hands up, ready to move me out.

"No! No! Miss." He grips my arm and tries to pull me out of the kitchen. "You can't be in here."

The hiss of meat in oil reaches me, along with the smell of frying food. If I weren't on a mission, I might offer myself up as a taster.

"Cameron," I call, refusing to get pushed from my spot. He looks over, anger filling his face.

"Get her out of here," he yells at the man holding me, who tries again. Cameron storms over, wiping his hands on his apron. "You're violating all kinds of health regulations," he hisses. "You need to leave."

"You need to speak with me," I say over the sound of pans clanking against the stove.

"Should I call the cops?" one of the chefs asks.

"No, no—" Cameron mumbles. "Follow me." He leads me around the perimeter of the kitchen and out the back door by a dumpster.

"I can't do this right now," he says. "I know you were friends with Alexa. But I'm barely holding on. Maybe we could talk next week—"

The smell of rotting food hangs in the hot, humid air, convincing me to get to the point.

"I know the police are speaking to you."

He blanches. "How do you know?" He processes what I said, folding his arms across his chest. "And why do you care?"

I pull out my sunglasses and put them on against the strong rays.

"Are you looking for a story?" he asks. "Because my hostess told me you're a television reporter. That's pretty shitty to take advantage of your past relationship with Alexa." Now that he's talking, he can't contain himself. "Is that why you came to the vigil? To prey on the mourners."

A delivery truck starts to back up to the loading area, and Cameron and I step out of its way. "I'm not here as a reporter. I'm here as Alexa's friend."

He shakes his head in disbelief.

"Did you know I'm the one who found her in the locker room?" I take off my sunglasses and wipe tears from my eyes.

"I didn't." His face softens slightly.

"I want to figure out what happened to Alexa," I say. "I owe her that."

He blinks at me. "Why do you owe her?"

The truck beeps as it backs up, stopping about five feet from us. Two men get out and open the doors.

"Give me a second." Cameron goes over and shakes hands with the older man. He points toward the kitchen before returning to my side. "Why do you owe her?" he asks, again.

"Did she ever tell you why she quit soccer?" I ask him.

"No—she didn't tell me why she quit soccer or why she broke up with me." He lowers himself to the curb, and I sit down next to him, despite the heat rising from the concrete. "She came back from that last national camp and just said we were done. I only found out she quit soccer from friends." He stares off into space, lost in a memory. "Do you know the reason?" He looks at me.

"I think I know," I say. "There was a pretty bad incident the last night of camp."

"What happened?"

I hesitate. This man remains a suspect, so I don't think I should tell him. But if he's cleared, he deserves to know the truth. "I can't tell you now," I reply. "But I will another time."

He doesn't push. "Did something happen to Alexa before camp started?" he asks.

"What do you mean?"

"She just seemed off the weeks leading up to the camp."

I think about what Mrs. Kane said to me before she gave me the diary—she believes the hazing incident was *one* of the things that happened to Alexa. Still, I remember how nervous I was leading up to camp. I kept having nightmares. One where I showed up to training naked. Another where Savy turned into a dragon and chased me under the bleachers.

"Could Alexa have just been nervous? I certainly was."

"When Alexa got nervous, she tended to talk about it. Not pull away," he says. He shakes his head. "I was crushed when she ended it. And without any reason."

"But you reconnected, didn't you?" I say, watching the deliverymen carrying crates of vegetables into the restaurant.

"Gossip sure travels around town." He gives a quick, bitter laugh. "We did. She came into the restaurant one Saturday and just sat down at the bar. I didn't even realize she was there at first. We hadn't spoken in decades."

He tells me how they started to catch up. "She came back the following Saturday. And then I started meeting her in the city. I'd been planning to open a restaurant in Tribeca. I signed a lease a few months before reconnecting with Alexa. It almost felt like our reconnection was predestined. The timing was so perfect."

"And then she broke up with you, again?" I ask, remembering Ginny's story about Cameron proposing just before the murder.

"Not at all. We planned to get married." He looks surprised. One of the men from the truck waves Cameron over. I watch him review a paper on a clipboard and then sign his name. I see what Alexa was attracted to in him. Cameron has boyish good looks and a sweetness about him.

He returns and sits back down on the curb. "Why do you think we broke up?" he asks.

"I heard you proposed, and she said no."

"I proposed, and she said to hold on to the ring and ask her again in a week. Which would have been today." He stands and turns his body.

He's shaking. I give him a moment of privacy. He turns back, wiping his eyes with the back of his arm.

"Do you know why she asked you to wait?" I stand up too.

"Alexa said there was something she had to put right before moving forward with her life." He rubs his fingers. "With *our* lives."

His words echo the email she sent me—*You don't know the whole story, but I'm ready to share it with the world.*

"I'm guessing she didn't tell you what that *thing* was?"

"Correct," he answers. "I asked. Alexa promised to tell me when she was done. I should have pushed." He shakes his head.

"Don't go there," I say. "Once you go down the second-guessing hole, it's hard to climb out. Did you tell the police?" I ask him. "This goes to motive."

They already know about my email. But her comment to Cameron corroborates her plan to take some kind of action. An action that someone seemed determined to foil.

"My weekend hostess told me not to talk to the authorities. She said I needed to get a lawyer before I did anything." He cracks his knuckles. "She kept talking about the man from the Atlanta Olympics who got wrongly blamed for the bombing." He rubs his face with his hands. "I'm not sure I did the right thing. I feel like it would have been better to share what I knew. Better for Alexa, for sure."

"It's not too late." I take out a pen and paper and write down Liam's direct number and tell Cameron to call immediately. "One last thing—" I say as I hand Cameron the paper. "Is your hostess Ginny?"

He blinks. "Yes. How did you know?"

"Lucky guess." I thank him and say goodbye.

CHAPTER 32

I replay my conversation with Cameron in my mind as I open the door to David's slick Mercedes. The car smells new; I have a vague recollection that he told me about buying it recently. My bracelet hugs my wrist, and I feel a dumb smile crossing my lips. *Too soon to start feeling giddy,* I tell myself.

Outside, two women with strollers walk down the street, sipping from iced drinks. Their kids wear matching pink-and-yellow dresses. One of the girls starts squealing with joy at the sight of a puppy.

I blast the air conditioner and dial Liam. "Running into a meeting, but I have a second. How are you?"

I give him a quick recap of my conversation with Cameron.

"Did you believe him?" he asks over chatter in the background. "One second," he says to someone on the other end.

"I think so," I answer, watching one of the little girls as she climbs out of the stroller to pet the puppy. "But it's troubling no one saw him at the restaurant. I'd feel better if he had an alibi."

Liam grunts his agreement.

The puppy starts licking the girl's face, and the mom picks her up, the little girl's fists pounding into the mom's back.

"We finally got that actress, Cassandra, to agree to speak with us. We want a better accounting of what she and Alexa were talking about during halftime."

"Do you think Cassandra gave Alexa the press pass?" I ask again.

"Maybe, sometimes these celebrities get access."

"Did Cassandra ever reappear on video after going to the bathroom?"

"She did, about ten minutes later."

"That's a long time—"

"I need to run; I'll call later." He hangs up before I can say anything else. I didn't have a chance to tell Liam about the diary, but I'm not sure I should. Mrs. Kane gave it to me. If she wanted the police to have it, she would have shared it with them. Besides, Mrs. Kane said Alexa wrote in code, so I might be the only one who can decipher it. If I find something relevant, I'll immediately tell Liam.

With that decided, I put the gear in drive and start to pull out, when my phone rings with a call from TRP.

I put the gear back in park and wince as Charlie's voice explodes through the speaker. "Where are you? We need you at the studio pronto."

"What's going on?" I pull the phone away from my ear.

"Have you been hiding under a rock?" Charlie barks. "Please tell me you're aware of what just happened on the women's team. Kate?"

"I'm sorry, I had something—" A person behind me honks and motions to ask if I'm pulling out of my spot. I shake my head.

"Quinn quit the national team, Kate. She quit!" Charlie yells.

Quinn quit the national team? No one quits the Olympics. "Are you sure?" I ask, not believing I heard correctly.

"Yes, I'm effing sure," Charlie yells. "And she's going to explain her decision to you. You! In an hour."

"What?" I'm completely confused by Charlie's statement. I check my phone to see if I missed any calls. Nothing pops up.

"Quinn went on Instagram and posted she will explain her decision to you at three p.m. At the studio. Where are you, Kate? It's one fifty-five p.m."

My stomach does a flip as I register the urgency. I set my GPS to TRP and pull out of the spot. "I'm driving now—and will get there at two forty-nine p.m., assuming traffic doesn't change. Could we push the announcement?"

"Not if we can help it. Everyone is going to turn on TRP at three p.m. It might be our highest-rated hour of the Olympics."

Ratings. Always ratings.

"Let's talk through how to make this work," Charlie says, his voice calming. "I'll have an intern meet you on the street and deal with your car. Next, are you TV ready?"

I glance down at my simple black dress, which will be fine for television. I need some jewelry, though—something so I won't look drab. "I have a necklace and earrings in my top drawer. Have someone grab them. And I don't have any foundation on."

I hear him whisper about the jewelry, and then he tells me hair and makeup will be standing by. I merge onto the Long Island Expressway and move to the left lane, keeping pace with the other cars speeding toward Manhattan. "Any idea why she would quit?" Charlie says. "And why she wants to talk to you?"

"No idea why she quit," I respond. "As for talking to me—I am the correspondent covering women's soccer." I hear the irritation in my voice, feeling a little insulted. But he's right to ask. *Why* me? Does her decision have anything to do with my past with Savy? Or the discovery of Alexa's body? I think back to when we found Alexa in the training room. Quinn asked if Savy and I knew her? Did Quinn pick up more than we thought? I frankly didn't think she was smart enough to tap into nuance. Maybe I misjudged her? But even if she picked up on our connection with Alexa, why in the world would that affect her decision to leave this team? It doesn't make sense.

"Kate?"

"I don't know, Charlie. I can't think of any reason to quit the Olympic team. Even if she was injured, she'd ride the bench." A car cuts me off, and I press my brakes. *Jerk.* "Maybe she's having a tantrum?"

"On the biggest stage during the biggest competition of her life?" Charlie asks. "Do you think she's having some emotional trauma after finding the body in the ice bath?"

"Maybe?" I think as someone flashes their brights, signaling a cop ahead. I move to the middle lane and slow to the speed limit. "Charlie, read me her post again."

He clears his throat: "I will no longer be giving my time to the national team. I quit. I will explain myself to Kate Green at 3:00 p.m."

I check the time on my dashboard—it shows 2:05 p.m. "I don't get it," I say.

"We'll know soon enough," Charlie says and tells me he needs to go. "Call back when you're close." Charlie clicks off.

Whatever Quinn's reason, this will be the biggest story I've ever covered. I flip on the news station and hear my name. *Stunning developments in women's soccer. The young superstar Quinn Price abruptly quit the team and announced it over social media. She is keeping mum about her reasons, saying she will explain in an exclusive interview with former soccer gold-medalist Kate Green.*

My phone rings with a not entirely surprising caller. "Kate." Savy's southern accent is strong. "You're going to give her airtime?"

"She came to me." I put my blinker on and take the exit for the Fifty-Ninth Street Bridge. "I didn't even know about it until my boss called. What happened?"

I hear Savy pacing. She must be in her office. The team plays in the semifinals the day after tomorrow. "On the record—Quinn wasn't the type of player for my team."

I glance at the dashboard, 2:38. "And off the record?"

"What do you think?" Savy snaps.

"I would guess you cut her and she's trying to spin the story."

Savy doesn't respond.

"If that's true," I say, feeling exasperated by all the cloak-and-dagger. "Why not just say it?"

"I don't want to dignify her games. My job is to win the Olympics, not fuel her drama."

"It's too late for that. This story has a life of its own." Savy doesn't say anything, but I hear her pacing back and forth, back and forth. "I need to go." She draws out the words.

"Wait!" I yell. "What were you doing in your office during halftime the day Alexa was killed? Why didn't you go out with the team?"

"My God, Kate," she says into the phone, and then I hear her tell whoever is in her office that she needs a moment. The door shuts before she speaks again. "You really think I killed Alexa? Knocked her out and dragged her into the ice bath in the few minutes I had before running out to the field?"

"How did you know she was knocked out?" I ask, holding my breath.

There's silence. "She had a bruise on her head, Kate. Don't you remember?"

I do but still make a note that in all the mayhem, it's a fact Savy registered. Did she *notice* it or *know* about it?

"I realize I made some mistakes back then—I was young and stupid. But I'd never have intentionally hurt someone. I'm not a monster," Savy says.

You were a monster, though, I think. *Your anger went well beyond the boundaries of normal. And you saw how scared Alexa was when she was gagged and blindfolded.* "I have a lot to be ashamed about, Savy, but you have so much more."

"You're a real shit, Kate," she says and hangs up.

The traffic slows as I cross Fifth Avenue at Forty-Ninth Street. Two blocks from TRP. The clock shows 2:46 p.m.

Private security guards direct traffic away from our building, waving me in front—nice to see Charlie putting the TRP security to use. I pull up as a young man with round glasses opens my door.

"Ms. Green, I'll park the car." He slides into the driver's seat as I step out. Two producers flank me and hustle me toward the building.

"Wait." I turn back to the car. "I left my bag." *And Alexa's diary.*

"The intern will bring it to you," one of the producers says and starts texting.

"I really need it." I hesitate.

"Six minutes," the other producer calls. "Come on, we need to hustle." She breaks into a light jog, and I follow, glancing as David's car disappears around the corner.

More security blocks the entrance to the building, where I see media pushed against barricades. Reporters yell questions.

"What will Quinn say?"

"Why did she quit?"

"Why did she decide to speak to you?"

"Four minutes." The producer hands me my necklace as we step inside the lobby. I secure it around my neck while we walk across the marble to studio A. They are having me report from the studio with windows visible from the street. *Great! More pressure.*

I step inside and fasten my earrings. "Two minutes," the stage manager yells.

"Kate." Quinn waves from behind the glass desk, dressed in a pale silk pantsuit, her face fully made up, her thin hair curled. "Bet you're happy with me—this is going to be your biggest story yet. Am I right?" She beams as I settle into the chair next to her. The makeup and hair teams start working on me.

"One minute," the stage manager calls from the floor while listening to directions over his large headphones.

"Any preview of what's going on?" I ask Quinn as the makeup artist mumbles for me to stay still.

"You'll have to wait like all the other bitches," she says with bravado, but I spot a glimmer of nerves.

"Thirty seconds, Kate," a voice says in my ear. "You're the top story."

"This will have to do," the makeup artist says and steps back with a shrug.

I rub my hands together, trying to warm up in the ice-cold studio. The stage manager grins from inside his winter coat as he points to the pedestal camera where I'll start. "Five, four, three . . ." He uses his fingers for the remainder of the countdown, and then the red light shines from the camera.

David's voice booms through my earpiece. He gives a short recap of the situation and then introduces me. "Kate Green is standing by with Quinn Price, who will explain her shocking decision to quit the Olympic soccer team. Kate."

"Thanks, David," I say and for a moment feel a flood of warmth, hearing his voice. I turn to Quinn, who gives a devilish smile.

"Quinn, welcome to our studio. Why don't we get right to it?" I say. "You posted on Instagram that you will no longer give your time to the national team. What happened?"

"It's very simple. Coach Savannah Baker is a terror to play for, and I needed to take a stand against her treatment of her players." Quinn raises her hands as she talks, and I see an Alexa Kane bracelet on her wrist.

"It's my understanding that Coach Baker cut you from the team," I say.

"That's a lie!" Quinn's cheeks flush. "Who told you that? If Coach Baker said that, she's lying. It was my decision. She doesn't appreciate me, and I won't stand for it." Quinn seems confused where to look. She stares into the camera in the middle, but that's a wide shot of us. Did the stage manager forget to tell Quinn to keep her eyes on me? She's not looking as poised as she imagines.

"Quinn." I call her attention toward me. She gets the hint and shifts her gaze.

"So it seems to be a question of she said, she said," I continue. "Do you think people are really going to believe you quit the Olympic team? Something you worked so hard to make?"

"I don't care if they believe it or not." She folds her arms over her chest. "It's the truth. You above anyone should believe me," she says.

"Why me?" I respond, surprised by her words.

"Because I know you don't like Coach Baker," Quinn says, as if that's the most obvious point in the world.

"First of all, whether I personally like Coach Baker—or you, or anyone I cover—is irrelevant."

"But you played with her. You know how mean she can be. How could I play for someone like that?" Quinn's voice quivers, and I wonder, at this moment, who is telling the truth. Both Savy and Quinn are capable of lying to make themselves look better. Savy completely reinvented herself as the *golden coach*.

"What are you going to do now?" I ask Quinn, changing the subject.

"I'm going to hope that the USSF comes to its senses and fires Coach Baker."

"And then you would return to the national team?"

"Absolutely."

"And you are sure a new coach would take you? Given all the—drama?"

"One hundred percent. I'm one of the most talented strikers in the world. Anyone would want me."

I turn back to the pedestal camera and announce that we will return with more of our interview after a quick break. As soon as the light goes out, I unclip my microphone and walk away from the desk. I'm sweating. Under the lights, it went from winter cold to summer hot in minutes.

Charlie runs into the studio. "Great interview. Everyone's watching. Incredible. Junior came down and is giddy." Charlie walks closer to me and whispers, "I might even agree with him that you should get the new show. Keep her going as long as you can. This is gold."

"One minute," the stage manager announcers to the studio. I move back to my seat.

Quinn puts her phone down. "Kate—we're blowing up on socials. It's going great even though you are being a little too tough on me. But I get it. You need to look impartial." She winks.

Ten seconds. Five seconds. Go . . .

"Welcome back to TRP. If you are just joining us, Quinn Price announced she's left the Olympic soccer team just before the semifinals, because of a conflict with Head Coach Baker."

"Not a conflict—there's nothing I did wrong. She's a bully. And she went too far."

"Can you give us more specifics? Does this have anything to do with being benched at the last game?"

"As you know, I got benched early in the last game. She said I didn't pull my weight. I was in good form. She was punishing me for being a leader on the team. She didn't like that my fellow players look to me for guidance. For strategy. She called me into her office today and said I either get on board with her program or leave. 'You are bringing morale down, and I don't like it. Shape up or pack up.'" Quinn mimics Savy's southern accent. This girl has a career in Hollywood if she's truly done with soccer.

I imagine Savy did say those things. But my money is on Savy ending by telling Quinn to clean out her locker.

"I'm not quitting soccer for good," Quinn says. "I just can't play for someone who doesn't appreciate me."

"So, this is a showdown—either you or Coach Baker?"

"Call it whatever you want." Quinn smiles.

The stage manager gives me the signal to wrap, and I throw it back to David. He starts to thank me, but I've already pulled my earpiece out and turned to look at Quinn as the lights go dark.

"So you plan to go head to head with Savy," I say once I'm sure the camera is off us.

She just smiles in response.

CHAPTER 33

David calls as I'm heading out of the studio. Picking up on the first ring, I say, "Aren't you on air?"

"Commercial break," he replies. "Which means I don't have a lot of time. Please don't go home tonight. I'm worried after this morning."

"That's sweet, but—"

He cuts me off. "Did the police find the person who vandalized your car?"

"Not that I heard," I admit.

"I'd feel so much better knowing you are safe at my place." David tells me he already called the doorman and told him to give me his keys. "I won't be there for a while, but you can hang out."

I consider his offer; I want to read Alexa's diary as soon as possible. Going to David's apartment means I can avoid rush hour traffic. Plus, the idea of sitting home alone, even with the alarm working, is not what I'd consider an ideal night. I'm so glad that Nikki and Jackson are away with their dad in the Hamptons even though I was annoyed at first when my ex sprang the idea of the last-minute trip.

"Sounds like an offer I can't refuse." I smile into the phone.

David's air-conditioned lobby is a welcome salve to the heavy heat of early evening.

"Ms. Green." The same young doorman from yesterday calls me over. "Here's the key to Mr. Lopez's apartment. And a package for him."

Inside David's apartment, I dump his package and keys onto the counter and flick on the lights. I've never been here by myself. Is this the next step in our relationship? Keys to one another's homes? *Don't get ahead of yourself, Kate.*

I like the cool vibe of the brick-and-glass open loft, with large rectangular windows, high ceilings, and exposed pipes.

My phone pings with a text from David telling me there's an open bottle of wine in the fridge along with cheese, crackers, and fruit.

My stomach rumbles in response to the information. After everything that went on today, I feel both hyped and exhausted. Something a little snack and glass of wine could fix. I prepare the snack and set it on the coffee table in front of David's deep velvet couch and then take my wine to the window, looking out at the view. Across Columbus Avenue a couple sits on a manicured roof deck with candles flickering on the table. So many hidden worlds in all the different crevices of Manhattan. It makes me feel small.

I return to the couch and retrieve Alexa's diary, skimming the entries of her classes, dinners with parents, and her weekly babysitting job, stopping at the next soccer entry.

> Dear Diary,
> Good news and bad news. I did great at the select showcase. I made it to the regional trials and got recruited to be on an Academy Girls Team. My dad is thrilled because the Academy Teams are free! The director explained that we're the girls they see heading for D1 soccer. And maybe the National Team. Could you imagine me playing in the Olympics? The bad news is no one else from my local soccer team made it to the next level and now they are saying I'm selfish. One girl drew a picture of me kissing the coach's butt and passed it around to everyone. My mom keeps asking what's wrong, but I can't tell her. If she knew about

the photo, she'd call all their moms and make it worse. I wish I could just share things with her without worrying she'll do something embarrassing.

My heart goes out to Mrs. Kane. Even though most teens get angry with their parents, that must have been a difficult entry for her to read. I turn the page and continue.

Dear Diary,
I'm glad to be done with the girls from my old soccer team. They were the worst. I've met some new girls in middle school, and we've been clicking. YAY!!!!!

I continue to read through her entries—many about the mean girls in her grade, her experience with the regional soccer program, and her issues with her mother. Her next entry makes me smile.

Dear Diary,
Oh my god. Oh My GOD. OH MY GOD!!!! I got invited to National Camp. THE national camp for soccer. I could SCREAM. I can't wait to go. There are girls from all over the country. I can't wait . . . I bet they'll be really nice. It will be exciting to play with people at my level and not worry about jealousy. I hope my roommate is nice.

I catch my breath on the word *roommate*, remembering our early days together. I'm about halfway through the notebook and stand up, realizing how stiff my body feels. I must have been reading for hours. I walk around the apartment, trying to loosen my muscles. Art posters hang on the walls. I recognize the Rothko and Monet but don't know the others. I realize family photographs are missing from the place. No pictures of David with his parents or siblings. No picture of the sister who passed away.

I stifle a yawn as I check the time: 9:00 p.m. David must have gotten stuck at work. The stretching only made me more tired, and I know I need to shut my eyes for a little while before I pass out. I set my alarm for 10:00 p.m., lie down on the couch, pull the throw blanket over me, and close my eyes. I feel myself drift off into welcome slumber.

———

I'm aware of noise coming from behind me, yet I know I'm asleep. I force my eyes open and take in the surroundings, remembering I'm at David's loft and not home. I push myself up and blink against the bright light pouring into the room.

"Morning, sunshine." David steps toward me from the kitchen, two cups of coffee in hand.

"What time is it?" I sit up on the couch and check my phone, 6:30 a.m. "I thought I set my alarm—"

"Your phone was beeping when I came in last night." He hands me a cup of coffee. "I figured if the noise didn't wake you, then you probably needed the sleep." He sits down next to me. "I hope that's all right?"

I gulp down the coffee. Grateful for the caffeine, mixed that David decided to let me sleep. What if there was an important reason I set my alarm? Shouldn't he have checked? I hear Nikki's voice in my head: *Stop looking for excuses to be critical.*

The notebook. I scan the area, finding it on the edge of the coffee table. Did I leave it on the table? Or had I tucked it into my bag?

I reach over to the notebook and put it into my tote, which sits at the edge of the couch.

"Is that super secret?" He smiles, and I can't tell if he's joking. He tells me he put scones out on the counter and that he's heading into the shower. "Take your time, I just need to get ready—Charlie wants me anchoring again this morning," he says, like he's complaining about getting too much money. *Poor me, I'm working so hard at this awesome thing that will advance my career. Boo-hoo.*

These anchoring shifts likely put him closer to hosting the new show. Does David realize we appear to be pawns in a standoff between Junior and Charlie?

He goes off to get dressed, and I pad into the kitchen area and pour myself a second cup of coffee. As the caffeine takes effect, I start to feel less ornery, becoming appreciative of the extra sleep. I pick up a scone and start eating, when the phone inside David's drawer vibrates again.

"Your super-secret phone is ringing," I tell David as he emerges dressed in khakis and a button-down.

"I'll deal with it later." He drapes a tie around his neck.

My phone vibrates with a text, as if the person trying to reach David decided to try me. "I think your cousin is calling me," I joke. David's eyes widen, not finding my comment funny. I remove my phone and unlock it as David walks toward me. I hear myself gasp.

"My car." I look at the photo on the screen of the scratches and flat tires. David walks toward me, and I show him the screen. Whoever did this has my phone number and is taunting me. Three dots appear . . . we watch and wait. I hear David's breathing grow heavy.

The words pop up on my screen, and I jump up and away from David.

"I can explain," he says.

"What does this mean?" I scream. "Why did the person write, 'Stay away from my *boyfriend*'?"

Another picture pops up, a selfie with David kissing a young blonde woman. The time stamp shows a few days ago.

My head spins. "You've been dating someone else?"

"No," he says. "I mean, yes. But no." He's fumbling for words. "We dated before you and I started. And, well, I just—I mean she was waiting for me outside the station a few nights ago. We grabbed a drink. She doesn't mean anything to me . . ."

"So, you kissed her?" I cut him off.

"It was a few drinks," David says. "I'm sorry. It was stupid. I wasn't sure we were exclusive." He hangs his head.

"Then you might have thought to ask," I yell back. "But that's not even the main point—the point is she's violent. Did you know she was dangerous?"

"She said I should stay away from you. I didn't think she meant—"

"I have kids," I say, terrified I put them in danger. "Who is this woman?"

"Someone I met online—a while ago," he mumbles. "Honestly, Kate, she means nothing to me. I was trying to end it. It's practically over. I won't see her anymore."

I rush out of the kitchen to gather my things.

David continues to speak, but I'm not listening as I grab my tote. "I don't love her," he says as I grab my phone from the counter, push past him into the hallway. "Kate, I really care about you. Please don't go." I jam my finger against the elevator button and squeeze in as soon as the doors start to part.

On the street, I can't breathe. Did he cancel our plans Thursday to be with her? Even if we weren't exclusive, this is still scummy.

I refuse to cry. *No crying.*

My phone rings with a call from Charlie. "Yes?" I say.

"Are you okay?" He actually sounds concerned.

"Fine. Allergies," I answer. "What's up?"

"We're changing our meeting from one p.m. to eleven a.m. Can you get here by then?"

"Yes."

"Anything new with Quinn or a response from the women's team?"

"Nothing yet," I say. "But I'll circle back with everyone this morning." We hang up, and I realize I need to stay on top of the story. I got so distracted by Alexa's diary. And I won't let David sabotage me. Thunder sounds, and a raindrop lands on my shoulder. I look up in the sky as dark clouds descend on the city.

What should I do? My car's not here. It wouldn't make sense to take a train back to Greenwich only to return shortly after. I have a change of clothes in my bag, something I've learned to carry as a reporter.

It's times like these, I wish my mom and stepfather were close. But I do have my dad.

I call Liam and ask if I can crash for a few hours. He agrees and gives me the address. As I'm in the taxi on the way to his apartment, I realize how strange it is that I've never seen his place.

I step out of the taxi and run to his building. The neighborhood feels familiar, right by Columbia University, and near where I spent the first six years of my life. I don't have many vivid memories, only flashes and images. Feelings.

Liam's building is a small brick structure with a single elevator and no doorman. I get out on the third floor and spot his head poking out from a door at the end of the hall.

He follows me inside, and I see concern in his eyes, but thankfully he doesn't ask me anything other than if I want coffee. I take the coffee and move to a square table, between a small kitchen and living area.

"Tough morning?" He sits across from me, dressed in a button-down and jeans. I nod my head and sip.

"How long have you lived here?" I ask.

"Thirty-seven years," he says. Since my mom, brother, and I left New York. His phone rings, and he excuses himself. I get up and study the pictures on a shelf next to the television. I lift a photo of me from the Olympics, standing on the podium just after receiving our gold medals. I return it to the shelf and pick up the one next to it—of my brother, Anthony, from when he graduated college.

"I need another half an hour." Liam's voice floats down the hallway. "Nonnegotiable," he says, then reappears.

"You don't have to stay. I'll be fine."

"I'm staying." He returns to the table. "Nonnegotiable." He gives a half smile. Too exhausted to argue, I sit back down.

"Do you want to talk about it?"

I shake my head.

"All right." He stretches his arms overhead. "Would you like me to update you on the case?"

"Yes," I reply, hearing how meek my voice sounds.

"Okay, but first—" He gets up, rumbles around in the kitchen, and then returns with Hostess cupcakes on a plate. I pick one up and peel off the icing, nibbling along the edges.

"We spoke to Cameron," Liam says and picks up the cake part of the cupcake I stripped of icing. "He seemed relieved to talk to us, actually." Liam takes a large bite, the white filling dripping onto his lip. He wipes it away and continues. "If he's telling the truth, then Alexa had something serious she wanted to share. We've now heard that twice. From Cameron. And from the email she sent you."

"And the fact she called me after I didn't respond to the email. She seemed very anxious to get in touch. Do you think she knew she was in danger?" I ask.

"Maybe," Liam says and then tells me the police spoke to Ginny.

"How'd that go?" I ask.

"She seemed thrilled to get questioned by the police—like it was the most exciting thing that ever happened to her."

"It might be," I reply.

"Anyway—her alibi is solid. She was helping her mom, who's sick, and a visiting nurse verified Ginny's presence at the house."

Liam shifts in his chair. I feel a tear on my cheek and wipe it away.

"You sure you don't want to talk about it?" he says again.

The words spill out. I recount my morning in fits and starts between outbursts of tears. I see his eyes get dark when he realizes this woman is the one who vandalized my car. But he lets me finish without interrupting.

"This isn't your fault," he says, handing me a tissue. "What you should be proud of is that you walked away. Knowing when to end something isn't easy."

"You sound like a fortune cookie," I reply, sniffing.

He laughs and checks his watch. "I do need to leave. Will you be all right?"

I nod my head. Liam goes into a kitchen drawer and pulls out a key hanging on a soccer-ball chain. "Take my extra set if you go out." He places it on the counter. "Consider my home your home, Kate." He flashes his half smile as he pulls on a raincoat. "And text me that woman's cell number and everything she sent. Even though you ended things with David, I want to check her out—she sounds unhinged."

"Thanks," I say.

"You never need to thank me," he says and leaves.

CHAPTER 34

Liam's apartment feels like a favorite worn leather jacket. I still have two hours before I need to leave for the TRP meeting and decide to shower and change before diving into Alexa's diary.

Under the hot spray of water, I let the morning wash away. I get what Liam is saying about ending it. But I still can't believe how I misjudged David. If I'm this upset, I can only imagine how Nikki's going to feel.

By the time I'm dressed in my brown top and black cotton skirt, I feel a tiny bit better and settle into Liam's recliner. One more task to check off before returning to Alexa's diary. I need to see if I can get an update on the Quinn drama. I pull up the news feeds and find Quinn's name blasted everywhere.

QUINN PRICE WALKS AWAY FROM THE OLYMPICS. QUINN ACCUSES THE GOLDEN COACH OF BEING A BULLY.

Not all headlines paint Quinn in a positive light. Or as the one who ended things.

SOURCES SAY COACH BAKER CUT QUINN FOR HER ANTICS. TEAMMATES SECRETLY TRASH QUINN AND SAY COACH BAKER KICKED QUINN OFF TEAM.

All the content rehashes my interview from yesterday. Quinn shockingly hasn't uttered another word or posted anything in over twenty hours. Does she even possess that kind of self-control? The United States Soccer Federation issued an official statement saying they won't comment on distractions and that they support Coach Savannah Baker's right to make decisions regarding her roster as she sees fit. In other words, Savy cut Quinn and Quinn went on a rage.

I try Quinn, straight to voicemail. I send a text, checking on her and asking if she wants to speak. Nothing.

Next, I turn to the other side and call Willow, the public relations officer for Savy and the team. Also, straight to voicemail. I send her a text asking for a comment.

Her response comes quickly: The women's team is focused on tomorrow's semifinal match and won't get distracted by side issues.

One more person to try: I dial the number and wait for it to go to voicemail.

"What do you want?" To my surprise Savy picks up.

"I'm calling in an official work capacity," I say. "Do you want to comment on Quinn's interview? And her accusations that you bullied her."

Savy sighs. She sounds tired. "I don't have any official comment," she says but doesn't hang up. "Can we talk off the record?"

"Sure," I answer and wait for her to speak.

"I didn't anticipate this Quinn thing would blow up into such a media frenzy," Savy says, in a shockingly candid admission. It makes me wonder if she has any friends, because I should be the last person Savy confides in.

"How is the team feeling—off the record?" I add. Through Liam's door, I hear footsteps in the hallway and a door shut. Thin walls.

"The team's had enough of Quinn's crap," she says. "They're furious at her behavior during the quarterfinals. And they're livid that she's adding to the distractions. Were we that juvenile?" she asks, her southern accent strong.

"I think we put up a better front," I answer, reaching for my coffee, which sits on the side table next to Liam's television remote. "We saved all our drama for behind closed doors. I do remember a certain player who broke a television when she was pulled from a game," I say.

"Yeah, but I was a kid." She laughs. "Still—fair point."

There's silence between us, and I hear muted conversations through Liam's walls again. I wonder if all the noise bothers him.

"I know what I did back then was terrible," Savy says, in a whisper. "Especially with Alexa. And I'm not making an excuse. I was just doing what the girls before me did to us. A tradition."

I don't say anything.

"I need to get going. See you tomorrow?"

"Yes. And don't blow off my interview after the game."

"I won't," she says. "I promise." I hang up, almost believing her. Can Savy change? It's the same question I asked about Liam last year, and he seems like he's managed it. I get up and walk around his small, neat living room. He's lived here thirty-seven years, yet there are no visible signs of junk. No piles of mail or papers. It's not sterile; Liam's imprint is all over the place, with the warm leather couch, wooden bookshelves, and retro turntable in the corner.

I glance at his albums, pulling out the Mamas & the Papas. Liam and my mom loved this album, and I remember them playing *California Dreamin'* over and over again. In fact, when Mom told my brother and me that we were moving out west, she said it was to the place mentioned in the song. She tried to make the trip sound fun, like an adventure. But she couldn't hide the simmering resentment bubbling up when she thought we weren't around. I close my eyes and think back to those hushed conversations between her and my dad. I always thought anger was the prevalent emotion. Now I wonder if what I picked up on was actually fear.

I put the record back and walk over to his bookshelf.

I run my finger along the worn spines. Most are memoirs and biographies. I scan the titles on the top shelf. Big, thick volumes that I can see my father methodically reading, from biographies of Thomas Jefferson to Theodore Roosevelt to Winston Churchill.

My eyes land on a book titled *My Father Was a Bad Man*. I pick it up and stare at the picture on the back, showing a young Marsha

Compton before she was mayor. I hardly recognize the stunning person in the photo—it shows the same intelligent eyes, but her hair and makeup are much more glamorous. I flip through the book and stop at a note she wrote to my father.

> Dearest Liam,
> I wouldn't have gotten here without you.
> All my love,
> Marsha

What does she mean by that? Did my father support her emotionally during this time? Or did he literally help with the operation to bring the older Compton to justice? I can't fight this nagging feeling that Mayor Marsha Compton and my father might have been romantically involved. Or, for that matter, are involved now. I think back to my encounter with Mayor Compton and how her eyes lit up at the mention of Liam.

If they are together, I bet there'd be some sign of her in the apartment. An extra toothbrush? Special shampoo? Does she have a drawer?

I return the book to the shelf, making a mental note to read it. I walk toward the other rooms, in search of clues. I search through the bathroom and find nothing incriminating—just a razor, shaving cream, Irish Spring soap. No fancy shampoos, or makeup remover, or even a hair dryer. I open the first closed door at the end of the hallway; it squeaks as I push. There's a desk by the window and a pullout couch facing a television. No papers sit on top of the desk. I certainly didn't inherit Liam's neat gene. I reach for the first drawer and open it. A small pile of bills sits in the drawer, along with a box of paper clips and a few pens.

I try the second drawer and find it locked. Why would Liam lock a drawer inside his apartment? Is it to keep nosy daughters from snooping through the contents? I reach under the desk, feeling around for a key.

Nothing. I look on the shelf and even behind the television. No luck. Reluctantly, I leave the room and go into Liam's bedroom.

The square, neat space smells like Liam's soap. He's made the bed, pulling the brown comforter up against the wooden headboard. I walk over to the dresser and place my hand on a drawer, then lower my arm. Suddenly I feel embarrassed. I've taken my snooping too far. Rummaging around in Liam's clothing definitely feels wrong. Even if Marsha does have a drawer, should that matter? Liam deserves some privacy.

I leave the room and pull the door closed behind me. Settling back into the recliner, I pick up Alexa's diary and turn to the next entry.

> Dear Diary,
> Soccer Camp was ok. The older girls were really mean, especially one they call Savannah Baker. She might be the meanest person I ever met. She physically kicked me off the bench with the bottom of her foot. Who does that?! I was so mad at myself for crying. My roommate Kate is super nice. Well, mostly nice. I just was a little upset the first night. She blew me off right after we made the first cut to the A team. I don't know if she did it because the older girls pressured her or because she didn't like me. We got closer over the rest of the days, so I think she likes me now.

I close the book, angry at my thirteen-year-old self. But, I mean, I was thirteen. Plus, I have a lot worse things to punish myself over regarding Alexa. I take another sip of coffee, which is cold at this point, and then continue reading.

> Dear Diary,
> I didn't get invited to the winter National Camp—my coach told me not to worry. But I feel miserable. My

coach says they only took the older girls at this one and he's sure I'll get invited to the next one. But I think he said that just to try and make me feel better. Kate didn't make it either. We've been writing to each other, and I decided I really like her.

I read through about forty more pages of entries, mostly detailing mundane things from the rest of her freshman and sophomore years. I stop at an entry from the middle of her junior year.

Dear Diary,
I was dreading returning to school after New Year's. But there's a new boy on the bus. He's also a junior and really cute. His name is Cameron.

The entries following are all variations on the Cameron theme. *He's so cute. He said hi to me today. We passed notes in study hall.* On. And on. Finally, she gets to an event I remember her describing to me during one of our phone calls. I can still hear the excitement in her voice as she recounted every single detail.

Dear Diary,
Cameron asked me out. We were getting off the bus and he asked if he could talk to me for a minute. He waited until everyone else walked away and then he asked me to a movie. He was so cute, he started stumbling like he was nervous. I still can't believe it. We are going on a date!! I'm so happy.

After that, the entries are only about Cameron. Full of teenage angst, jumping from Alexa's confidence that he really likes her to entries where she's convinced he's into someone else. It takes about two months before she seems to settle into the relationship.

Dear Diary,
Things are sooooooo amazing!! He asked me to Junior Prom! Cameron and I are together. I HAVE A BOYFRIEND.

The next entry is predictably about her prom dress.

I found the most amazing lavender dress for prom. It's gorgeous. But it's expensive. Mom's saying I have to pay for it myself if I want to buy it. She's so clueless. UGH! I don't really want to keep babysitting but now I have to. The kids are all right and the dad's hardly around, but the mom is really bossy and snobby. She acts like she's better than me. Just cuz you're richer doesn't mean you're better, Bitch. Cameron is trying to teach me to stand up for myself.

I close the diary and think back to my conversations with Alexa about babysitting. I remember she would complain about the family. I never gave it much thought. I equated it with my complaining about watching my brother—for free. *At least you get paid,* I'd always point out. But maybe it was worse than I realized. I look for other babysitting entries and find a really long one.

Dear Diary,
More babysitting drama. The mom called in a panic begging me to come over. Her husband was supposed to be home, but something came up. She had her book club and didn't want to miss it. I almost said no even though I was free. But I really need the money. The kids were so happy when I got there. I wonder if anyone gives them attention? The Yankee game was on, so we watched together. The older one has become

a huge Yankees fan, thanks to me. At least, I've been a positive influence on his baseball choices. He even made me a picture of the two of us watching a game in the stands. He told me the Yankees are his favorite team. It was all going fine. The Yankees even won. Then, the dad showed up. I've only seen him once before and he's really scary. I might even understand why the wife is a bitch. Who wouldn't be married to him. The second he walked in the door he started screaming at the older kid for leaving his jacket on the bench instead of hung up. I mean—it's a jacket. He called him all kinds of horrible names—useless, stupid. He's not mean like my mom. He's nasty mean. I wouldn't be surprised if he hits the kids. Then he noticed me standing by the couch and he tried to be extra nice, like he was embarrassed I saw that. He gave me an extra $20.00—and made a comment about how he's sure I'd never leave my stuff around. As if.

The parents sound awful. I wonder what happened to those kids and if Alexa continued to watch them. The following pages are, once again, all about Cameron. I skim through until I find a soccer entry.

Dear Diary,
This is everything Kate and I have worked to get. For more than three years, we wanted to reach the U-17 World Cup. WORLD CUP!!!!!!!!!! We knew we'd get called to the camp. One more step and we'll make the team. I feel really excited about this. I can't believe how well things are going in my life. I'm kind of shocked. Cameron is amazing. I'm on the verge of getting everything I want with soccer. School isn't even that bad and I've made some nice friends.

My mom would be so mad if she saw this. She'd say I'm going to jinx everything. Don't tell her.

I remember Alexa telling me how superstitious Mrs. Kane was and how her mom would say things like *poo, poo, poo*, thinking it would keep the bad away. I get up to stretch my legs and look out the window, where the rain is still coming down in heavy sheets. Someone crosses and steps right into the middle of a puddle, jerking their leg back too late. Looking at all the umbrellas makes me shiver.

I step back and walk into the kitchen area in search of more coffee.

Liam has a basic coffee maker, but I'm surprised to find a full bag of gourmet dark roast next to the machine. The coffee smells rich and strong. I pick it up and see the purchase date was this morning. Liam must have run out when I called. I can't help but feel touched by the gesture.

I take my steaming cup of coffee and return to my seat. The next entry in the diary is dated a few weeks before the World Cup camp.

Dear Diary,

I was babysitting again today, and the father came home unexpectedly. He threw a book at the older son. It hit him in the ear and he was bleeding! I went to help him when the father grabbed my arm, shoved money in my hand and told me if I said anything I'd regret it. His eyes reminded me of a bear. I know he could feel me shaking. And, I swear, he smiled at my fear. Meanwhile, both kids were crying silent tears like they knew if they made a noise things would only get worse. I'm absolutely not going back to that house ever again. I wonder if I should report the dad for his abuse? I might need to tell my parents.

The next entry is dated the following day and is very troubling.

Dear Diary,
I feel completely manipulated and don't know what to do. I spent all night thinking about telling my parents about what happened while I was babysitting. I decided I was going to tell them at dinner. Then, my father said the awful dad reached out to him and asked if my dad would be his accountant. My dad said he's been trying to get Mr. H as a client for years and all of a sudden Mr. H's secretary called him out of the blue and said I had spoken so highly of my father, Mr. H thought he should use my dad. My dad said this would mean life changing money. Paying off the mortgage, a splurge vacation. He was so happy; I didn't have the heart to say anything.

I read the passage again, a prickly feeling entering my brain that I might, in fact, know the family Alexa is talking about. The next passage confirms my suspicion.

Dear Diary,
I didn't know what to do on Friday. My dad answered a call from Mrs. Hutchinson and said she needed an emergency babysitter. I heard him say I was free. He looked so happy, I didn't have the heart to tell him how much Mr. Hutchinson scared me so I agreed to go but told my dad, with the World Cup camp only two weeks away, I really shouldn't babysit anymore after today. Thankfully, he agreed.

Mr. Hutchinson. I can't believe the coincidence. Although, on some level it fits. And it was what went through my mind when I read the reference to Mr. H. It explains the reason Curls was at the candlelight vigil. But it raises significant red flags as to why Junior lied about knowing Alexa. Clearly, Junior is the older brother Alexa keeps mentioning.

I think back to my encounter with Junior at Yankee Stadium. I asked him why his brother, Curls, was at the candlelight vigil for Alexa. He acted like he'd never heard her name. Did he think his father would overhear us discussing Alexa? But after all these years, why would that matter?

And if Junior was the son closer to Alexa, as the diary suggests, why didn't *he* attend the vigil? Maybe something else happened between Alexa and Junior?

I google *Great Neck home/Wyatt Hutchinson* and watch the estate with the gingerbread cabanas pop up on my screen. The mega mansion that I admired belongs to the Hutchinson family. And it was just blocks from Alexa's home. I pick up the diary and continue.

The next entry is dated after the World Cup camp, which means she didn't write anything after babysitting for the Hutchinson family that night. These entries are equally troubling and recount, in detail, the hazing incident and my part in it. My eyes linger over her final paragraph.

> I feel alone in the world. My parents don't understand me. Cameron keeps bothering me. And after all these years, Kate didn't even stand up for me. I'm not sure it's worth going on.

There's no date, but I imagine this entry might have been from around the time when Alexa tried to kill herself. I feel sick. The following pages are blank, as if echoing her despair, followed by the coded entries Mrs. Kane mentioned.

These bubble letters are foreign to me—jagged, sharp, angry looking compared to our usual cloudlike, rounded style. The words are alarming—*Disgust, Hate, Vile*.

Mrs. Kane told me she believes the hazing incident was *one* thing that happened. She believes something else awful occurred and it's hidden inside these letters.

I check my watch to see if I have time to decipher the hidden messages. I'm already running late. With great reluctance, I pack Alexa's diary into my bag, clean my mug, and head out the door, grabbing the extra set of keys and an umbrella on my way out.

CHAPTER 35

I find an empty seat in the conference room toward the back, not in much of a mood to socialize. I'm hoping that David will be on anchor duty and miss the meeting. The idea of seeing him makes me physically ill.

Charlie walks in with not one, but two Hutchinsons. Their presence sucks the air right out of the room. The producer next to me glances in my direction, raising a brow. I shrug in response. While Junior rarely shows his face, Wyatt almost never does. In fact, the only time I saw Wyatt here was when NetWorld gobbled up a slew of local television stations after a big battle with the government over antitrust regulations.

"Don't get alarmed." Wyatt's smooth voice rings through the air as he steps to the head of the table, dressed in a tan suit and beige tie. All I hear is the voice of the monster in Alexa's diary. The man who brutalized his children and terrified Alexa. Behind his poised demeanor, I search for signs of the sadistic father and spot them in the edges of his tight smile and accusatory stare.

I move my gaze to Junior, searching for the fragile child Alexa described. He's there in Junior's hunched shoulders and side glances toward his father, as if still searching for approval. But there's also an arrogance within Junior. "I'd like to sit here," he says to the assignment editor already settled next to Wyatt.

As the woman starts to stand, Wyatt motions for her to sit back down. "Junior, sit over there." Wyatt points to the empty seat next to me. Junior's face flushes, either in anger or in embarrassment, as he obeys his father and walks toward me.

"Hi, Kate," he says, keeping his eyes on his father. I nod hello but hold my tongue, despite my desperation to ask Junior why he lied about his relationship with Alexa.

"Let's get to it." Charlie starts right in. "Mr. Hutchinson wants to speak to you."

Charlie gestures toward Wyatt, who grasps his hands in front of himself. "Ladies and gentlemen, I have the greatest admiration for all of you." He looks around the room, attempting eye contact with us. "But—"

"Here it comes," the producer near me mumbles, not caring that Junior snaps his head and leers at him.

"I'm troubled by *your* ratings."

What a choice of words. If the ratings were good, they'd be *our* ratings.

A universal groan fills the air as Wyatt blames us for a predicted outcome. When Wyatt outbid his competitors, including NBC, most speculated he paid too much. But he insisted TRP would breathe new life into the Olympics. This should be a Wyatt Hutchinson problem. Not a staff problem.

"Only one event is outdoing projections—women's soccer." Wyatt turns in my direction. "Good job, Kate."

I feel angry eyes on me as Wyatt smiles across the table. I'm not stupid enough to think I'm the reason for the fortuitous ratings. I know that my scintillating reporting isn't bringing in the viewers—I'm just riding the drama wave. A thought that makes me feel sad about viewers in general.

"So, here's the story," Wyatt says. "All of you need to do a better job. I expect ratings to improve during this final week of the games. Questions?"

"We can't do anything more than we are," an old, grizzled producer calls out. "Do you want blood from us?"

"If it will drive up ratings, then that's exactly what I want," Wyatt says with a straight face. Most people wouldn't be so blunt, but the old guard doesn't take bullshit from people like Wyatt, and rarely does it cost them their jobs.

The door to the conference room opens, and David walks in. All eyes turn to him, and I almost feel sorry for him. Almost.

"You're late!" Wyatt yells.

"I was anchoring—" David starts to explain, not reading the room.

"You're late," Wyatt roars. "Sit."

David scurries around the table, and everyone watches him slink into the only empty chair, which is, of course, on the other side of me. I wish I could disappear under the table or find an invisibility cloak to hide under.

"What's going on?" He makes the mistake of whispering in my direction.

"You want to know what's going on?" Junior leans over me, his suit jacket brushing my elbow. "If you're coverage doesn't improve, heads are going to roll."

I feel David's eyes on me but refuse to meet them.

"Save the dramatics, Junior. I think everyone got the message." Wyatt stands and motions to Junior, who obediently follows his father out the door. No one speaks until the men are out of sight; then the room explodes with questions.

"What else do they want us to do?" one reporter yells.

"Working my butt off isn't enough?" another howls.

"For fuck's sake, are we supposed to manufacture a repeat of Tonya Harding and Nancy Kerrigan?" a third voice rings out.

"Everyone." Charlie raises his hands to try and gain control of the room. "Pretend that didn't happen and the meeting is just starting. You're all doing fine. Whatever's going on there is beyond all of our pay grades."

The buzz dies down as everyone looks at Charlie, not quite understanding his meaning.

"There's something stirring upstairs." He shrugs. "Just do your jobs, and I will protect you as best I can."

We all love Charlie for saying that. But we also know there's nothing he can do if the Hutchinsons decide to fire us.

———

I'm so happy to see Jackson and Nikki, I could scream. "How were the Hamptons?" I ask, plopping down on the couch as Jackson flips off the television.

"Fine," Nikki says. "Dad has a new girlfriend."

"She's practically our age." Jackson shakes his head. "Well, not our age, but early twenties, for sure."

"And so stuck up." Nikki rolls her eyes. "She's the worst—not like David." Nikki smiles and asks if David told me she called him.

"He did. That was very sweet of you," I say. "But the truth is— *David* might be the worst."

They both stare at me as I tell them that I discovered David was seeing someone else while we were together. I leave out the part about the woman being a stalker.

The color drains from Nikki's face as if he mistreated her. She comes over to me and starts apologizing. "I shouldn't have pushed you to keep giving him chances." Tears appear in her eyes.

"Nikki." I take her hands in mine. "Don't be silly. It was good to get out there again. And really, I'm fine. And I'm glad I found out now and not before it went further." I repeat Liam's words to them.

"Men," Nikki grumbles and gives me a hug.

"Hey!" Jackson responds.

"Men—except for you." She sits back down, giving him a sly smile. "You know what this calls for, right?"

"Not grilled cheese," Jackson moans. "I can't eat that again."

I laugh, telling him I agree. "How about if I pick up some pizza and ice cream?"

"Sounds great!" Nikki responds. "But we can get it."

"No. I'll get it. I insist," I say. "But I need to borrow your car. Mine is at the shop. I got a couple of flat tires." I don't mention the part where my tires were slashed.

Nikki gives me her keys, and I head out the door, feeling a little bad about keeping the vandalism thing from them. But technically I didn't lie. My car did have flats. Liam also assured me there's nothing more to worry about regarding the woman. She's been properly scared by the police. And, for good measure, informed that David and I are no longer together.

After I get back, we sit around the kitchen counter, shoveling cheesy pizza into our mouths. I didn't realize how starving I was. "Tell me more about Dad's girlfriend," I ask, looking for a good distraction.

"OMG! Do you know she always has makeup on?" Nikki laughs. "Always! She comes down to breakfast dressed like she's going to a nightclub. It's gross."

"And all she does is name-drop," Jackson adds. "Apparently, she's from some wealthy tech family or something. But she's really needy. She holds on to Dad like she's going to fall if she lets go."

"Honestly, I give it a month. Tops," Nikki says.

Jackson clears the pizza boxes and plates, and I take out the ice cream, along with the chocolate sauce, Marshmallow Fluff, and sprinkles that I picked up.

"You went all out!" Jackson smiles. "Nikki—you going to partake?"

"Yes!" She squeals. I've noticed she's been more open to treating herself to fun food recently and take that as a good sign. Not that I'm against her healthy eating, but everyone needs to indulge once in a while.

I dig into my ice cream with the layers of toppings and feel the dessert relax me. Moments like these with my kids feel sacred, and I want to bottle them up and save them.

"This is so good," Nikki says, shoveling another spoonful into her mouth.

"What's on your agendas for the rest of the week?" I ask them.

"Nothing much, now that camp is over," Jackson says. "I really enjoyed it this year. It was fun working with the kids."

I look at Nikki and ask if it got more tolerable since the last time we spoke.

"Yeah, it got better. A few of the kids actually turned out to be decent tennis players."

We finish up, and Jackson heads to his room. Nikki loiters at the counter, and I get the feeling she wants to talk about something. I sit back down and ask what's on her mind.

"I was wondering about your dad—" She squirms in her chair. "It doesn't feel right to call him Grandpa. Is that all right?"

"Of course that's all right." I reach for her hands and give them a squeeze. "I sometimes have trouble referring to him as *dad*. Half the time I call him Liam."

She starts nibbling on her lip as a car outside pulls onto our street. For a second, I worry it's the blue Honda, but I see through the window it's our neighbor.

"What's troubling you?" I ask her.

"Is Grandpa Lou," she says, referring to my stepfather. "Is he upset about all this? Does he feel like we're replacing him?"

I smile at her, so taken with her empathy. "It's a great question, and I had a long talk with him about Liam. He just wants us to be happy, and adding someone else to our lives doesn't take away our affection for Grandpa Lou."

"It's just hard to get used to," she says.

"I know," I respond. "We can take all the time we need. Feel better?"

"I guess." She shrugs.

"You can call Grandpa Lou and discuss it with him. I know he's always happy to talk things through."

Her face brightens at the suggestion, and she hops off the stool and says she's going to do that. "I think it could help."

"Great!" I say, watching her run off to talk with my stepdad. I wish this conversation was the hardest thing on my agenda tonight, but now I need to return to Alexa's diary and whatever message she hid. I settle onto the couch in the family room, watching the sky change colors as the sun disappears behind the houses. Pink and orange threads line the sky, with just the hint of the moon poking out.

I pull Alexa's diary from my bag, along with a handheld mirror I retrieved from the bathroom, and start writing down the letters hidden within the bubbles.

If dbnf . . . Some of the words I quickly recognize. *If* stands for *He*, and it's mentioned a few times. It's a long passage, and it takes me about an hour to figure out the words. Even as I read it, I can't quite grasp the ramifications.

"Mom." Nikki startles me. She's standing at the stairs in her pink sweats and T-shirt. "Are you all right?"

I realize I'm crying and wipe away a tear.

She comes over and gives me a hug as I turn the paper over. "Don't be upset about David," she says, assuming that's why I'm sad. "There are more fish in the sea."

I hug her back and tell her that of course, she's right.

"Grandpa Lou made me feel a lot better," she says. "Thanks for the suggestion." She walks to the stairs, stopping again to study me. "You sure you're all right?"

"I promise you I won't let what happened with David bother me," I say and force a smile. She walks upstairs as I reread the words Alexa hid within the jagged letters. My mind moves to my conversation with Cameron. He told me Alexa wanted to put things right before moving on with her life and getting engaged. Now I understand what she meant. And what I now believe was the real motive for her death.

I tuck the paper in my tote and put the diary in a safe spot. Then I take out my phone and call Liam.

CHAPTER 36

"Where's your cameraman?" The security guard stationed at the media entrance for Yankee Stadium looks up from his newspaper.

"He'll be here soon," I reply.

He squints his eyes. "You do know there isn't a single reporter here yet. The teams aren't due till the afternoon. The field isn't even set up yet. It's a night game—you know that, right?"

"I do," I reply. The subway across the street rumbles above, taking morning commuters to work. It's early. I get that. But I'm here for a different reason. And one I can't share.

He shrugs. "No rule says I can't let you in. Gonna tell me what you're doing here so early?"

"Looking for inspiration," I say, sharing the first thing that pops into my brain. He snorts but tells me to step through and let him check my bag.

"Granola bars and a thermos of coffee. Like always."

"Like always." I smile and take one of the bars and hand it to him. "Your favorite—peanut butter and chocolate."

"Thanks, Kate." He rips the top off. "Go get inspired." He turns back to his newspaper, and I step into the wide cavernous space, feeling like I'm inside a modern version of the Roman Colosseum, images of the movie *Gladiator* flashing through my brain.

My heels click-clack against the concrete, echoing off the limestone and steel of the Great Hall, where I pass the larger-than-life banners of past and present Yankees superstars. A franchise steeped in history and glory—will Alexa's murder be more than a footnote? A lone police officer nods at me as he leads a bomb-sniffing dog in the other direction.

I find the elevator and press suite level. The doors open, and I step into the nearly empty hallway—with a cleaning crew mopping the floor and a few security guards scattered about. Nerves ping through my body, and I start to second-guess the plan—even though it is *my* plan. *Keep going,* I tell myself and take the ten paces needed to reach the platinum luxury box. This morning's destination.

A single security guard dressed in a suit stands by the door, listening to AirPods. He removes one to greet me.

"Ms. Green." The guard nods. "He's expecting you."

The guard opens the door, and I step inside to the same spot I visited when it all began. It feels like an out-of-body experience—a carbon copy of last week, minus the revelry. The globe-shaped chandeliers cast a yellow glow over empty food carts lined up at the ready for caterers to fill with scrumptious treats. Tufted couches and lounge chairs wait to hold spectators. It's like seeing the bride without her dress and makeup. Or a clown without the costume.

"Kate." His voice rings with warmth as he steps from behind the bar, holding a tall crystal glass with a celery stalk bobbing up and down in red liquid that makes me think of blood. He's wearing a polo shirt and khakis, the most casual I've seen him. "Can I get you a drink? I'm having a Bloody Mary."

He closes the distance between us and reaches to shake my hand but doesn't release it. His fingers are hot and clammy. I force myself to remain still, not wanting him to sense the change in my feelings. The disgust.

"I wouldn't say no to coffee." I ease my hand from his and force my lips into a smile.

"Milk or sugar?" he asks, walking to a table where there's a tray with porcelain cups and a stainless steel carafe.

"Neither." I step in that direction too. He pours the liquid into the cup, and I can tell by the smell, the coffee will be disappointingly weak. "Thanks." I sip the watery liquid. "It's a bit strange to see this place so empty," I say, once again scanning the vast space.

"You said you wanted to meet away from work. Seemed like a good option." He waves his arm around, his face brimming with pride. *Look at me and all I control.* "Let's go outside and take advantage of the dip in humidity." He steps in the direction of the door leading to the plush stadium seats only available to those with luxury boxes.

Outside isn't part of the plan. "Would you mind if we talk here? The air-conditioning feels so good."

"Suit yourself." He shrugs and points to two tufted chairs facing one another. "So, how can I help you? Why did you want to speak in private?" He flashes a smile, his overly bright teeth reminding me of a vampire. "I'm intrigued." He crosses one leg over the other, bouncing his leather shoe up and down. "I bet I know what it's about."

Doubt that, I think, although I'm not surprised that he believes he knows everything. The hubris of an insecure man.

"You want to talk about David Lopez." He smiles wide, thinking himself so smart. "I'm assuming there's an issue and you don't feel comfortable going to Human Resources." He uncrosses his leg and leans toward me. His breath smells of liquor and spearmint. "We're friends, Kate. I'm glad you feel comfortable coming directly to me." His arrogance should astound me, but, really, it's almost predictable.

"Frankly," he continues, "I've never been a fan of Lopez." He presses his lips together. "You could do much better." He puts his hand on mine.

"I don't know what to say," I respond, pulling my hand away slowly so he doesn't get suspicious.

Outside his father's presence, Junior's shoulders are back, and his chest puffed up like a peacock. "You're wondering how I found out about you and David." He says it as a statement, not a question.

"I'm assuming you went through some HR files," I suggest, keeping my emotions in check. Human Resource violations are not the reason I'm here.

"Not *your* files." He winks conspiratorially. "Never yours. David's." He smiles, smug satisfaction showing. "Charlie's been pushing David to host the sports-magazine show, but, well, you know, he's not my first choice."

I hear a plane in the distance and look through the window, watching the stream of white clouds in its wake. This conversation has veered off course, and I need to steer it in a new direction.

"I appreciate you looking out for me." I force a smile. "But that's not actually what I wanted to talk to you about."

"Well, color me intrigued." Junior chuckles. "But first, I need another drink. You sure I can't get you anything stronger?" He looks at my coffee. "I won't tell your boss." He winks, like he's just told the funniest joke.

"I'm fine for now."

"Suit yourself." He walks to the bar. I stand, too, and step over to the photographs on the wall, a running display of big moments in Yankee history, from Don Mattingly to Derek Jeter.

Junior returns and stands next to me. Too close. "Man, that Jeter," he says, and I feel his breath on my cheek. "He's definitely one of my favorites."

"You a Yankee fan?" I ask, seeing an opportunity.

"Biggest Yankee fan there is," he says. "Since I was a kid, in fact."

Junior might make this easier than I imagined. I carefully consider my next question.

"How did you become a Yankee fan?" I ask. "Your dad doesn't strike me as someone who would be a super sports fan—" I stop, hoping he'll take the bait and mention Alexa.

"Could you imagine Wyatt Hutchinson cheering over a home run?" He laughs at the thought. *Good.* "Actually, one of my babysitters turned me on to the team."

Yes. Here we go.

"Really—" I begin but am interrupted by a knock at the door. Junior calls for them to come in, and a waiter enters, carrying a tray of pastries, cheeses, and fruit. Junior points to the table, and we move back to the tufted seats we were in a few minutes ago, the tray of food between us.

He picks up a few grapes and pops them in his mouth.

"You were saying a babysitter turned you on to the Yankees." I return to the conversation.

"Ummm, yeah." He sounds distracted. "Excuse me a minute." He picks up his phone, which must have been on vibrate because I didn't hear it ring. I watch him—his shoulders sag as he nods his head, throwing in a *yes* and *uh-huh*. He clicks off. "Sorry about that."

"Wyatt?" I ask.

"How'd you know?" He tilts his head, appearing embarrassed.

"Just a guess." I shrug.

Junior clears his throat, no longer smiling. "I hate to rush you, but I need to take care of something. What is it you wanted to talk about?"

To know if you or your father killed Alexa. Last night, after I figured out the message in Alexa's diary, I realized the phone call Alexa made to TRP the morning of her death might not have been for me. Originally, I thought she called to speak with me when I didn't immediately respond to her email. But now I think she might have tried to reach Junior. Knowing how thoughtful Alexa was, she probably wanted to tell Junior of her plan to go public. From the diary, it seemed like she truly cared about him. If she was going to expose what Wyatt did to her, she could have decided to first warn Junior. She likely still thought of Junior as the scared child from her years as his babysitter.

"I'm here because of the babysitter who made you a Yankee fan," I say, watching his face closely. Junior twitches at my comment but doesn't speak.

I continue. "It was Alexa Kane. Right?"

He stares at me but remains quiet, and I wonder if he's smarter than I gave him credit for.

"It's a funny coincidence." I keep my tone light, hoping to put him at ease. "Alexa and I played soccer together as kids."

His shoulders loosen, and he nods his head. "Right, I remember she used to play soccer at a high level. Yes, she was the babysitter who turned me on to the Yankees. Why? Are you planning a sports story on me?" He forces a chuckle. "Assuming you get the job—which, as you know, I'm pushing for."

I ignore the gross attempt at manipulation and continue. "I'm confused about something. A few days ago, I asked you why your brother Curls went to Alexa Kane's candlelight vigil. You acted like you never heard of her."

He folds his arms across his chest. I sense I'm losing him. "Was it because of your dad?" I ask, leaning close in a conspiratorial motion. "He didn't like Alexa—did he?"

"He didn't," Junior says quickly, and I glimpse the little boy who feared his father and worshipped Alexa.

"I know how much you meant to Alexa," I tell him.

"She told you that?" he asks, his eyes misty.

I nod my head, technically not a lie since writing is a form of telling.

He rubs his chin, lost in thought. "She was a great babysitter. But she stopped coming. They all did." He hangs his head—still the wounded child.

"I need some air." He stands and walks toward the door leading to the outside seats. I hesitate. I know I'm supposed to remain inside, but I'm so close to getting Junior to open up. I can feel it.

I follow him outside, using my hand to shield my eyes from the blazing sun. I don't feel any dip in humidity, despite what Junior suggested earlier, the muggy heat causing my silk tank top to stick to my skin.

He motions me to the front row as he slides over, patting the cushioned stadium seat next to him. "Best seats in the house," he says, the proud child who believes he owns the world.

"It is a great view," I say, looking down at the ground crew laying the sod for the soccer match as they convert the baseball field into a soccer pitch.

"This process used to take three days." He turns to me. "Now these crews get it done in less than twenty-four hours." He smiles as if this is his achievement. *You don't own the stadium or the team, dude.* "Look over there—about a hundred feet down." He points to a man driving a golf cart on the field. "He's the head groundskeeper. Best in the business." I stare at the cart below us, and see a man with salt-and-pepper hair in the driver's seat.

"You're not scared of heights—are you?" Junior gives me a nudge. "My brother won't sit in this row, worried about falling." As if to make his point, Junior bends his body over the metal bar to stare at the steep drop. He straightens up and curls his lips.

"So, why the questions about Alexa?" Junior asks, his expression appearing benign but his tone menacing.

"Alexa reached out to me the day she was murdered," I say, watching for a reaction. He gives away nothing. "I wondered if she reached out to you?"

"To me?" He tries to appear surprised, but something slips, a blink of his eye. "Why would she reach out to me?"

I pull out the folded paper I've been keeping in my pocket and straighten it. "Because of this." I hold up the lined sheet. He crosses his arms over his chest, his eyes narrowing.

"She kept a diary when she was young," I continue. "Some of it was written in a code Alexa and I used as kids. I thought she might have wanted to tell you about this." I point to the paper. "I think she planned to go public with this information."

I pause, hoping he'll say something. He doesn't. Does he know what's coming? I clear my throat and start reading.

"*He came home early. Junior jumped out of his seat, spilling juice on the rug. Mr. Hutchinson slapped Junior, who ran and hid behind me, and I tried to protect him.*"

I glance up and see Junior's fists clenched. I continue.

"*That made Mr. Hutchinson even madder. He grabbed my arm and dragged me into the hallway. 'You think you're better than me?' He growled as he put his sweaty hand over my mouth and nose. He reached for my pants and pulled them down. 'I'll show you what a bitch you really are.' He kept his hand over my face, and I could barely get in a breath as he pushed his body against me. When he was done, he told me he'd kill me if I said a word. 'Besides,'—he laughed, zipping up his pants—'who would believe a silly girl like you?'*"

"That's a lie," Junior says, his voice so low, I need to lean toward him. "She lied." His face flushes red as his breath quickens. "Where's the diary?"

"Why do you want to know?" I say.

"Because obviously she's lying."

Gone is the scared child, replaced by a caged bull. I flinch. It makes him smile.

"Kate, I don't want vicious rumors to spread about my father," he says as if it's the most logical explanation in the world. "Do you know how that could hurt our company?"

Our company?

"Why would Alexa lie about a rape?" I give him my best *you can trust me* look.

"My father would never hurt anyone. I mean, he can be gruff," Junior says with a forced chuckle. "But rape? Never. I told Alexa—" He stops, realizing his mistake.

"When did you tell Alexa? When you saw her at halftime?" I ask, knowing how close I am to getting a confession.

The color drains from his face. The sound of a microphone check blasts from the stadium speakers. "Check one two, check one two, check—"

241

"Kate." He leans toward me, his head inches from mine. Across the way, on the Jumbotron, photos of the USA players flash across the screen. Hazel, smiling out at us, a soccer ball in hand. I turn back toward Junior, whose face is flushed.

"Kate," he repeats, the artery in his neck pulsating. "Please, tell me where the diary is."

I see my opportunity. "I will tell you where the diary is if you tell me what happened between you and Alexa."

"Why do you want to know?" he asks, weighing my offer.

"She was my friend," I respond.

He scans the stadium and then looks over the edge. If he killed Alexa, he won't have any qualms about killing me. I imagine he's calculating how to get the diary, destroy it, and then dispose of me. We are playing a game of chicken on the edge of a deadly drop with only concrete, metal, and rigid seats to cushion the fall.

Junior relaxes his body and leans back in his chair. "Fine. I'll tell you what happened—then you tell me where she kept that silly diary."

I nod in agreement.

"But this is just between us, Kate," he says, as if I believe he won't go after me next.

"Of course," I reply. "I just need to know, and then you can have the diary. I don't want it."

He searches my face. I can tell he wants to believe me, like I might hold the power to absolve him.

"You better not be lying to me." He knits his brows together.

"I only want to understand what happened. Really." I put my hand on his arm, trying to assure him.

He nods his head, looking surprisingly relieved. "Alexa did call me the morning she died. I was excited to hear from her. She *was* my favorite babysitter."

A smile crosses his lips, and I can almost see the little boy Alexa wrote about.

"I thought I could give her a backstage tour of the stadium. Even had my secretary courier her an all-access pass, and we agreed to meet at halftime."

"What happened?" I ask in a whisper.

His eyes radiate betrayal. "Alexa told me the same lie she wrote in that diary."

"That must have truly upset you."

He draws his brows together. "She accused my dad of rape," he says, his voice distant. When he looks up, I no longer see an enraged man, but a young boy who's scared and confused.

"And you didn't believe her," I say, leading him along.

"Of course not," Junior snaps. "My father may have been rough, but he'd never do something like that." He holds my gaze. "All I tried to do was make her realize how misguided it was for her to go public with this lie." He swallows hard. "I was holding on to her shoulders, and she pulled away, I didn't mean to—" Junior seems lost in the memory.

"I hear you," I say, trying to sound sympathetic.

"It was her fault. *Alexa* pulled away and banged herself against the cinder blocks. She was lifeless."

"That must have been awful." I force the words out, still trying to maintain his trust for a minute longer. "Did you try to get help?"

"I wanted to," he says, nodding, like he believes I understand his reasoning. "But she was dead. It wasn't my fault. You see that?"

"What a terrible situation," I say, keeping my voice soft. "What did you do next?"

His lips press together in a scowl, and the little boy is gone. "What could I do? I would be blamed, the company ruined, all for her lies. I had to move the body."

I have what I need and can no longer suppress my disgust. "The autopsy showed she died from drowning. She was alive when you put her in the ice bath. You could have saved her."

"I don't believe you," he says, mouth twisted as his nostrils flare. He grabs my arm and jerks me closer. "You're a lying bitch, just like Alexa."

I try to pull away, but he's stronger than I expect. He smashes me against the rail—pain shoots through my lower back. "Where's the diary?" He leans, his lips inches from my face. "Tell me now—"

"And if I don't—"

"I'll find it either way. And destroy it. If you don't tell me now—" He looks down at the field and then at me. "Poor Kate, pressure got too much, and she jumped—" He pushes my shoulders back, bending me over the bar as thunderous footsteps explode behind us. I can't help smiling, knowing what's about to happen.

"Hands up," multiple voices yell. Junior releases his grip, shock crossing his face. I rush behind the police officers with guns pointed at him.

"You set me up?" His eyes go wide with betrayal. He was going to kill me, and he's surprised I made a move against him.

"I did." I remove the wire from my shirt and hold it up for him to see. "For Alexa, who did nothing more than try to protect you."

CHAPTER 37

A police technician takes the wire from me as Liam wraps his arm around my shoulder as if to shield me from danger. I'm now inside the suite, but can see Junior as the cops place handcuffs around his wrists.

"Let's sit down." Liam leads me to a corner couch.

"Did you hear everything?" I ask him, dropping onto the cushion.

"We heard everything." He gives me his half smile, but his eyes reflect worry.

"You're bleeding." He reaches for my right arm and turns it, pointing to my elbow.

"It's nothing." I look at the scrape, which must have happened while Junior pushed me against the railing. Liam brings me a wet napkin, and I dab the cut and then apply pressure. We sit on the tufted ottomans as more officers rush about. The policeman with the bomb-sniffing dog approaches us.

"You did a great job," he says to me.

"Thanks for having my back," I reply.

The officer walks off, and I refocus on Liam.

"Why do you seem upset?" I ask, concerned I did something wrong. I replay my interaction with Junior. He clearly stated he murdered Alexa.

"You don't know why I'm upset?" He actually laughs.

"I'm assuming something went awry. But what? You're arresting him—"

Our conversation is interrupted as the door from outside opens and five officers escort Junior past. His face is red, his head high, and his voice loud as he yells for them to let him call his attorney.

Junior turns his head, eyes finding mine. "This isn't over, Kate Green. Not by a long shot."

Liam's shoulders tighten, but he controls himself as the officers jerk Junior out of our view and into the concourse. "I was worried, Kate. About *you*."

I put the napkin down, reach for his hand, and squeeze it. "I'm okay. Really. And we got him."

"We did." Liam nods.

"Will you be able to charge Wyatt?" I ask, worried that while Junior will be charged with murder, his rapist of a father could walk free.

"It's going to be hard," Liam says. "The statute of limitations has run out."

"That's not fair." I hear the anger in my voice. "Wyatt Hutchinson needs to pay."

Liam looks down at the ground. "I know. It isn't fair."

"Detective Murphy," an officer calls from the door. "Coming with us?"

Liam stands and tells me he needs to go. "A lot is going to unfold quickly now." He reaches down and wraps me in a big hug. A full hug. A non-Liam hug. "I'll call you later." He starts toward the door and then turns back. "Kate"—he gives his half smile—"we make a good team."

"We do." I smile, too, even though I'm still seething about Wyatt.

I watch Liam and then get up and step outside, where I sit in the back row—far away from the drop to the field.

A clip of Frank Sinatra's "New York, New York" blasts through the speaker. On the field, the grounds crews are raking the edges of the grass. We got Junior, but we may not get Wyatt. The thought makes me sick.

I take a deep breath and call Charlie, knowing I need to fill him in.

"Where are you?" Charlie answers as soon as I say hi.

"Hello to you," I respond.

"Seriously, Kate, what's that music?"

"I'm at Yankee Stadium," I say and then tell him what happened.

"Oh, shit," he says as the bright-green track loader whirs to action on the field, chugging over the newly laid sod. Charlie asks me to hold a second as someone enters his office. I hear them telling Charlie about Junior's arrest.

"Still there?" Charlie asks.

"Yup," I respond.

"I need to run into a meeting about this exact thing," Charlie says. "Wow, Junior Hutchinson! I'm surprised. But I'm also not."

"I know what you mean," I say, leaning back in my seat.

"Are you going to be all right to cover the game tonight?"

"You couldn't tear me away from it," I tell Charlie. "But I need to leave here and take care of something first."

"As long as you're back tonight," he says.

"I will be." We hang up. I finish my coffee and am ready to leave when my phone rings again. The caller ID shows a number from Westchester.

"Hello," I answer, stepping inside.

"Kate Green?" a woman says, her voice soft.

"Yes." I push the phone closer to my ear, wondering if this is the call I've been waiting for.

"This is Nancy Hall," she says, explaining she's the daughter of the 911 operator I've been trying to reach. As if I might have forgotten.

"Nancy," I say, "I'm glad you called."

"Well, my mother passed away a few days ago. We had the funeral yesterday—"

"I'm so sorry for your loss," I add.

"Thank you. I appreciate your patience." She takes a deep breath. "But I'm ready to meet with you. Should we say this afternoon?"

A million thoughts run through my mind. I desperately want to leave to go speak with Nancy this second. But there's something I need to do first. For Alexa.

"Could we speak tomorrow instead?" I ask.

"Umm, sure." She sends me the address of her mom's nursing home, explaining she needs to clean out her mother's things. We agree to meet tomorrow morning.

"Leaving already?" The security guard at the stadium exit gives me a knowing smile. "Guess you found what you were looking for?"

"You could say that." I smile. "See you later for the game."

"See you later, Kate." He returns to his newspaper.

Traffic to Long Island is heavier than expected. I turn on the radio news, where stories of Junior's arrest top the news cycle. The anchor reports that Junior was arrested at Yankee Stadium. Thankfully, there's no mention of me, although if this goes to trial, I know I'll have to testify as a witness.

I get off at the exit for Great Neck and wind my way toward Kings Point. Two security officers stand in front of the Hutchinson estate. I imagine they are readying themselves for a media frenzy, although this home is one of many owned by the Hutchinson family.

I turn and pull in front of Mrs. Kane's home. She answers the door in a terry cloth robe belted across her waist, flowered pajama top and pants peeking out. Without a word, she beckons me inside, and I follow her into the living room, where I sit on the chair across from the couch, a glass table with a framed picture of Alexa between us.

"I'm assuming you heard about the arrest?" I say.

"A detective called me with the basics," she replies. "In my mind, Junior Hutchinson is still the little kid who used to worship Alexa." She looks past me as if seeing them in her hallway. "It's hard to believe." She hugs her arms into her chest.

I reach into my tote and pull out Alexa's diary. Her doorbell rings. Through the window I spot a news van.

"Want me to get rid of them?" I ask her.

"The police are already on their way to the house. They predict it will be crazy. We keep refusing to give interviews, but like flies, they keep returning," she says. "I'm getting to the point where I don't even hear them, like white noise, or something."

She looks from me to my hands, which hold the black-and-white marbled diary. I place it on the table and slide it toward her.

"Do you want to know what the coded message said?" I ask her. "I imagine the police told you something?"

"I want to know Alexa's exact words," she says, stretching her lips into a thin line. I take the folded paper and hold it out to her. With shaking fingers, she unfolds the note and peers down. I stare out the window, trying to give her a bit of privacy as she learns the details of her daughter's rape. A blue jay jeers at a sparrow, scaring the small bird away from the feeder. I remember my stepfather telling me how vicious the beautiful blue birds can be.

"Will he get punished?" Mrs. Kane's voice pulls me back to the room, and I turn as she wipes a tear from her cheek.

"I don't know," I say. She bites her lower lip and stands. I get up, too, and she walks me to the back door, which is clear of reporters.

She opens the door and leans against the frame. She looks so fragile; I wonder if she should be alone. But I also know we aren't friends and it's not my place to ask.

"Goodbye, Mrs. Kane."

She nods as I step onto the stoop.

"Thank you, Kate," she says so softly, I wonder if I imagined it. I hear the door shut behind me. The reporters ignore me—probably assuming I was there for the same reason as them. I get into my car and drive to my second stop in Alexa's hometown.

CHAPTER 38

The door to Cameron's Place is locked, and the sign in the window says OPEN AT NOON. It's 11:30 a.m. I peek through the glass and see waitstaff in the back—I try knocking, but they ignore me. I walk around to the back of the restaurant, where Cameron and I spoke a few days ago. A squat delivery worker stacks crates of tomato paste onto a hand truck. He tilts the device and wheels it toward the open kitchen door.

"Hey." I walk up to him. "Is Cameron inside?"

"Yeah." He nods. "Who are you?"

"I don't want to barge into the kitchen," I say. "Could you tell him Kate Green is out here?"

The man shrugs, pushes the hand truck up a metal ramp, and disappears inside. A minute later, Cameron steps out, rubbing his hands against a white apron. "Kate?" He walks down the ramp and stops. I step toward him, glimpsing the action in the kitchen. A few chefs at the back stove, mixing steaming food inside large aluminum pots. Behind them, another group of chefs chops vegetables at stainless steel stations.

"Did you hear about the arrest?" I ask.

"No." His eyes go wide. "I've been prepping all morning."

The deliveryman slides past us, closes up the truck, and yells goodbye. Cameron doesn't register him, his eyes still on mine.

"Please," Cameron says. "Tell me."

"Junior Hutchinson confessed to killing Alexa," I say over the beeping of the truck backing up.

"She used to babysit for him," Cameron says, his right hand pulling on his left knuckles. "Why would he do that?"

"Chef." A young woman comes out, her face flushed. "We got a problem with the sauce—"

He cuts her off. "You handle it." She starts to protest, but he walks away and sits on the concrete stoop, head in hands. She stares at him a moment, then disappears back into the kitchen.

I walk over to where Cameron sits, thinking if I meet with him again, we need to find a better spot to talk than beside the dumpster. I lower myself down.

"Why?" he mumbles. "Why would Junior Hutchinson do that?" He raises his face and looks at me with his sad eyes. I tell him everything, including the hazing incident.

Cameron remains on the curb, staring across the street. A group of men and women walk through the door of a small studio, Yoga Goga, with mats tucked under their arms. I don't think he notices them, but a few look over, shaking their heads in sympathy. Everyone must know about Alexa's killer by now. I stand up and move in front of him, casually trying to block their view. No reason Cameron should become a spectacle.

The group gets the hint and disperses. I sit back down as Cameron turns to me. "I was so hurt when she broke up with me in high school, I didn't consider she'd suffered a trauma of her own." He runs his hand through his hair. "I wish I hadn't been so selfish."

I would tell him not to feel guilty, but how can I say that when I feel the same way?

"What will happen to the older Hutchinson?" Cameron asks. "Will they charge him with rape?"

"I don't think they'll be able to because of the statute of limitations."

"Cameron." Ginny's voice reaches us before we see her. Footsteps move closer, and I turn to see her glaring at me. "What's going on here?" Her tone is accusatory.

"Ginny." He wipes his eyes, and we stand.

"Why are you with her?"

A flash of anger crosses Cameron's face. "My sister was so right about you." He grimaces. "I can't believe I didn't see it."

She stops, like her feet hit glue. "No, Cameron. Your sister hates me. She tries to make you think bad things about me."

"Stop," he yells.

"Cameron." She finds her footing and steps closer, reaching for his arm.

He pulls away like she's burned his skin. "Ginny." His voice shakes. "I know you've been spinning tales and telling lies about Alexa."

Ginny glances at me and then back at Cameron. "That's not true—"

"You told the police Alexa called off our engagement? Which completely misled them."

"You proposed and she said no."

"She said *not yet*," Cameron spits. "And you knew that. We discussed it. You pretended to support me."

"You're wrong, Cameron. You remember it wrong." She rocks up and down on her heels.

"Not only that, I found out from the police you sent Alexa a threatening message the day she died." His voice shakes. *You better back down or else.*

Liam shared the same information with me a few days ago. They tracked the threatening text to a burner phone purchased by Ginny. It was smart of Liam to also tell Cameron. It probably helped convince Cameron to cooperate with the authorities.

"She didn't deserve you," Ginny whines.

"I asked you to come by to tell you that you're fired," he says, his voice barely a whisper.

"You can't fire me." She starts fumbling her words. "I'm sorry." She sobs. "You are right, I did lie. I'm so sorry, Cameron. Please, this is the only place I'm happy."

"My decision is final." He puts out his hand. "Can I please have the keys?"

"I don't have them," she replies, folding her arms across her chest as if this fact gives her the upper hand.

"Suit yourself. I already called the locksmith, so don't bother returning." He turns to go. "Kate, want me to walk you to your car?"

"I'm fine," I say. "Goodbye."

"Goodbye," he says and walks to the kitchen.

Ginny and I watch him disappear, and then she bounds toward me like an angry child. "What lies did you tell him to make him turn on me?"

"It wasn't anything I said," I reply. "It was what you did."

She raises a hand like she's going to slap me. I step closer to her, inches from her face, and stare into her eyes. She hesitates and drops her arm. "I'll get him back."

"No, you won't," I say and walk around her to my car.

I have a soccer game to cover.

CHAPTER 39

Yankee Stadium feels electric, fans packed into the stands. Once word of Junior's arrest circulated, the spectators returned in droves to watch the Women's National Team in the semifinals. I'm so happy for the team—they worked hard to get here and deserve to compete on a big stage packed with fans.

"Ladies and gentleman, please welcome your USA Women's National Team," the announcer calls over the sound system. Cheers erupt as the women walk out of the tunnel holding hands with kids dressed in USA soccer jerseys that reach down to their knees. Bringing little kids out for the pregame festivities is one of my favorite traditions in sports.

"You fangirling again?" Bill watches me, a cigarette dangling from his mouth.

"Don't you think it's sweet to see the young girls standing out there with the players?"

He scoffs and takes a puff of his cigarette, blowing the smoke to the side. "I'm not in a *sweet* mood," he grumbles.

"Are you still mad at me?" I ask.

"You could have been killed. Liam never should have let you confront Junior," Bill says as the kids are escorted off the pitch. Earlier, Bill gave me a piece of his mind when he heard of my involvement in the arrest. *It was actually sweet,* I think.

The referee blows the starting whistle, and the game begins. I feel a burst of adrenaline as the USA takes possession and scores an early goal. The crowd roars its appreciation. I scan the stadium, thrilled to see the happy fans. Bill nudges me and hands me his phone. I read the headlines, thrilled to see word leaked about Wyatt Hutchinson's connection to Alexa.

WYATT HUTCHINSON RAPIST. JUNIOR KILLER.

CHAIR OF NETWORLD CORP ACCUSED OF BRUTALIZING BABYSITTER.

THE DEEPER YOU DIG, THE MORE DIRT AND DISGUST SURFACES OVER HUTCHINSON FAMILY.

And there's more. News reports say that earlier this afternoon, NetWorld Corp held an emergency board meeting and voted Wyatt off the board. It's hard to imagine Wyatt surviving this from a PR standpoint. But he'll still live a life of luxury. A fact that guts me to the core.

One story that got completely upstaged is the Quinn controversy. No one seems to care much about whether Savy cut Quinn or the other way around. And if the USA women's team wins today, the Quinn drama will fade even more.

As the second half begins, Gayle sends a great pass to a winger and the US goes ahead 2–0. When the final whistle blows, the girls rush to the middle of the field, embracing in a hug as fireworks shoot off into the night sky.

Bill hands me the microphone, and we run onto the field to interview Gayle.

"What a game," I say, smiling at her. "How do you feel?"

"I can't believe it," she gushes, as a teammate runs over and douses Gayle with water from a squeeze bottle. I laugh, not even minding getting wet in the process. Gayle pushes her damp hair away from her eyes. "I want to be serious for a minute," she says, looking at me. "Our team is dedicating this win to Alexa Kane and the victims of the stampede. They are foremost in our minds."

I ask her a few more questions before she heads off to the locker room.

"My turn?" Savy walks over, hands crossed over her chest.

"I'm so happy to speak with you," I say, a little surprised she kept her word about the postgame interview. "How does it feel to be one step closer to gold?"

"Well, Kate," she starts, her southern accent strong. "You know how amazing it is to make it to the finals of the Olympics. Nothing quite like it, other than winning that gold medal." She winks. "And that's what we hope will happen at the next game."

We wrap up the interview, and I hand the microphone back to Bill, who heads off to get video of the players celebrating. Savy remains next to me, staring across the pitch.

"I can't believe everything Alexa went through," Savy says, her toe pointing into the ground.

"It's heartbreaking," I say.

"It is. It truly is—after the last game, I was thinking maybe I need to face my own past—"

"What do you mean—" I start. But before I can finish my sentence, the players surround Savy, dumping Gatorade over her head.

CHAPTER 40

I wake with a start, the whistle of the train jarring me from sleep. Edges of a nightmare dissipate like smoke. Closing my eyes, I reach for the dream—Liam shot in front of a brownstone. Mayor Tony Compton, standing over Liam with a gun, demanding my father look him in the eye. Then my father does something. But what? I can't get there. It recedes from my grasp.

I push myself against my headboard, listening for a disturbance. It's 5:00 a.m. What woke me? All I hear is the purr of the air conditioner inside the window. My body aches after yesterday's encounter with Junior.

I get up and pad to the bathroom to retrieve two Advil. I don't think there's any chance I'll get back to sleep. Outside my bedroom window, the streetlamps cast a warm glow over my neighbors' homes. What a week this has been. And now, I'm hours away from speaking with Nancy Hall, the daughter of the 911 operator who received the distress call right before my father got shot.

I step around the folding partition in my bedroom that blocks my bulletin board bearing my research on Liam. I reread the article from the police blotter that was in the paper the morning after Liam was shot that cold January evening when I was six years old.

Two police officers responded to a domestic violence call in Washington Heights, NY. Emergency operators received a call at 11:48 PM from a woman crying that her boyfriend was beating her with a coffeepot.

What I'm desperate to learn today is whether the 911 operator asked about guns on the scene. Because the next day, the NYPD reported that Liam and his partner had walked in on a massive drug ring with large quantities of crack and an arsenal of guns.

The response to a call regarding an arsenal of guns would have been much different than a domestic fight with a coffeepot. If guns were mentioned, more police units would have been dispatched to the scene. Either the 911 operator totally screwed up or someone deliberately put Liam and his partner, Harley, in danger. The idea makes me shudder. I wrap a shawl around my shoulders, despite the heat, as I think back to my conversation with Theresa—the woman who lived in the basement apartment of the brownstone. She referred to the building as drug infested and claimed it was still dangerous to discuss what happened.

I now understand why you have been trying to contact my mother. Nancy Hall's message flashes across my brain. I check my phone; a few more hours and I will learn the truth. I head downstairs and make some coffee, ready to check another line of inquiry. I turn on my computer and search for books on Mayor Marsha Compton. In the rush of events around the Hutchinsons, I forgot about my discovery of her book and the message to Liam.

I wouldn't have gotten here without you. All my love, Marsha

A lot of titles come up when I google *Marsha Compton books.* The first is the one I saw on Liam's shelf, *My Father Was a Bad Man.* I add the book to my cart and scan the other options. There are a few written by journalists—*The Complicated Compton Family: How a Young Girl Tackled a Mayor.* Most titles appear complimentary toward Marsha. But one suggests a different narrative. The title reads *Like Mayor, Like Daughter.* I scan the description:

Everyone thinks that Marsha Compton, then a young woman, cooperated with investigators to bring her father down because she was "appalled" by his corrupt practices. That's the story she wants you to believe. The truth is much more complicated and damning.

Well, that's certainly one way to sell a book. I add it to the cart and then check out as I hear footsteps on the stairs.

"What are you doing up so early?" Jackson saunters into the kitchen, rubbing his eyes.

"I could ask you the same question." I smile and offer him coffee.

He waves it off, walks around the counter, and grabs a glass, then fills it with water. "I'm going back to bed. I was just thirsty."

"You should sleep in today. Camp's over, and your senior year starts soon."

"Tell me about it." He yawns. "Will you be around today?"

"I have one errand to run this morning, and then I'll be back for the rest of the day."

"Maybe we can have a movie night," he says, suggesting one of my absolute favorite pastimes.

"Yes!" I respond. "With lots of candy and buttered popcorn."

"Nikki will go nuts, but absolutely." He shuffles off, and I listen to his steps up the stairs. I smile to myself, feeling as if things might start returning to normal soon.

———

The trip to the nursing home is surprisingly easy. I turn onto a long driveway that wraps around a shopping center and then down a hill. The buildings are along the Hudson River. A receptionist directs me down a hall, and I knock at the door marked room 1221.

The woman who opens the door looks exhausted, with dark circles under her eyes. She's thin and in yoga pants and a zip-up sweatshirt. "I'm Nancy," she says and moves aside for me to enter.

"Kate." I step around some boxes to enter the single room with a stripped bed and strong smell of Lysol.

"Thanks for meeting me here," Nancy says, sitting on the edge of the bed and motioning for me to take the chair. "I'm trying to get everything of Mom's packed up today."

"I'm sorry for your loss," I tell her again. I pick up a photo of a striking young woman with a headset from the table next to me. "Is this your mom?"

"It's from her time as a 911 operator. She loved the job, but left shortly after that, umm, call."

I put the photo back on the table and thank her again for speaking with me.

She pulls at her hair, seeming nervous. "My sister was here yesterday, and I told her what Mom had whispered to me. She does not want me to talk with you." She pauses and looks down at her hands. "She's worried it will stir up trouble."

I want to scream, but I remain silent. Nancy seems like she has more to say, and I don't want to protest too soon.

"But, well, I really believe Mom would want you to know. Why else would she have bothered to tell me?" Nancy sighs and stands up, walking to the window, with a beautiful view of the Hudson River. "We made sure Mom had a room with a river view. She loved the water. We used to boat as kids. It was the place she seemed most happy."

Nancy stays by the window, so I get up and move next to her.

"This spot actually gets nice afternoon sunlight." Nancy gazes outside. "Cancer is tough," she says, more to herself than me. "The last months were tough. But she led a good life."

"You said she enjoyed working as a 911 operator?" I say, trying to steer the conversation.

"She used to love that job. But that all changed." Nancy looks back out the window.

"What happened?" I prod.

"After your emails and my mom's *confession*, I started to put some pieces together from my past. I remember a huge fight my parents had when I was ten. Now I realize it took place just after that 911 call involving your father."

I keep very still, not wanting to spook her, as if she were a bird that could fly away at any second.

"I remember my dad yelling at my mom to 'stay quiet.' I never knew what it was about. But I remember him repeating that she'd hurt our family if she didn't toe the line."

Nancy continues to look out the window. I notice a tugboat on the river, pulling a wide barge. A woman knocks on the door and enters the room, asking if Nancy needs any help with the boxes. Nancy says yes but asks for a few minutes.

Once the door closes, she turns to me. "Knowing what I know now, I'm not sure my father was wrong. He was looking out for us. But the secret gnawed at my mom. I realize that."

"Can you tell me what your mom said?" I ask.

She pulls at the ends of her hair as she begins. "The 911 call that came in was for a domestic disturbance," she says, looking at the floor. "The caller said her boyfriend hit her with a coffeepot."

Nancy tilts her face up toward mine, looking in my eyes. I can tell what she says next will be important.

"My mom asked if there were any guns in the apartment, and the caller said no. My mom says she asked the question twice and the caller, a woman, insisted there were no guns."

This is exactly the information I wanted, but hearing it makes me sick to my stomach because it suggests the caller lied. Did she know that my father and Harley would be dispatched? Was she trying to get my father and Harley killed? Or was it a general setup against the NYPD?

Nancy says, "My mom was really upset when she heard about the guns on the scene. Not only that, according to witnesses, there wasn't a woman at the apartment, even though Mom swears the 911 call was made by a woman."

Nancy stops as a staffer returns with a few workers to help with the packing.

Nancy leans over and whispers to me, "After the funeral, my sister and I started cleaning out this room. We found a file box under the bed with your father's name on it."

"Can I have it?" I ask, holding my breath.

"My sister took it to her house. I wanted her to give it to you, but she said no. I can try and ask her again, but she's stubborn."

One step forward, two steps back, I think, wondering what could be in the box.

"There's one more thing," Nancy says, offering to walk me out so we can continue speaking in private. We step around the boxes into the hallway, where we are once again alone.

"Some strangers came to the house right after the call and threatened my mom. They told her she needed to forget the 911 call and never talk about it again. A few weeks later, ten thousand dollars showed up in her bank account. That was a lot for us. And the very fact that it was there made my mom appear complicit. No one would believe she didn't take the money as a payoff to keep quiet. Which in fact, kept her quiet."

A person peeks her head into the hallway and calls to Nancy, asking where to put the photos.

"I need to finish up here," she says.

"Thank you," I say and reach for her arm. "And could you please ask your sister again about the box? Please."

"Yes. I'll try," she says and scurries away.

I step outside and put on my sunglasses, squinting against the bright rays beating down. The more I learn, the more questions I have. If Nancy's information is correct, then the 911 call was a trap. The next question is whether the setup was directed at Liam and Harley or the NYPD in general. And why? Why!

CHAPTER 41

"Welcome to TRP's *Behind the Game,* our new sports-magazine show." David smiles into the camera. "Kate Green and I are happy to be here with you."

"Thanks, David." I smile back, despite having to sit next to my lying, cheating cohost. "Our weekly sports-magazine show will feature in-depth stories and interviews from within the sports world."

David speaks next, reading from the teleprompter. "And for our first episode, Kate has an exclusive interview with one of the biggest stars in sports."

"That's right, all coming up after the break."

The stage manager signals clear, and I drop the smile, unclipping my microphone so I can move to the interview area with the two large chairs. My heels echo in the cavernous studio, the only noise besides a soft whir of equipment.

"Two minutes," the stage manager calls, holding one hand against her headphones. I sit across from Savannah Baker and ask her if she's ready.

"Ready as I'll ever be." She shrugs. Hair and makeup approach and touch up my eyes.

"You missed a spot." Bill steps forward and takes the powder puff from the makeup person, who laughs at him. Bill leans down, the smell of cigarettes wafting off him, and dabs the puff against my nose.

"You missed your calling," I say to Bill as he hands the powder puff back to the makeup artist.

"Ha ha," he responds. "So far so good?" He raises a brow and motions in David's direction. Bill knows the whole story and is worried about me as usual. He wants me to get on a dating app. I'm not ready, thank you very much. But I'll get out there at some point.

The stage manager announces one minute.

"Bill," I call as he starts to step behind the studio cameras. "Thanks for being here."

"Always." He gives a fake bow and disappears.

"Thirty seconds," the stage manager yells. I straighten up and look over at Savy.

She's digging her toe into the rug. Her nervous tell. But she tries to make conversation, asking if it's always so cold in the studio.

"Yes." I explain they need to keep the temperature low so the equipment doesn't overheat.

"You'd think someone could figure a fix for that," she says and takes a deep breath. I wonder if she's having second thoughts. Last week, Savy called me, saying she wanted to go public with the hazing incident. *I thought it would have come out with the media scrutiny during the Olympics,* she said. *I was finally ready to talk about it.* Yet despite the attention on women's soccer that followed Alexa's murder and the Quinn drama, the hazing incident never came to light. Savy didn't say much more to me on the phone, except that she wanted to clear the air.

The stage manager signals ten seconds and then counts me down. The red light goes on above the camera, and I begin.

"Welcome back to TRP's *Behind the Game*." I smile into the light. "Joining me tonight is the head coach of the Women's National Soccer Team, Savannah Baker. But she's not here to talk about leading the USA women's team to Olympic gold, which was quite a feat," I say, taking a moment to acknowledge that accomplishment.

"Thanks, Kate," she says.

"You're here to talk about your past." I clear my throat. "Our past."

I turn to face Savy as the camera switches to a shot of both of us. "One would think you would be on top of the world, leading the women's team to gold." She nods her head. "But there have been issues. The murder of Alexa Kane during the last game of the group round. And Quinn Price's abrupt departure and public attacks on you personally."

"Let's start with Quinn—because I think that one is less important," Savy says, always able to cut someone down. "No matter how talented a single player is, if they can't be a team player, it's not good for the whole. Quinn is an incredibly talented soccer player. There's no question about that. But what she's not, is a team player. The proof is in our results. Look how much better we did when she left."

"Your results certainly tell that story," I say, crossing one leg over another and leaning toward her. "Do you see a pathway forward for Quinn and U.S. Soccer?"

"I will hold no grudges. I want what's best for the team. If she can adjust her attitude, I'd be happy to reconsider."

"Meanwhile, she's criticized you, accusing you of being hard on her and the other players. Although, your other players seem to have rallied behind you."

Savy laughs. "Can you ever imagine a scenario where every player is happy with their coach? But the players still need to respect their coach. And, more importantly, their teammates."

I look back into the camera, saying that after the commercial break, Savy has something from her past she will share.

"Clear," the stage manager yells. "Two minutes."

Hair and makeup return, and I'm handed a towel to dab my face. Under the hot lights, I've started sweating. Savy too. I see Charlie standing by the camera. He catches my eye and waves me over.

"What's going on?" I whisper.

"I wanted you to hear it from me before it leaks." He rubs his chin. "Junior Hutchinson was the 'source' of the fake post about the crazed man on the loose at Yankee Stadium. They tracked the message to a burner phone he hid in his home."

"The irony," I respond. Alexa's murderer posted about a fake murderer running around Yankee Stadium with a knife.

"He's a despicable human being," Charlie says.

"Thirty seconds," the stage manager calls. Charlie confirms Junior is getting charged for the lie and motions for me to return to the set.

"Ten seconds," the stage manager calls. I stare into the camera, forcing myself to focus on Savy. Junior doesn't deserve my time. Or anger. He'll pay in court for what he did to Alexa and the people killed or hurt in the stampede.

The camera light turns red, and I welcome the viewers back. "Our next topic has to do with something that took place decades ago when we were in our teens and playing for the U.S. Youth National Team."

"That's right, Kate," Savy says, holding my eyes. "I feel very ashamed of my behavior back then, and I want to share what happened to the world. I owe it to Alexa Kane. Not many people know that she was one of our teammates on the national team. And my behavior toward her, and you, was inexcusable."

The camera pushes in to a close-up of Savy as she discloses her leading role in hazing and bullying Alexa and other players, including me. She doesn't hold back, sharing every single detail. When she finishes, she crosses one leg over the other and takes a deep breath.

"My first question is *why* did you do those things?" I ask, always wondering about that.

"I did what was done to me. When I was the younger player, the older kids did the same to me and my teammates. I thought it was just how things were supposed to go. And I don't mean that as an excuse. I was wrong. And I shouldn't have continued the rituals. It's not like anyone would have come and said, *Savy, why were you nice to Alexa. Or Kate?* But I was young and immature and stupid."

"Why go public now? Surely there will be consequences for telling the world."

"I feel like I owe Alexa Kane. Even though her murder had nothing to do with our history, I'm gutted that I never got the chance to apologize to her. At least, I can apologize in person to you. I also hope that younger players can learn from my mistakes."

"And the consequences?" I prompt.

Savy sighs. "I told my players yesterday, and I offered to resign. But they rallied around me and said they want me to stay."

"But how many players are going to tell their coach they don't want them around?"

"Still with the tough questions, Kate." She laughs. "Yes, that's true. I'm sure the United States Soccer Federation will conduct a complete investigation of this and will deliberate on my fate."

"One last question before we wrap up," I say. "How do you feel now that you've shared all this information?"

"I feel lighter," she says, her southern accent strong.

"Thanks, Savy," I say. "And I, for one, forgive you."

CHAPTER 42

The grilled-cheese brigade agreed to take a hiatus and allow me to cook tonight's dinner. They weren't as keen on my second request—allowing Liam to join. But they caved when I explained that it would mean a lot to me. "Just give him a chance," I said. "No pressure."

Nikki and Jackson were excited about our other guests. Virginia Dell, the girl injured in the stampede, and her mother. From the kitchen I hear the doorbell. Nikki's feet clomp down the stairs as she yells that she'll answer it. I cut the Italian bread in half and slather butter inside, before adding fresh garlic.

"It's Virginia and her mom," Nikki yells excitedly from the hallway. I hear Jackson bound down the stairs and greet our guests.

They all enter the kitchen as I place the garlic bread into the oven. I wipe my hands on my apron and walk over to give them each a hug. "What can we get you?" I ask, offering Virginia juice and her mom wine.

As I sauté the broccoli, Virginia tells me about her progress in physical therapy. "I won't be able to play soccer this fall," she says, looking sad. "But I should be back for the spring season."

"That's great." I give her a hug. "Every soccer player has to deal with setbacks. But you'll be good as new. Would it be all right if I came to your first game?"

Her eyes light up as she says yes.

I pull the lasagna and garlic bread out, checking the clock. Liam is fifteen minutes late, and I know what the kids are thinking. He's going to be a no-show.

"I'm starving," Jackson says. "Should we start without him?"

"Let's give him a few more minutes," I say, asking Jackson and Nikki to bring the food to the table. They exchange a not-so-subtle look that confers their agreement that inviting Liam was, in fact, a mistake. But I believe they are wrong.

When I asked Liam to join us for dinner, he was close to giddy. He actually cracked a full smile. Or as close as he could come to one.

The doorbell rings. I take off my apron and go to answer it. Liam holds up a container of chocolate ice cream.

"You come bearing gifts," I say, taking the ice cream from him. He leans down, his T-shirt rubbing against my chin.

"That's the little gift. Ready for the big one?"

I close the door.

"Mom," Jackson calls. "Dinner's on the table."

"One second," I reply and look at Liam. "Want to wait until after dinner for the second thing? Or does it need to go in the freezer too?"

"It doesn't." He laughs at my joke. "But it's information you will be happy to hear."

I shut the door behind him, and we remain in the hallway.

"The reason I'm late is that I just got a call from the office. Five women came forward and formally accused Wyatt Hutchinson of raping them within the last ten years."

I let that information sink in. "Within the statute of limitations," I say slowly.

He nods. "They all told the prosecutor that reading about Alexa's ordeal made them decide to come forward."

"That's great news," I say. "Wyatt Hutchinson will pay for what he did."

"That's right." Liam pats my back. "And you helped make that happen by uncovering what Wyatt had done to Alexa."

"There's something I want to ask you too," I say, thinking about all the information I uncovered recently. There are so many new questions I have for Liam, and enough information that I don't think he can dodge me any longer.

"Mom," Jackson calls again. "Everyone is waiting."

"What is it?" Liam asks me.

I hesitate. "We can talk about it another day," I reply, deciding not to put a damper on tonight's dinner.

"After you." Liam puts his hand out, and I lead him through the kitchen, into the dining room, and to his first family dinner with us. It feels good to all be together. Like a new beginning. Hopefully, a happy one.

ACKNOWLEDGMENTS

I want to start by thanking all of you—the readers—who have embraced Kate Green. Without readers like you, I wouldn't be lucky enough to do what I love. So, from the bottom of my heart, know that I am deeply, deeply appreciative of all of you. To the Instagrammers, bloggers, podcasters, content producers, and reviewers—thank you for giving this series a chance and sharing your insights with the world.

To my agent, Liza Fleissig of Liza Royce Agency, you are the best agent in the world!! Thank you for being a fierce advocate and tireless champion. And to Ginger Harris-Dontzin and the rest of the LRA team—thank you for your steadfast support and incredible advice.

To my editor extraordinaire—Liz Pearsons—thank you for embracing this series and bringing Kate Green into the world. You are brilliant at your job, and I love working with you! A huge thank-you to Grace Doyle, Nicole Burns-Ascue, Andrea Hurst, Alicia Lea, Jenna Justice, and the rest of the incredible team at Thomas & Mercer for your steadfast support and guidance. Thank you to Erin Mitchell, a guiding light in all things marketing. I'm thrilled to be working with you.

In creating *Dangerous Play*, I sought guidance from four talented women who personally experienced the world of competitive soccer. Thank you, Kat Jordan, Nata Ramirez, Rachel Benz, and Maura Walsh. This book wouldn't exist without your insight. Thank you to legal expert Audrey Felsen, police expert Greg Saroka, stylist Sarah Burns, and sports producer Bryan Schwartz for always answering my questions. I want to thank my cousin Alanna Nodelman, an extraordinary jewelry designer and the inspiration for Alexa's profession.

I am lucky enough to have wonderfully talented beta readers. Huge thanks to Linda Copolla, who has been reading my manuscripts from the beginning. I wouldn't be here without you! My dear friend Naana Obeng-Marnu, I love our plotting sessions, and I value your sharp edits and insights. To Tessa Wegert, my phone-a-friend for all things book related—thank you for your keen insights, advice, and friendship. To my mom, Joyce Hartstein, for her thoughtful input. And to my husband, Rob, who reads all my drafts and provides feedback that has made this book so much better.

To Michelle and Greg Marrinan, Tracy and Michael Kellaher, Rachel Sherman, and Ben Kessler—thank you for your steadfast support and love. Thank you to my dear friends and brainstorming buddies, Cindy and Gregg Schwartz. And to my incredible friends Gigi Georges, Pam Gerla, Stacy Novoshelski, Jayden Tabor, and Anne Strahm—for your constant support of my series and me.

A big thank-you to the mystery-and-thriller writing community—one of the most generous groups of people I've ever met. You have made me feel welcome and supported. I am also deeply grateful to the communities I have found within Sisters in Crime, the Sisters in Crime Connecticut chapter, as well as Mystery Writers of America, International Thriller Writers, Bouchercon, and Readers Take Denver. I also want to thank Friends of Key West Library for welcoming me into their community.

I am so lucky to have such a wonderful extended family who continues to support my series and me. You've enthusiastically embraced Kate Green and shouted her existence to the world. Thank you to the Hartsteins, Grays, Tulletts, Hochbergs, Kipnesses, Kalverts, and Richmans. Shout-out to Abi Tullet for her help with TikTok and Diana Beinart and Gigi Georges for the fabulous book event. To my mother-in-law, Dorothy Kipness, and Larry Broder—thank you for your support and love. To my aunt Sylvia Moss and father-in-law, Irwin Kipness, you are always with me.

Thank you to Michelle Zelin for being a constant in my life. I couldn't have wished for a better "sister" than you. To my parents, Joyce and Marvin Hartstein, thank you for teaching me to believe in myself. I'm lucky to have such supportive and caring parents. A huge thank-you to my sons, Justin and Ryan, for believing in their mom and cheering me on at every turn. Love you tons! And to my husband, Rob, who does everything from reading my drafts, to creating graphics, to tattooing his arm with the titles of my thrillers. Okay, henna tattoos. But still! You are the absolute best, and I love you.

ABOUT THE AUTHOR

Photo © 2018 Adam Regan

Elise Hart Kipness is a television sports reporter turned crime fiction writer. *Dangerous Play* is based on Elise's experience in the high-pressure, adrenaline-pumping world of live TV. Like her protagonist, Elise chased marquee athletes through the tunnels of Madison Square Garden and stood before glaring lights reporting to national audiences.

In addition to reporting for Fox Sports Network, Elise was a reporter at New York's WNBC-TV, News 12 Long Island, and the Associated Press. She is currently copresident of Sisters in Crime Connecticut. When not writing, Elise loves reading and binge-watching thrillers, and she will fight you for the last scoop of coffee ice cream.

A graduate of Brown University, Elise has two college-age sons. Elise, her husband, and their three labradoodles split time between Key West, Florida, and Stamford, Connecticut.